T0146880

RIVER
OF
DENIAL

RIVER
OF
DENIAL

A SAMANTHA GRANT MYSTERY

LEA BRADEN

RIVER OF DENIAL
A SAMANTHA GRANT MYSTERY

This is a work of fiction. All of the characters, names, incidents,
organizations, and dialogue in this novel are either the products
of the author's imagination or are used fictitiously.

iUniverse books may be ordered through booksellers or by contacting:

iUniverse
1663 Liberty Drive
Bloomington, IN 47403
www.iuniverse.com
1-800-Authors (1-800-288-4677)

ISBN: 978-1-5320-0361-5 (sc)
ISBN: 978-1-5320-0362-2 (hc)
ISBN: 978-1-5320-0363-9 (e)

Library of Congress Control Number: 2016912677

Print information available on the last page.

iUniverse rev. date: 04/03/2017

River of Denial is dedicated to Norman Parks, my father
and Grant Ackerman, my husband.
Love and miss both of you.

PROLOGUE

In Pied Piper fashion, Superintendent Worthington lured River Bend's non-descript teachers to a meeting at the Board of Education building. Like the children in the tale they followed the tune of hope. They hoped and prayed the meeting meant they had been selected as a candidate for the prestigious award of Teacher of the Year.

These followers were the quiet, dedicated teachers with the firm belief that their sole purpose in life was to educate children. Their lives reflected their passion, everything they did centered on their students, yet they were overlooked year after year for any professional acknowledgment. When they received a personal call from the superintendent it had to mean that they were finally being recognized for their dedication. Quietly, they left their classrooms after school and floated on a cloud of optimism to the District's Board of Education building.

One excited teacher called home, "Hello dear, I am calling to inform you that I will be late coming home tonight." Modestly she patted her plump chest, to calm away her tears of joy. "I have good news, the Superintendent called and asked me to come to the board office after school for a meeting with her. You know, it is Teacher of the Year time. After thirty-plus years with the district, maybe they are nominating me. I would be so happy just to be nominated."

"Why would they nominate you? They don't nominate old cows!" A shriek of laughter blasted through her phone.

"It is based on state test scores and I have the highest scores in the district. I just know it is my turn to be nominated." She stopped and remembered she needed to put him first or later she would get his fist. "Oh, I am sorry, I forgot to ask you. How was your cardiologist appointment today?"

Her husband whined. "Just won-der-ful... Now, don't waste your time going to the Board Office. Get home. I'm hungry."

"Honey, I just told you, I must attend my interview. It would be rude not to attend and it would ruin my chances of being nominated. After my interview I will be home and prepare a special dinner tonight. I love you, goodbye."

She turned off her phone and placed it carefully in the pocket of her purse. "He is just in a bad mood. The doctor probably told him to lose weight, again. If I get nominated, then maybe he will forget to punish me."

As she drove to the interview she rehearsed her speech about being a valuable teacher and all that entailed. For example, when her husband had a heart-attack she had driven back and forth to the school in order to discuss with her substitute about the students' work, daily. All of her hard work and sleepless nights had paid off. Her students had scored the highest in the state on their assessments. If she repeated that she was valuable often enough, then it would be true. She was a valued teacher.

Shyly she scuttled into the Board's office, settled in a discreet place and waited for her turn. She watched familiar faces stumble out of Superintendent Worthington's office. A soft smile spread across her homely face. Finally, the school board had decided to focus on the teachers with seniority for the nomination of Teacher of the Year, how wonderful. She busily brushed off her suit skirt that stretched across her plump thighs. She pulled her compact out of her purse and checked for spots on her blouse. The worn white blouse had survived another day without a blemish. Thank goodness the superintendent called the meeting on Wednesday. Every Wednesday she wore her faithful navy blue suit. After all these years it still looked so professional.

Curiously the woman scanned the reception area to find others from her building. There were none. She knew the superintendent's secretary, a former student of hers, Janet Monroe. Even in sixth grade Janet always looked so neat and proper and today was no different. A perfect example of River Bend's fine educational system. Nervously she glanced at the secretary's desk and hoped for a brief and friendly chat with Janet. Janet had disappeared. She checked her Timex watch, noting it was fifteen after five. Oh, her husband would be in a state tonight. She should leave so she could prepare the promised perfect meal for him. No, she thought. I am here. This is my chance. Politely she waited and hoped the superintendent had saved the best for last.

As the room thinned out, the nervous woman noticed with disdain that the beige–on–beige reception area needed a makeover. Appearance was so important when trying to make a good impression on visitors or dignitaries. She reexamined her suit and removed a small piece of thread.

IT IS ALL ABOUT APPEARANCE

Superintendent Worthington emerged from her office followed by a pale and shaking teacher. Worthington looked for her next victim, she meant teacher, and hoped it was the last one. *Oh great*, she thought when she spied the Pillsbury dough-woman partially hidden beside the fake plant. Worthington pointed and said nothing, but just pointed at the woman. The timid teacher rose, patted her hair, brushed off her clothes and tapped her chest. Superintendent Worthington pointed at her *Cartier* watch and said, "Come along, now, you are wasting my time."

The woman scurried to the superintendent's office; stopped short, caught her breath and staggered into the office. Her image ricocheted off the shined glass, polished chrome and mirrored surfaces. Her head spun from the kaleidoscope of reflections that rotated with each of her movements. Superintendent Worthington, positioned at her desk, studied the woman's reaction in the reflective surface. The poor woman's stunned expression bemused Worthington. She denied her inner voice that said this was beyond cruel, even for her.

Superintendent Worthington rotated on a stiletto-like chair. "Hurry up and sit down before you fall down. I don't need a lawsuit. Sit next to me so you can hear me clearly."

"You have served USD 555 efficiently for years." Worthington rolled her eyes back towards her perfectly arched brows as she droned on with her mental script. Worthington inhaled a small breath.

The woman assumed Superintendent Worthington had stopped talking, so she started her practiced speech. "I would like to take this time to thank you for interviewing me for the Teacher of the Year award. I feel I am worthy of this nomination because..."

Superintendent Worthington interrupted her speech with a loud harsh laugh. Her hand shot up, flat in the 'stop right now' position. Her head riveted back to the computer screen. Superintendent Worthington continued. "You aren't here to be nominated for anything. We are changing the school district's imagine. We need young blood in the district. We'll try to find you and all the others that were here tonight a place in the rural area of the district, a less visible site."

Humiliated, the teacher lowered her head and sobbed, "I– I thought – I was here for – the Teacher of the Year nomination. Superintendent Worthington, I have entered the turnstile of my career. I entered your office as a teacher and will leave as a – what?"

Superintendent Worthington with her lips curled in a despicable smile, laughed so hard she almost choked. "Don't you see? You are – what fifty something years old. You are too old for the Teacher of the Year award and too old for your position in our prime school building. It's all about appearances. You aren't a good visual."

Numbly the woman stood up. "Thank you for your time." She reached into her purse for her keys and gloves. She staggered toward the chrome door and left.

Superintendent Worthington's breath caught and held. Her ears strained to detected source of the sound. Quickly she finished writing *Samantha Grant* on a sticky-note and slid it under her keyboard.

Worthington poised her hands over the keyboard to conceal her latest mischief. She heard another snap of static electricity. Someone had entered her domain. She trembled in anticipation. Leisurely her eyes lifted to view the intruder.

"Oh, it's you again. What did you forget this time?"

A wicked smile greeted the guest. Relaxed, Worthington decided to toy with her unexpected visitor. They locked eyes. Superintendent Worthington thought she controlled the game. So fixed on the sport, she ignored the visitor's slow advancement towards her. So preoccupied with her mind-game, she missed the visitor's movement. Their eyes locked everything disappeared for Worthington except the game. A hand slid around Superintendent Worthington and stabbed Worthington's long skinny neck in the jugular vein. Pushing until 'POP', pierced the silence. Time stopped. Worthington's smirk froze and her hands paused over the keyboard motionless.

The reflective walls held Worthington's flawless beauty and sadistic smile. Not a spot of blood showed on her luxurious black cowl neck sweater. The hand straightened the strand of Worthington's hair that was out of place. The visitor whispered into her ear, "Better"

The moon peeked through the window shade and added its silver face to the collage of faces wallpapering the room.

1

BEAUTIFUL DAY FOR
A DISASTER

Samantha opened her front door and let Bo out to do his business. The crisp apple breeze dashed passed her into the house. The early morning pinkish-orange glow shed enough light to watch the fog magically drift along the road and up the hill of the old dusty road. She closed her eyes and let the beauty of the day wash over her.

Samantha answered her phone in fast forward. "Katherine... I am – am ready to leave. Sorry, I was just thinking of missing today and all the bedlam, but then I remembered it was bring your planet day, a big day for my students. So, I decided to bring a plastic trash bag to wear over my new 'professional' suit so when the parents start throwing things at us, my suit will stay nice and professional looking."

She listened to Katherine, her best friend and fellow teacher and responded, "Sorry, but, what do you plan to tell the parents when they ask about happened to the new computers, the new heating and air conditioning that was promised in the bond issue? They will go ballistic and demand answers from us while we are trying to teach in our rooms. It will go on all day. Only our superintendent would plan an Open House on a Thursday during the regular school day. And to think I used to like Thursdays. Sorry, but there will be a scene when our parents find out their Twenty Million Dollar Bond Issue only got them fresh coat of paint on the same old walls. Oh, and some new trees."

"Yes, I know I am yelling. Yes, I know I am already on Superintendent Worthington's '*not good enough*' list. I know I need to watch my questions, my appearance and my whatever. I will have her know that I'm also on the '*not good enough list*' of my ex-husband and my grandmother. But, our parents deserve what they were promised to them."

"Katherine, I am surprised that you, old Miss Tight Money pants, don't have concerns about the costs. I'm telling you there will be trouble today. I feel it. Oh, I'll bring a trash bag for you, too." Samantha quickly ended the call.

Bo had finished marking his zillionth blade of grass and stood listening to Samantha's conversation with a quizzical look. Samantha bent down and picked him up, ruffling his furry head. "Bo, I think we need to start a new investigation. I know there was a crime committed either by that out- of - town Construction Company or Superintendent Worthington. We need to find out if our Superintendent Worthington was taken to the cleaners by that Construction Company, or did she take River Bend to the cleaners?"

Samantha shut the front door. She felt the tightening in her head. "Oh, no, have to get control of this. Breath - just inhale and exhale relax. I don't have time for this insanity. Today, I am Cleopatra, the Queen of Denial. As the Queen I will deny the headaches, Porta Potty on my porch and the Open House at school. I'm in total denial of all things unfixable."

"Bo, hop into our chariot and let's be gone."

2

A BEAUTIFUL DAY

Ramon's long legs crunched through fall's gift on his way to work. The early morning rays touched the frost and created a glittering effect across the landscape. He loved this time of year. He envisioned his little son Rey wadding through the leaves on his short two year old legs. He smiled. The smile disappeared. "Better get the leaves cleaned up before the wicked witch fires me for letting the grounds look messy."

Ramon loved his job, but hated his boss. He made good money, enough money to send some to his family in Mexico. He was a citizen of this wonderful country. Life was good, or had been, until Superintendent Worthington held that Christmas party for the district's office staff. Ramon remembered every detail of that life changing day. He had brought his beautiful wife, Angela, and their son Rey. It hadn't dawned on him that he shouldn't bring Angela, that it could cause problems for them. But, the Monday after the party Superintendent Worthington called him to her office. He figured she just wanted to chase him around her desk. He was prepared this time and stood with his back pressed beside the door for a quick getaway and his utility flashlight in front of him ready to swing.

"Ramon, everyone remarked about your beautiful wife." Superintendent Worthington's voice was syrupy sweet. She paused. Her red nails tapped on her Lucite desk a rhythm like a cat's tail makes when focused on its prey. "She doesn't speak English well, does she?"

Worthington paused. "And I bet she doesn't have a green card, either?" She saw a flicker of fear in Ramon's eyes. She slapped the desk with her long white fingers and snorted. "Got ya'!"

Fear seized him more, but he just stood there tapping the flashlight against his hand and looked down at his shoes. What was she going to do? She was the type of a woman who would do something mean just because she could.

Twirling around and facing him as she played with a strand of her smooth black hair. "Ramon, it would be a shame if I had to call the immigration people. You know I'm obligated to do that. Then I thought to myself. I just bought a new house and I desperately need a housekeeper. And you need me to keep my mouth shut. I am giving you a wonderful opportunity to save your wife. Do you understand me?"

Superintendent Worthington's dark grey eyes had drilled holes into Ramon's heart. Her chiseled porcelain features showed no emotion. He continued to stare at his shoes. Now fear plus anger burned through him. He couldn't believe his ears. He had two choices. One choice was let Superintendent Worthington send Angela back to Mexico, or his second choice let Angela be used as her servant. If Angela went back to Mexico, her family would never let her come back to him. If Angela's family found out she was a servant, they would disown her. "They were right. I'm not good enough for Angela."

Ramon decided on the lesser of two evils. Angela would spend ten hours each week cleaning Superintendent Worthington's house, cooking her meals and ironing her expensive clothes in exchange for her silence.

Just the memory of Worthington taking advantage of Angela made his blood boil. He jerked the massive key ring out of his pocket to unlock the front door of the building but, when he pulled the door slightly to put the key in it swung open.

"Worthington, that stupid woman, didn't lock the door again. We're going to get robbed, and then she will blame it on me." Ramon's muscular hands opened and shut in his anger. He fumed, "The lights are still on, maybe someone arrived early to get a start on something? Hello, anyone here?"

4

Ramon unhooked the large utility flashlight from his work belt and listened. All was quiet. Armed with only his flashlight and phone, he checked the conference room and found it empty. Stealthy he crossed the reception area to the Superintendents' area.

Ramon listened at the door of Vice Superintendent, Mickey Sims's office then he tapped on the door. There was no response. He looked inside and found Sims's lights were on and the room reeked of cigarette smoke. Ramon just shook his head. "Superintendent Worthington will fire you Mickey if she finds out."

Ramon opened the window enough to air out the room and turned off the lights on his way out. "Now, no one will know."

Ramon tiptoed to Superintendent Worthington's domain and prayed she wasn't there. He would rather deal with an intruder than Worthington any day of the week. He listened at the door and then tapped. He slowly turned the handle and peeked in before he entered. The lights were on and he scanned the room using the mirror like surfaces. The reflections told him everything he needed to know. Superintendent Worthington was seated quietly at her computer with her head bent down. She appeared to be working. In the reflection she looked normal but something wasn't right. The way her back wasn't in its usual erect state in that thing she called a chair. Superintendent Worthington never ever slumped. Ramon entered and gently let the door close. He whispered her name, but she didn't move or growl. "Are you asleep, Superintendent Worthington?"

No answer. He knew he had to be brave and wake her. She was a proud woman who wanted everyone to think she was super hero, not a person who fell asleep at work. Maybe she would feel indebted to him and end her threat against his family. With that thought in his mind, he slowly crept up to her. Her hands were on the keyboard and he lightly touched her shoulder.

"Ms. Worthington, it's time to wake up. People will be here soon. Come on now, wake up." He nudged her a little harder. She slipped sideways and dropped to the thick black carpet. Without checking her pulse. He knew. She was dead.

"Roger, this is Ramon. I just found Superintendent Worthington - dead." Panic raised his deep voice a pitch or two higher than normal and Roger barely recognized Ramon on the phone.

Roger deep gruff voice answered. "Ramon, stay with her. I'm calling the police. I'll be there in a minute. Just stay with her and don't let anyone in her office, understand?"

3

A QUIET THURSDAY

River Bend's police department loved Thursdays. Nothing major ever happened in their quiet picturesque town on Thursday. It was the one day of the week when there were donuts and fresh coffee and unread newspapers scattered around. The handful of River Bend's police force worked quietly, finishing their paperwork. The shrill ring of the emergency phone startled all of them, especially the dispatcher, Shelia. Shelia had bragged many times that she could tell by sound of the ring the seriousness of the situation. She listened to the phone's ring. Sniffing, she pinched her red lips and pulled a pencil out of her frizzy grey hair. "This one is bad, just mark my words."

"Yes, River Bend Police Department, state your problem and then your name," She listened, pencil poised ready to write all the information. "At the Board Office, Worthington . . . now Roger, who's with the body? Who is? Tell him not to touch anything. Please, lock up the building until we show up. I'll have our men there immediately."

Sheila walked back to Police Chief Patterson's office and looked into the room, her hand flew to her mouth as she pretended to be shocked he wasn't there yet. She turned her attention to the second in command, Detective Jim Murphy. "Jim, you and your partner need to go to the Board Office. They found the Superintendent dead in her office. Where's Patterson? The police chief should be there for this one." Sheila snapped at the men as she penciled on the F-73-A form the time, who, where and when. Later the officers could fill in all the data about the incident.

"You call him, Sheila he's afraid of you. We're leaving. Please put the form on my desk, thank you." Detective Jim Murphy grabbed his notebook, his gun, a donut and left with a smile on his face. He muttered to his partner, "We have a case, I hope."

Sheila flipped Jim her special one finger salute as he left and grudgingly called the Police Chief. With one hand on her boney hip, she gave her gum a few more chomps then picked her teeth with the point end of her pencil. She used the eraser end to dial his number.

"Patterson, this is Sheila your dispatcher, I'm at work. Thought you needed to know since you weren't here, that one of the maintenance men found the superintendent of our school district dead in her office. You need to meet Jim at the board office, now." She slammed the phone down.

Patterson rolled out of bed. From being in the military he got ready in thirty seconds and headed out the door. He grabbed a protein bar and bottle of water, his typical breakfast of late. His house was closer than the police station to the school board office so he could arrive about the same time as Jim. He had been slacking lately. Now was not the time to slack. He called the River Bend's coroner, Dr. Flanigan. He needed to make sure the coroner was able to work.

"Dr. Flanigan, Police Chief Patterson here, we have a body. I need to know if you have had a drink in the last forty-eight hours. Don't lie to me."

"Flanigan, I can't use you on this case. Hey, get some medical help. I need you."

Patterson clicked off and dialed Dr. Ackerman, the City's coroner, who had helped on his other cases.

"Ackerman, we got a body, and we need you now."

"Where is it?" Ackerman growled.

"Board of Education building located two blocks west of Al Roth's office. Remember?" Patterson talked as he cautiously drove down the street. Unconsciously he had stopped rubbing the back of his neck the second he knew that Dr. Ackerman would handle this case.

"Are there school kids?" Ackerman's voice became high pitched whine, "I don't like kids. Nasty little germy creatures, do not let them near the body or I won't touch it."

"The Board office isn't close to the schools. No children are around the body or the building. Are you coming?"

"Yes, see you in a few minutes." Ackerman clicked off.

Patterson arrived before his men, allowing him a moment to check out the area. The Board of Education building shared a huge parking lot with the football stadium. In daylight the area was okay, he counted only six light posts. Not enough light to see as you walked to your car at night unless there was a game. Then the lights from the stadium would light the parking lot. Patterson thought, *I bet Samantha and her crazy teacher friends would have tales about the parking lot and about Superintendent Worthington. If this was a wrongful death case, Samantha and her friends, the good, the bad and the scary, would be of help with it. Between the three of them they knew everyone in River Bend's school district. If this was a case, then he would have an excuse to see Samantha again.* Patterson hoped there was a case.

Detective Jim Murray's truck squealed to a stop. He and his partner Henry hopped out of the truck and joined Patterson. A tall, heavyset man with the word Maintenance over his pocket and a smile on his face walked towards them. "Man, am I glad to see you guys. I'm Roger, the head of maintenance. She's inside, and Ramon, my assistant, is guarding her. I'll show you where."

Patterson stopped mid stride turned to Officer Henry. "We need you to stay out here. Keep your eyes open for anything unusual. Talk to the maintenance guy. Find out what he knows. They always know the low down on everything and everyone. Don't let anyone in this building unless they are the City's Coroner's group. If anyone comes and wants in the building, ask for their picture identification and write down information. Ask their business here. Then send them to their car to wait."

To himself, "Damn I don't have a drill sergeant anymore. Need to train these guys myself. Procedure rules, civilians hate procedure. Damn, I hate civilian life. Don't fit- in."

9

Roger walked the Police Chief and Detective Jim Murphy to the superintendent's door he paused and wiped his feet on the mat. Roger giggled as he stepped aside to allow Police Chief Patterson and Detective Jim Murphy through. The morning sun crashed into their eyes as the sunlight deflected from chrome, to mirrors, to glass windows. The ricocheting light blinded them from multiple directions.

Patterson dazed. "Are there shades for the windows?"

Roger puffed out his chest, "Of course she had shades. Only the best for Superintendent Worthington. Ramon, lower the shade."

Ramon nodded. Relief showed on his face as his eyes moved from the body. He slid around to the side of the desk and pressed the button. Shades appeared from beneath the wood trim and inched their way down the windows, slowly and quietly in unison.

"So that is where our tax dollars go. They pay for expensive toys!" Anger erupted from Police Chief Patterson. "The money spent on that contraption would have paid for bullet proof vests for my men."

Roger smiled, "Oh, not tax dollars. Her mommy and daddy paid for the shades. They're the same Worthingtons who built the new football field. We have a state of the art football field for everyone to see. Of course our poor football players don't have uniforms, but our football field is something else."

"Hum, Ramon, we need you to assist us in here." Patterson scribbled in his notebook.

"Roger, we'll talk to you later. Please, go outside and assist Officer Henry. Thank you for your help." Patterson shook Roger's hand. It's dry and steady, a sign of an innocent person, at least in the military.

Patterson jotted down his observations. He turned to Jim. "What's the story is on Ramon? He's nervous or something? And a heads up that mustache you are trying to grow, get rid of it. It looks more like a 'Got Milk' mustache."

Jim didn't look up from his work just rubbed his mustache. "He's just scared."

"Scared, scared of what. When I was in the army my men were in dangerous situation. They never acted like that. Their chins were out and strong, shoulders squared. They looked me straight in the eye."

"They were in the army. You taught them how to act. Poor Ramon wasn't trained on how to not act scared. He's just scared. His boss is dead. He was in the room either before she died or after she died. He is our prime suspect and he knows it."

Patterson listened to Jim while he wrote notes about the victim, just in case this turned into a case.

Jim opened and closed Superintendent Worthington's desk drawers. He moved to the computer and searched around and under the computer. Under the computer he found a sticky note stuck on the desk with just Samantha Grant's name on it. He carefully removed it and showed it to Patterson. "Samantha's name but nothing else, I bet Worthington's secretary knows why. It's odd that Worthington left a note, so out of place. Judging from this room and the rest of the building, a pen out of place would stick out like a sore thumb. I would put a bet on her secretary knowing if anything else is out of place."

Patterson put the piece of paper in a protective sheath and placed it in his notebook, and worried. *What had Samantha gotten into now? First, he had to take care of things here then he would talk to her. It was time to interview his prime suspect, Ramon.*

"Ramon, tell me how you found the building this morning when you arrived."

"The main door wasn't locked. The lights were on and Superintendent Worthington would fire anyone who left the lights on at the end of the day. She would have blamed me. I thought that someone had come in early to work. I checked all the rooms before I checked her office. I thought she was asleep. I touched her she fell over. I called Roger."

"Thank you, Ramon that helps us." Patterson wrote down the statement and noted that Ramon's eyes darted around, but lingered on the Superintendent's body. Ramon was a tall, dark and handsome young man. Superintendent Worthington had been a breathtakingly beautiful woman. Had Ramon and Worthington been lovers? That brought the issue of Worthington and her relationships with her other co-workers. Did anyone have an issue with this beautiful woman?

Patterson stared down at Superintendent Worthington. She reminded him of his ex-wife, Jillian, who was beautiful but deadly.

Worthington was beautiful and dead. Jillian dined on men like Ramon, gorgeous nobodies. Jillian used her money and beauty to wrap them around her little finger. Her people skills were simple. If you were of some use to her. You were fine. When you were no longer useful, then you were gone. Jillian had set her heart on being an Army officer's wife. When he refused to become an officer like his father. He was gone out of her life. Had Ramon killed Superintendent Worthington because she no longer desired him?

Patterson was jolted back to reality when the City's coroner and his crew marched into the room. He turned to Dr. Ackerman and feigned anger, "How many speeding tickets do I get to pay for this time?" Ackerman and his crew had arrived from the City, located over twenty-five miles away. It had taken them less than fifteen minutes to drive to River Bend.

Ackerman scoffed back, "Three coming, and we'll find out how many going. I swear the police wait for us. They had their ticket pads out and ready." The Ackerman's well trained forensic crew immediately started collecting evidence from every surface even the victim's trash.

Dr. Ackerman snapped, crackled and popped when he bent down to examine the body. He tried not to move her until they had taken all of the pictures. He questioned. *Heart attack?*

Detective Jim Murphy and the coroner assistant finished photographing the victim. Dr. Ackerman gently turned the body over and started a quick examine for an obvious cause of death - still nothing. When he straightened her head that was tilted awkwardly he felt something damp and sticky in the thick cowl-neck sweater. He removed a neatly folded white handkerchief out of his pocket and blotted the neck of black sweater. Then he tapped with the tip of his handkerchief on the thick black carpet both had a red damp sticky substance on them. Gently he pulled the collar away from her long slender neck. There was a good size bruise with tiny line blood next to a small hole in her neck. The victim had been stabbed. "Hey, Patterson, found what may have killed this woman."

Patterson joined him. "That's the jugular vein, right?"

He re-examined the area under the desk and questioned. "No blood splatters anywhere. Where's the blood? Streams of it should have shot out, but there isn't anything?"

"Because this is a Worthington and you don't have a full lab, I better take the body to my lab. I will tell you what caused her death after I run some tests. I have an idea, but I need proof first, not a guess. Make sure you guys check all of the carpet for blood in case we have a bloody shoe prints from the killer." Dr. Ackerman wiped the sweat off his forehead. "It's hot in here?"

Patterson nodded in agreement. "I've been in steam rooms that were cooler than this office. Our tax payers' money has gone up in steam just to keep her office like a sauna."

Dr. Ackerman gently covered the body with a white sheet, loaded the evidence, and headed out.

Patterson stared at the floor and reflected, the superintendent had been a beautiful rich young woman with a strong personality, judging from her office. Who wanted her dead? He hadn't heard anything negative about her. He turned and put his hand on Ramon's shoulder the young man about jumped out of his skin. "I'm sorry Ramon, but I need your help. We need the door locked. Then put yellow tape across the superintendent's office door."

Ramon nodded his head, relieved just to get out of the room. As he quickly walked away his mind raced. *Oh, my beautiful Angela was free from that monster. Truly this is a beautiful day. A small smile slipped sideways across his face. Better be careful not to show how happy I am that Superintendent Worthington is dead.*

4

THE ROOM TOLD

Alone Patterson studied the superintendent's office. A person's office told so much about the person. In the army he could tell the type of person my new commanding officer was just by looking in his office. Most commanding officers put very few things in their office. But, what they put in it said a lot about them. Family pictures meant a good solid steady leader. Awards, diplomas, meant an ego tripping leader, not a good thing. What did this room say about Superintendent Worthington? She liked expensive things. Jillian, his ex-wife, had a chair just like Worthington's. A sleek, plastic super modern useless pieces of shit chair. No pictures of family or friends, nothing personal, yet, this office was very personal. The comfort level had to be hers alone with the reflective surfaced walls and the humid heat. Even old cantankerous Dr. Ackerman noticed the heat. On the last case the temperature was one hundred and ten degrees' in the shade. It hadn't bother him.

"Jim, do you see a thermostat in this room? I can't find it."

Jim inspected each wall carefully. "Nope."

Patterson whipped a neatly folded white handkerchief out of his pocket and mopped his clammy face. "Jim, let's get out of here. I feel like I've been on a roller coaster in July after eating a whole pizza. Roger said that Worthington's parents paid for remodeling of that room. Right?"

Jim nodded.

Patterson stopped at the door took one more look around, his brows knitted together. "You wrote down or collected everything. Did you find Superintendent Worthington's stuff? Her phone, or her purse, or her car keys? Or a storage area?"

Jim read his notes to make sure he hadn't forgotten and shook his head. "Nope, nothing, I checked that small file cabinet by her desk. It had chewing gum and purchase orders, which I have with me. Could this have been a robbery gone wrong?"

"No, they left her expensive computer. Maybe robbery interrupted? We are taking the computer. Maybe you can find something on it that will give us a lead."

They left Ramon placing the yellow tape across the outside of the superintendent's office door. The police chief's facial expression was walled up. Detective Jim Murphy smiled and a bounce to his step until he got slapped on the back of his head by Patterson.

"Why did you do that?"

"You are just too happy about having a case." A smile curled on Patterson's lips. "Always wanted to do that. Hum"

5

INTERVIEW WITH A CHESHIRE CAT

The reception area was crowded with slender, well-dressed, every hair in place, women in business suits whispering to each other while a handful of bewildered equally well-dressed men paced back and forth.

"They look like Superintendent Worthington clones." Jim whispered to Patterson as they stepped out of the superintendent's office. The clones turned and stared at them.

The clones parted as a woman, with a cheesy smile greeted the police. Police Chief Patterson only saw the smile, not the person, just the smile, as she marched towards him with her hand extended.

"I'm Mrs. Steinem. How may I help you?" She reminded Patterson of the Cheshire cat from <u>Alice in Wonderland</u> in the scene when only the cat's grin was visible.

When Mrs. Steinem spoke the bee hive sound ceased. Silence permeated the room. Patterson paused, steeled himself against this formidable creature. The room stared at them. Their behavior told him the Cheshire cat was a very important person in the school system's hierarchy. The room waited.

Patterson spoke first. "Superintendent Worthington's secretary?"

She smiled coldly, "Oh, my, no I'm Vice - Superintendent Mickey Sims's secretary. I'm too, ah; well, I'm not up to Superintendent Worthington's standards. Again, may I help you?"

Before he answered her, he scribbled notes regarding Mrs. Steinem's comment about not being good enough to be Superintendent Worthington's secretary. Yet, to him she appeared to be the icon for the perfect secretary. She appeared smart, efficient, personable - flawless; nothing like his receptionist, Shelia, ninety-nine pounds of bad attitude with steel wool hair. "Yes. Could I talk with you someplace more – private?" Mrs. Steinem's mind whirled as she led him to the conference room. Just keep the smile on your face. The moment he leaves double check everything to find what needs fixed before the police started looking closer into things. The conference room had plenty of space and privacy. She hoped he was as lazy as old Police Chief Vernon.

When Patterson saw the conference room his nerves tingled with anticipation. What was she going to tell him? Who the killer was? No, she didn't know that Worthington was dead. Maybe she had some lethal gossip...

Mrs. Steinem flipped on the light switch and her smile at the same time. She had turned on only one block of lights. She navigated to the table under the lights and sat down, motioned for him to join her. The lights cast shadows that partially hid her face added an aura of mystery about her.

For one second, Patterson considered a mental dance with Mrs. Steinem, but that would have put her in the advantage seat. He instinctively clicked his heels and mentally stepped into his military mode and prepared to interrogate. "I need the names of the people who worked here from four to about seven yesterday evening. Plus, the names of all personnel with a key and the access code to this building."

The smile and Mrs. Steinem faded into the shadows. She pictured in her mind last night's activities. She had moved into Vice Superintendent Sims office to work because of the meeting Worthington had with a group of teachers. They were a chatty group at first. One of them said something about it being the meeting for the Teacher of the Year nominations. Janet Monroe stayed at her desk. Sims had been out of the office for personal reasons. She left after Janet about five o'clock all that remained was the teachers meeting with Worthington.

Mrs. Steinem moved into the light and smiled her Cheshire cat smile. She gave him the names and the timeline of the last ones in the building. She explained, "Janet left before me. Superintendent Worthington and some teachers were still in the building when I left the office. In fact, when I drove by around ten, Superintendent Worthington was still here."

Patterson had been writing down her statement, stopped and looked at her. "You knew she was here, how? Was her car still here?" Maybe, Patterson hoped, this had been a robbery. Someone came in; threatened Worthington at knife point demanded her keys in order to steal the car. She refused. They stabbed her. Took the keys, purse, phones, car and drove off. That would work.

"Superintendent Worthington didn't have her car here yesterday. She rode to work with Sterling Bender, a board member and her neighbor. They commute together often. I knew she was still here because the lights were on in her office. She was a stickler for being energy efficient. If her lights were on, she was in her office. The lights were on in her office and in the reception area."

"Were there any vehicles in the parking lot when you drove by at ten?"

Her smile faded as she visualized the parking lot. It had been empty. She had driven around the building to make sure Bunny Worthington was safe. She assumed no one was around and that meant Bunny Worthington was fine. Would her sister, Mrs. Lana Worthington, blame her for whatever happened to Bunny? But, all, Mrs. Steinem said, "There were no cars in the lots."

"Fine, can you tell me about the meeting with the teachers. What was the purpose?"

Patterson had missed the concerned look on Steinem's face but noted that she had hidden longer on the parking lot question.

Oddly, she didn't dissolve into the shadow this time and promptly answered. "You need to talk to Superintendent Worthington's secretary, Janet Monroe. I was not privy to the purpose. She isn't here yet. This is very unusual for that young lady. May I ask you a question, please?"

"Yes, of course." He used the fading act and thought, *how dangerous can a group of teachers be?* Then he remembered Samantha and her group of teacher friends. Samantha the good, Katherine the scary, and Gin the bad. Dangerous…

"What happened to Superintendent Worthington? Was it an accident or a heart attack?"

"It was an accident." Patterson moved into the shadows. He couldn't reveal anything about the accident. Like Superintendent Worthington had accidentally stabbed herself in the neck with a candlestick in the library. He changed the subject.

He asked, "Would you assist us with the interviews? I need you to organize all the employees into the reception area. Detective Jim Murphy will do interviews in the Vice Superintendent's office."

One perfectly arched eyebrow raised it told him she would gladly rein over the other employees. "Well of course, I am delighted to help. This will be in a supervisory position. Am I correct?"

Patterson nodded and stepped aside for her to exit. As she stepped beside him.

He asked another question just to see her reaction. "Was Worthington working on anything controversial? Were there threats to her or the school district?"

She smiled and lied. "No, of course not, this is a public school district. We are here to serve our patrons. We have very happy patrons, happy staff, happy teachers, and happy superintendents. Everyone is happy, happy, and happy."

Mrs. Steinem maintained her arrogant appearance but felt a panic attack. Muttering under her breath. "What has that spoiled brat Worthington done this time? What have I missed? I have paid off, covered up and just made things disappear in order to make sure the school district appeared to be in the hands of a great leader. It's all about appearances. Deny any wrong doing that involved Superintendent Bunny Worthington. That was what Superintendent Bunny Worthington's parents pay me to do."

Patterson asked. "Where did Superintendent Worthington keep her cell phone and purse?"

A ten second response, "Her work iPhone and purse should be in the file cabinet with a glass front beside her desk. She never has her personal phone with her. Why?"

"We didn't find any of them in the room or on her. Hum, could you take a look. See if you can find them. Thank you for your help."

Patterson stood in a military at-ease stance and watched her take charge of her peers. He made a note of her mouth moving, but he heard no words.

Mrs. Steinem waited for the Police Chief to leave... *Hum-m-m, I need to find Worthington's phones and clean up anything that shouldn't be on them before I hand them over to the police. I will be that police chief best little helper and then I will find out what he knows.*

6
THE MOON

"Inhale and now exhale, the migraine is starting again. This is stupid I'm letting my fear of what Edward Wooten will do in class cause my headaches. But - I can't take him to the office. The last and only time I took Edward Wooten to the office for disciplinary reasons it blew up in my face. I can still hear Principal Moore crow, how I needed to learn how to handle spirited boys. All little Eddie needed was candy. 'Doesn't hims'." Talking to herself didn't help.

Samantha remembered when she told Katherine about Principal Moore treating her as if she was in trouble. Katherine laughed and told her not to worry. That Moore needed to what her behavior. Rumor had it that Ms. Moore liked males of all sizes and ages. That was the reason Moore had been sent to River Bend Middle School. Superintendent Worthington wanted Moore close to the Board Office in order to keep an eye on her. And, Worthington told Principal Moore that the middle school was her last chance. Something about keeping the lid on the pot of scandal that Moore had caused. And – that she (Worthington) had covered up. Katherine had heard that first hand.

Still, Samantha did not want to deal with Principal Moore today. After all she was Cleopatra the Queen of denial.

Today was 'Bring in Your Planet Day'. The sun was in its place in the center of the room. Several classes planets were up and floating on fishing wire. Samantha hoped that Edward Wooten would leave them alone.

The shrill bell rang to announce time to change class. The migraine increased in pain behind her left eye. Samantha scanned the hall. No Edward Wooten. She opened the door wider and she smiled wider. Eliza May was the first one into the classroom with her Saturn. Shyly she looked up. "Ms. Grant, Edward is in the principal's office." Quietly Eliza May moved to her seat in the back of the classroom.

The entire class simultaneously said, "No Edward Wooten." Peace filled the room.

Seconds later the peace was shattered when the door slammed open. "I'm here and I have my planet, too." Edward Wooten whirled around, dropped his pants, and mooned the class. Piercing screams could be heard in the next county. Seventh grade girls deny they practiced that eardrum splitting scream, but they have to practice to get it just right.

Speechless, Samantha raced toward the door prepared to block Edward and to remove him. As she reached the door, a grey shadow grabbed the back of Edward's tee shirt and pulled him into the hall. Samantha followed Edward and found the stoic Police Chief Path Patterson. He continued to hold Edward by the shirt as he ordered Edward to pull up his pants.

"Sorry, can you watch him while I call someone to cover my class, so I can take him to the office?" The thought of having to go to the office with Edward made her head hurt worse.

"No. I saw it. I'm taking him." Police Chief Patterson straightened up, clicked his heels and marched the distasteful beast to the office.

7

PATTERSON AND THE MOON

Patterson walked intently past the Principal Moore's secretary whose job was to protect the principal from unwanted guests. The Chief of Police ranked high in the unwanted list department. He left the secretary sniveling in his wake. "Don't go in there, Principal Moore will be upset."

He could care less if she was upset; he marched to the principal's door, knocked once and entered into the office.

"I'm Police Chief Patterson. I was in the building trying to consult with one of your teachers on a case. As I walked up to her room this young man, Edward Wooten, I believe is his name, bounced off me and went to the door of the classroom. Then, I observed him mooning the class."

"Well, let's work together to fix this." She reached out to shake his hand. He knew the moment his hand touched hers, he would be sorry. He just didn't know how sorry. Principal Moore latched on, lovingly stroked his arm while she coos up at him. Finally, he pulled his arm from her firm grip.

With both of his hands on Edward's shoulder, he moved towards the door. "I'm taking him to the police station and then home. Or, do you have a punishment, appropriate for Edward?"

"I'll put him in detention after school." She batted her sparse eyelashes at him, smiling as if he was a calorie-free donut. Frantic, Principal Moore thought, *I have to come up with something to prevent this hunk of a man from taking Edward to the police station. The police will notify the Board office. That bitch of a superintendent promised me this was my last chance. If I lose this job, I will lose my husband and my home.* "Not enough. Send him home and I'll take him there." Patterson advanced to the door dragging Edward Wooten with him.

Desperate not to go home, Edward's thin frame shook when he spoke in fast forward, "I'll go to the mean gym teacher's office. I won't do anything, but work. Please don't take me home. My mom will beat me."

Both Principal Moore and Police Chief Patterson nodded in agreement.

Patterson and Edward sprinted out of Principal Moore's office. Neither one looked back. Principal Moore stared at the retreating body of Police Chief and licked her lips.

8

LIGHTNING ROLLS AND MIGRAINES STRIKE

Lightning rolled in Samantha Grant's head and erupted behind her eyes. She closed her eyes for a millisecond and hoped it would depressurize the pain. But, when she opened them, her vision was gone. Can't panic. Must wait for the class to end. Then find Katherine. She'll make this go away. The bell buzzed the end of class. The class rose and rushed pass her and out the door.

Samantha stood still trying to decide which way to go. She was lost in her own classroom. A hand touched her arm. Who touched her? She flinched and the hand quickly retract.

"I'm sorry." It was the timid, high pitched voice of Eliza May.

"Oh, Eliza" Hope filled Samantha, Eliza May would take her to Katherine's room.

"I – I thought maybe you needed help. You have a migraine don't you?" Eliza's normal grating little girl voice sounded smooth like an adult.

"Could you take me to Mrs. Jones' room? Please."

Gently Eliza May seized Samantha's arm and guided her to the door. Quietly they moved down the hall. The sound of kids running caused Samantha to stop. She heard the nasal screechy voice of Principal Moore as she rode her broomstick down the hall. "Now, my darlings it's time to get to class."

Anxiously Samantha whispered, "Run, run to your class so Principal Moore won't punish you for being late."

Eliza May ran to Katherine Jones' room and told her that Ms. Grant needed help. Katherine rushed into the hall and seized Samantha's arm. Katherine knew that Principal Moore was closing in on Samantha. Quickly thinking, Katherine asked in a louder than normal voice. "Samantha, did you hurt your back moving those text books for Principal Moore? You know I would have helped you if you had only asked me."

"Is Samantha okay?" Bob Douglas's voice boomed from down the hall.

Katherine shushed and motioned for him to come and help her. Each one grabbed a limp arm and hauled Samantha into Katherine's classroom. The hall was quiet except for the squeak of Samantha tennis shoes, the tap of Katherine's heels, the thump of Bob's therapeutic shoes and the swish of Principal Moore's broom.

"Samantha what's wrong?" Katherine gently guided Samantha to her classroom.

"My head is killing me. I can't see. I think I am having a stroke or something. Eliza May said it was a migraine, but I think it's more serious than that. I've been having headaches lately, but, thought they were cause by Edward Wooten. But this one started before I left for school and Edward only lasted two minutes in my class. He mooned the class, Police Chief Patterson saw him do it. So he marched Edward to Principal Moore's office. I only hope Patterson got out without being attacked by her."

"Ah-hum, Samantha you changed the subject. The subject is your headaches. Did the headache get worse or better after Patterson marched precious Wooten to the principal's office?" Katherine leaned forward intent on getting an honest answer.

"Worse" Samantha smoothed her clothes as she readjusted the ice pack on her head. "Thank you for the ice pack, but we need to talk about our unit. Just because I can't see doesn't mean we can't work."

Bob, Katherine and Samantha were seated working on their subject areas when Police Chief Patterson walked into the Katherine's classroom. He clicked his heels ready for business. He had made a list of what to say to keep in on the professional level. When he looked up from his notes and saw Samantha with an ice pack on her head and her tear stained face. He stopped.

Katherine saw his facial change and shook her head 'no' smoothly covered the awkward moment. "Hey, Patterson, what brings you to our fair school? Have you been invited to the Open House to help us celebrate of our newly remodeled school's official opening?"

Slowly, he approached the group, "No, I came here to talk to Samantha, but got to meet the principal instead. How do you put up with kids like Edward Wooten? How do you put up with that principal?" He shivered as he remembered Principal Devora Moore's hands all over him.

The three just smiled and nodded. When Patterson asked. "What can you tell me about Superintendent Worthington?"

Their smiles disappeared

Two pairs of eyes looked up at him and three voices in unison defensively asked, "Why?"

Patterson couldn't share the information about her death. But, he needed an honest opinion about her. "Hum, she had a scare today. Just wanted to know how she got along with her peers?"

Bob Douglass blurted out, "You mean her inferiors, don't you? The common people. Well, if you kiss her behind, then you get along fine" Bob looked away, red faced, and sweating. "I hate and fear Superintendent Worthington. She is after my job. She called and told me I had to attend that meeting last night. The loser's meeting with all the other old, overweight, and 'not a good visual' teachers."

Katherine piped up, "She's hard on everyone, Bob. But, Samantha and I get along with her. We gave a tea for her when she became our new superintendent. She loved it. We played nice on purpose."

Patterson just stared at Samantha. His hand went out to touch her then he stopped mid-air. He opened his mouth; stopped and started to dial his phone instead. Katherine jumped up and guided him out of the room. His finger poised over the connect button. He hissed. "Where is the ambulance? I thought you were her friend. Yet, you let her sit there in pain. You didn't even call the nurse?"

"We can't call an ambulance unless there is a lot of blood or heart attack. The nurse only takes care of the students. Teachers aren't in her job description. Our principal would have Samantha's job if we called either one. Plus, who would cover her class? No one. This is the best for everyone concerned. You are correct Samantha does need to go to the doctor. She has been having migraines. That's what wrong with her now. It's that Principal Moore. She just keeps twisting her thumb on Samantha's head, metaphorically speaking."

Patterson started to reach for his handcuffs, "Want me to arrest Moore?"

"Yes, but the superintendent wants Moore's head. Definitely tell Superintendent Worthington about Principal Moore. She'll get rid of her and have pleasure of doing it. And -Worthington likes her little pleasures."

Patterson mentally wrote down the information about Bob Douglas' and Principal Moore's relationship with Worthington. "Whose Samantha's doctor?"

"She doesn't have one, she doesn't believe in them."

Patterson closed and then reopened his phone punched a button, "Police Chief Patterson, here. I need to talk to Dr. Evans now."

Katherine started to explain that a vet couldn't and wouldn't help Samantha, but it was so sweet. Patterson's behavior was the opposite of Samantha's ex-husband, Robert Grant. Robert Grant never did a thing for Samantha but give her his name.

"Dr. Evans, Samantha is having headaches. When can you see her?" He listened, "Why not? Fine" He opened the phone and punched another number, "Dr. Ackerman, Patterson here. I need your help. My friend Samantha Grant is having bad headaches. She needs a doctor. Doesn't have one." After a moment he continued, "You'll take care of it. Let me know when? Thank you, sir" Patterson closed his phone.

"Hum" Patterson clicked his heels and went into military mode. He opened his notebook and pulled out a green sticky note. "Found this on Worthington's desk. Do you know any reason Worthington would write Samantha's name down on a sticky note?"

Katherine brushed and picked at imaginary specks on her dress. "There is only one reason for Worthington to have Samantha's name on her desk. Worthington planned to get rid of Samantha."

"Why get rid of Samantha? I thought you said you and Samantha got along with Superintendent Worthington."

Red faced Katherine said, "We did, then a few weeks ago Worthington told me Samantha wasn't the right image for her school district. She probably wanted to hire some stud muffin to replace Samantha. Or..."

Katherine stopped and vigorously brushed her dress. "Samantha asked her too many questions about the bond issue monies. She wanted proof of how the money was spent on the remodeling. Superintendent doesn't appreciate being question about anything that she does."

Katherine went silent. "Oh, thank you for taking care of Samantha's doctor's problem." Katherine moved towards the door. "We better go back in or Samantha will suspect something."

Katherine and Patterson entered the classroom all smiles. Samantha had already figured out they were up to something. "What have you two been up to?"

Patterson went over and kissed her on the head. "See you tonight. I'll bring dinner out to your place. Okay?"

"Sure, that would be great." She spoke to the air. He was gone. Her headache had eased into a bearable pain. She thought about Patterson's visit. *He doesn't just randomly ask about anyone unless something had happened to that person. Worst case scenario Superintendent was murdered.* Samantha opened her crime notebook and started a page on Worthington and wrote some down facts - like the fact Worthington wanted to fire Bob Douglas. Samantha needed to collect more information. Just in case - there was a case.

9

PATTERSON TO THE RESCUE

Samantha placed her head on her desk. *Finally, this day has ended and I don't have to worry about dinner. I can dream about what I could do if I had water. Never dreamt that a septic tank backing up into my basement would cause such a mess. Think I will have the people who cleaned up after my disaster come back to clean the basement again after the plumber finishes. I'll make a wish I wish the new sewer line attached to my house. Oh, to have indoor plumbing, again.*

The tapping sound of high heels gave Samantha a warning that Katherine was on her way to visit. She raised her head, smoothed her hair, and pinched her cheeks just seconds before Katherine entered her room. The old saying that opposites attract is the only explanation why Katherine and Samantha were best friends. Katherine was confident with every hair in place. Samantha was insecure with wild curly hair.

Samantha asked. "Katherine, what were you and Patterson talking about in the hall?"

"That's why I'm here. Patterson made an appointment for you at City General. They will run tests and find out what is causing your migraines. He plans to go with you." Katherine chewed on the inside of her mouth, while she busily brushed nonexistent particles from her retro style dress, to stop from smiling. If only, Samantha and Patterson would stop denying they are perfect for each other.

30

"He doesn't need to go with me. I'll call the sub finder and make lesson plans for the sub." Samantha picked up her phone to speed-dial the sub finder.

"Stop! Patterson called Principal Moore and told her the police needed you for a top secret police business. Told her she had to find a sub for you." Katherine giggled and did a tap dance, "And she did it. She called me and asked what I knew about you and this police business. I told Principal Moore that Gin, you and I were police consultants when needed. Oh, I told her to send your sub to the library and send Gin up here for your class. We'll be fine."

A dreamy look passed over their faces and simultaneously they said, "Wouldn't it be grand if we did have another case to solve?"

Katherine glowed and Samantha was pain-free for a few fleeting minutes. Samantha said, "You know Katherine, I think something happened to Superintendent Worthington. Patterson never causally asks about anyone without a reason. Maybe someone threatened her or tried to kill her. I started a list of things I know or heard about Worthington."

Katherine read the list and added more things. They were busy on the list when they heard the Principal Moore screech. "Ms. Grant, I need to talk to you."

Katherine hissed, "Look busy, I'll handle this. Yes, Ms. Moore, we are in here working. How may we help you?" Katherine elegantly ushered the principal into the room. Then she paused with her hands placed primly front of her and one leg out as if she were a model from a Fifty's fashion magazine.

Katherine intimidated Principal Moore. But, Principal Moore loved to bully and berate Samantha. "Ms. Grant, what is this foolishness about you working as a consultant for the police department?"

Samantha raised one eyebrow at Principal Moore. "As a science teacher I use my scientific knowledge, logic and power of deduction to reason out solutions. I have been highly successful. One hundred percent of all my cases were solved."

Katherine nodded her head in total agreement with Samantha.

"What poppycock. What crime has happened in this 'no postal envy' town?" Principal Moore sneered at them.

"I can't tell you." Samantha continued with her work. I hoped that Moore flies away and dies. On second thought I hoped nothing ever happened to Devora Moore, because I would be suspect number one.

Samantha looked up at Principal Moore. "Principal Moore, you of all people should understand with all of our education, we capable to using our knowledge in many different ways. Plus, we are like Secret Service people. We have to be observant, detail oriented and willing to put our self between our students and danger. That's why I'm a consultant for the police department. Now, excuse me, I need to work on police business."

10

SURPRISE

Police Chief Patterson left the school with a smile on his face until he remembered he needed to meet with Superintendent Worthington's parents. As he called their number he hoped they were in town. After numerous rings someone answered the phone in voice of an elderly person. Patterson asked. "Am I speaking to Mr. Worthington?"

"No, whom may I say is calling?" the wobbly voice asked in a now strange accent.

"I'm Police Chief Path Patterson." He couldn't tell if the person was a woman with a mustache or a wizardly old very effeminate man. With his luck, the person's name would be either Pat or Chris.

"They are traveling in Europe right now. May I tell them the purpose of your call?" A brittle voice asked.

"It is extremely important that I speak with Mr. Worthington." Irritated, Patterson wanted to keep the mystery person on the phone until he arrived at Worthington's house.

"I'll tell them you called. They will get back to you, Mr. Path." The voice slammed the phone down.

"Thank you" Patterson said to the air. Something wasn't right. Without a siren, he sped to the old money section of River Bend with its large mansions, winding driveways and manicured yards. Upper income families from the city had moved into the area and had revitalized some of the homes. Worthington's home was a Gothic Revival and appeared to be well maintained. He left his car down on the street and jogged up the drive to the house. He was in military mode ready to attack. Ornate glass panels dressed the sides of the heavy paneled wood front door. When he peeked through the distorted glass, he was shocked. A scantily dressed very young woman romantically locked in the arms of a middle aged man. The strong jawed man resembled Superintendent Worthington with deep-set eyes and straight black hair. His bronze surfer's complexion was different from Worthington's pale porcelain complexion. Surely the young lady wasn't the Superintendent Worthington's mother, maybe a step-mother. The man looked too young to be the Superintendent's father. So who were these people?

Patterson pushed the button and the sound of great cathedral bells boomed interrupting the couple. The woman scurried off wearing what looked like a training bra and short-shorts. The man grabbed his shirt. Neither one glanced at the door. Patterson positioned himself in front of the wood door in an at-ease stance and waited. Finally, the door opened slightly. The man assessed Patterson with a smug look on his handsome face. Patterson could tell at first sight the man with rugged good looks and skunk breath had a problem or two. One, the age of his girlfriend and two, what right did he have to be in the Worthington's house?

Snobbery and disgust combined in his voice as he asked. "What do you want? Collecting for the Policemen's Ball?"

This angered Patterson more, "I'm here to talk to Mr. or Mrs. Timmons Worthington about their daughter."

"What has Bunny done now?" The man uttered a harsh laugh.

"Who are you, the butler?" Patterson felt for his handcuffs and hoped he got to use them.

"No, I'm Lana Worthington's nephew, her sister's only child, Nick Chase, of the Chase Manhattan Bank Chases. That is all you, a small, backward town cop needs to know. Plus, I'm her professional house sitter." He patted his puffed chest and giggled.

Patterson clicked his heels and reached for his gun. "I need proof that you have the right to be here. You either get your aunt on the phone and let me talk to her or I'm taking you to jail. You will be there until I find out the truth. It is my duty to protect the people and the property of River Bend."

Placing his hand on the door jamb to steady himself. Nick Chase bent in laughter. "I am not showing you anything. I told you who I am Nicolas Chase of Chase Manhattan Bank. That is all you need to know." "Well, this small town cop is taking you and your friend to the police station." Patterson snapped the cuffs on Nick's arm and flipped him to the wall. He followed the same routine and handcuffed the scantly clothed girlfriend. He led them down the driveway and into his car. He called Sheila and asked her to send officers Alex and J.T. out to process the Worthington's house.

When the officers arrived he explained. "This is a home invasion case. Collect fingerprints and photograph any areas that shows missing objects. Don't let anyone in the house. Don't forget the silver drawer. Stay here until I return. Don't let anyone in the house."

Patterson drove off with his two prisoners wedged in the backseat of his Nissan Frontier truck. By the time Nick and his girlfriend arrived at the police station, Nick begged Patterson to take all of his information, but, it was too late. He gave Nick Chase and his girlfriend the complete common criminal treatment. He took their fingerprints, their mug shots and gave them each a jail designer outfit. He reminded them at every opportunity they were getting the top end jail spa treatment and they were now shabby chic. He knew he could only hold them legally for twenty-four hours. That would give him time to find answers, hopefully. Sheila was to call him immediately if she got Worthington's parents on the phone.

Patterson called Alex to check on their progress.

"Well, Patterson, the investigation revealed that as far as we can tell only small items are missing. There are about ten areas on the walls that showed paintings had once hung there\ until recently. The area were the paintings hung is much darker the rest of the wall, shows recent removal. The bookshelves had spaces between antique books that were dust free, as if books were recently removed from the shelf. We found three large bags of recreational drugs. Apparently Nick Chase has been holding daily Open Drug House at the Worthingtons."

"Close the house and the grounds to the visitors for the next twenty-four hours. I need you and J.T. to photograph the visitors and their license plates before you turn them away. This will help us identify

Nick's associates. I plan to send all of the photographs to Mr. and Mrs. Worthington."

Patterson's conspiracy theory: *Nick, the cousin, killed Superintendent Worthington to keep her quiet about his stealing from her parents and to cut her out of her father's estate.*

11

LOST IN TRANSLATION

Sitting straight backed Patterson inhaled the smell of freshly cut hay as he drove down the road to Pretty Prairie. He loved the smell. It reminded him of summers with his grandparents eating freshly cut watermelon. It was the best of times during his childhood and the worst of times. With his arm out the window, he let the warm fall air calm him. It reminded him of Samantha. How she showed him how to be aware of his total environment by using all his senses. That he could discover clues by being more cognizant of the surroundings. *I'm getting soft. Civilian life is all touchy feely – but Samantha does find clues. Need to focus.*

He called Sheila, the stick with a Brillo pad dispatcher. "Sheila, would you call AAA Home Guard Company? Tell them to turn off the alarm to Worthington's house at 34 Sunflower Drive in Pretty Prairie. Call me back to confirm."

A moment later his phone beeped, "Yes"

"Sheila, your dispatcher here. The *Triple-A* guy will meet you at the house in a few minutes. They have to do a visual check before they turn off the alarm."

"Okay. Did Nick Chase give you usable phone number?" Patterson asked.

"Yes, but the phone number that idiot gave me was to a hotel in Italy. I called the hotel. The hotel manager said Mr. and Mrs. Worthington had been there but left just hours ago. They were on a tour and would be back sometime next week." Sheila paused to catch her breath.

Patterson jumped in, "Did they give you a phone number or a place where you can reach them?"

"No. They told me they were not a small motel. Hung up on me. I told him I was the police in the United States. He didn't care. Speaking of police, the girl that's with Nick Chase is an under aged runaway from Sage county. Old Nick is dating a milk carton kid." She hung up on Patterson.

A bright yellow truck with flashing lights roared down the street. AAA Home Guard was written in extra-large black letters on the side of the truck. A big burly man lumbered out of the truck with his phone to his ear. "Yep, it's the police. Sure I'm sure. Okay, turn the alarm off." He walked up to the door and nodded to Patterson. He placed his body between Patterson and the door and punched in the code. He stepped back, "I'll be in the truck until you're done, then I'll lock up."

Superintendent Worthington's house was one of the newer houses in the Pretty Prairie development. Sharp lines in a profile similar to that of a well-made paper airplane. Worthington's minimalist taste manifested itself in the house's design. Startling white with a zillion windows, the house visually snapped, crackled and popped. On a sunny day a person could see the glow from the sun hitting the windows from everywhere. Patterson listened for the sound of the doorbell. It was a simple, deep, very audible reverberated 'bong'. No one answered. He gingerly opened the door and placed one foot over the threshold.

"Hello, anyone here? This is the police. Anyone here?"

Gradually Patterson entered the house his hand on his gun, ready. The entrance had stark white marble with white carpeting in the main living area. Should I take my shoes off? He wondered. Cautiously, he listened for any sound. Faintly he heard humming and the sound of a vacuum somewhere to the right. Could it be the killer cleaning up after himself? Or someone else house sitting? Stealthily he crept along the wall of windows. He needed a plan. His plan was to sneak up and see why there was a person in the house. A nice, clean, one-man plan. A single door separated him from a potential killer. Silently he pushed it open. A statuesque young woman with long shimmering black hair with earphones hummed and swayed to the music as she vacuumed the floor. What to do now? She didn't know he was in the house. She could be armed and dangerous. His mother told him never trust a woman with a vacuum. He decided to jog around to the back of the house and knocked on the window.

After several knocks, the woman looked at the window and saw Police Chief Patterson. She looked like somebody that had been struck by lightning. She froze as if paralyzed at first. Then looked both directions as if she wanted to run. Her luminous black eyes wide and innocent revealed her inner fear as she bravely opened the door. Fear enhanced her accent when she spoke. "Yes, May I help you?"

"I'm Police Chief Patterson I am here to -" But he never finished his sentence before her hysteric started.

"No, oh, No, you are here to send me to Mexico. She told you to come and get me. Yes?" Tears flowed. The woman's body shook. Her beautiful face twisted in anguish.

Patterson quickly assessed the situation. She worked illegally for Worthington. So what did she mean by 'she told you to come and get me?'

The woman repeated over and over, "Oh, my Ramon works at the school building. Important job."

"Henry, I need you to bring Ramon to Superintendent Worthington's house. Now Please. The address is 34 Sunflower Drive in the Pretty Prairie. Call me if you get lost. Henry blasts the siren, put the lights on. Speed out here." Patterson hoped hadn't Henry heard his panic.

Patterson tried to inspect while he waited. By all appearances, everything had a place and nothing appeared out of place. '*Clean. Very clean.*' A quote from the movie: Lawrence of Arabia came into his mind: *Bentley asked, 'What is it, Major Lawrence, that attracts you personally to the desert?' Lawrence replies, 'It's clean.' Bentley: 'Well, now, that's a very illuminating answer.'*

Minutes felt like hours as he checked each room looking for clues. Ramon's wife followed him crying. In between sob he heard, "No, please. No, Mexico."

Ramon jumped out of the still moving car and sprinted into the house. He folded his wife into his arms and spoke soothingly to her.

Henry followed Ramon, listened to the couple and then spoke in rapid Spanish.

Patterson wrote down a need to know list and handed it to Henry. *Who knows that Angela worked at Worthington's on Thursday? How about the neighbors? Any problems with anyone? Was Angela an American citizen? Did this have anything to do with Worthington's death?*

Henry asked the questions. When he had finished with the questions he grabbed Patterson's elbow and walked with Patterson to his truck. "Ramon said Worthington was blackmailing them because Angela isn't legal. First, Worthington made his wife into her non-paid house-keeper. Later, Worthington tried to bully Angela into having a baby for her. Angela kept saying, 'No'. Worthington threatened to call immigration. Ramon begged me not to tell, because you would think he had a reason to kill Worthington."

"Well, he is correct, Henry. But, he was already a suspect. He supposedly found the body. Now he and his wife are both suspects. You need to find out their alibi for Wednesday night."

Patterson drove off. Focused on the landscape as he drove through Pretty Prairie. "What did Samantha say about Pretty Prairie? Oh, yes, their yards looked like they were painted from a child watercolor box. All the women were skinny, all the men cheated and all the children looked alike. Or something liked that. Who's your daddy? Snobby civilians. And I have to stop talking to myself."

12

COVERT DINING

Normally, Samantha worked while she ate at her desk during lunch. But, today she dined with the other teachers in hopes of hearing gossip about Superintendent Worthington. Today was her lucky day she found two sixth grade teachers eating in the teachers' lounge. They smiled and said 'hello' to her and continued their talk.

One of the teachers had been Samantha's sixth grade teacher. She remembered with fondness Mrs. Brown had been very kind when she started school in the middle of the year. Mrs. Brown had been a first year teacher. Then her name had been Miss Adams. The kids nicknamed her Miss Horse-face. Mrs. Brown continued telling Ms. Long. "I'm not ready to retire. I don't want to relocate. I can't help it if I'm not a good visual. I don't want to be replaced. That's what Worthington said to me, 'you're not a good visual we plan to replace you.' My son's a lawyer and I'm talking to him about Wednesday night's meeting. See if I have any chance against that evil woman."

Ms. Long patted her friend's hand and smirked. "I heard Bess Burton had an appointment with the superintendent, too. She just knew she had been nominated for the Teacher of the Year award. I wonder how she handled being told the district had nominated her to be relocated or retired instead."

"She wasn't the only one who thought they had been nominated for that award. We all thought that, too. What a slap in our faces. Hate that bitch…" Mrs. Brown wiped a tear away from her thin concave face and changed the subject to a student with academic problems.

Samantha sent Patterson a text with the information about Wednesday night's teacher's meeting.

13

WHO DIDN'T KILL SUPERINTENDENT WORTHINGTON?

After reading the text Patterson contemplated the people who had reasons to kill Superintendent Worthington? On that note, he decided to call Jim and to check on things.

Jim spoke in fast forward. "Yes, sir, I have interviewed and finger printed everyone who works in this building, except for the Superintendent's secretary. Henry and Ramon finally made it back. Mrs. Steinem seems upset that Janet isn't here. No one knows anything about Janet. Like where she lives or anything. Also, you know the question you asked me to ask everyone about how Worthington got along with others. Most of them as look away then look back with a smile pasted on their faces. And tell me how much they loved Superintendent Worthington. She's the best --"

Patterson wrote and then shook his head. "Fingerprinted? Why?"

"Well, sir, it did happen in the building. Also, we have all of the teachers' fingerprints in our system. It's a state requirement. So, I thought we needed to have office staff, too. Doctor Ackerman's assistant will take all of the new finger prints and compare them with the ones they found in Worthington's office. So, we can narrow down who had been in Worthington's office."

"On target, Jim. Keep me up to date on your findings. I'm heading to Janet Monroe's mother's house. I hope it won't be like the last two places. It was crazy. I have simple questions. All I need are with simple answers."

The address placed Janet Monroe's house in the poorest of River Bend's poor areas. Located north of the old warehouse area. The area had once been where the workers from the brick factories, river boats workers and the general laborers built their homes. Back then it had been the poor but good hard working families' area. Now, it was the poor barely working families' area. The Monroe's house backed up to the cliff overlooking the river. The yard needed mowing. The house needed painting. Garbage needed picked up, and there were parts of toys everywhere. But the view was breath taking.

Out of habit Patterson placed his hand on his gun and knocked on the door. A small thin woman with bright red lipstick and dirty blonde hair pulled up into a loose bun opened the door. Her blouse slipped provocatively off her bony shoulder.

"Are you Posey Jones, the mother of Janet Monroe?" Patterson tried to appear friendly. He was trying to act less military and more civilian in hopes this woman would cooperate with him.

"Yes, I am. Oh, my, I haven't had the police here since Vernon was police chief. Purely social, you know...." She beamed up with a gaping hole in her teeth. "Is this social call, too?" She ogled him up and down like a cat ready to pounce on an injured bird.

Patterson did a quick heel snap which snapped him back into military mode. "No, Ma'am. I'm here to talk to your daughter Janet Monroe. May I speak with her now?"

A cackle erupted from the woman. "Janet doesn't live here anymore. If you expect a good time with my little Janet, you better just stay here with me. She would shoot you if you tried anything. Didn't like my line of work. But dear girl sends me money every month."

"Do you know where she lives?" Patterson was taken back by Posey Jones being a prostitute and a mother. He had never dealt with a prostitute in the army. Thought they were a big city problem. He realized it would cost him to find out her daughter's address.

"How much for that information?" He pulled out his wallet.

"Well, let me see." She smiled up at him and held out her hand.

"Is twenty dollars enough?" He asked.

"Sure, if you promise to come back to play later."

He placed the twenty on her hand. He asked again, "The address, please."

In a flash, she stepped back and slammed the door closed. Through the closed door she hooted. "Got-ya- Don't know her address. She won't give it to me. Afraid I'll move in and bring all my kids with me."

Patterson clenched his teeth and started to march back to his car. As he stepped down his foot slid. A vomit smell drifted up. He looked down. He had stepped on a used diaper. Yuck squirted out of the diaper hidden under sticks and leaves on the ground. "Who would leave a diaper full of poop hidden in the yard? That crazy woman inside that house who took twenty dollars from me, that's who. Her idea of a burglar alarm. I am not in the army anymore, hum."

What next? Patterson pulled off his shoe and hopped into his truck. Some of the poop had splattered on his pants legs. He felt slimed. He needed The Poop Busters.

14

A SECRET AND A WHISPER

Samantha drove the Escalade over the hills, through the woods and across the streams straight to her house on Seven Sisters' Road. It was lovely fall day, the trees were changing color and the air had a crisp earthy smell. Samantha patted Bo as she chatted about her day. "Patterson is taking me to the city tomorrow to have my brain, I mean my migraine, checked out. He made old Mrs. Moore find a sub for me. Told her it was police business. That means you and I can sleep-in tomorrow. Plus, he is bringing us dinner tonight. Yes, Bo food for you, too."

Samantha looked down at Bo and saw his teary eyes. His little leg was extended as far as it could reach, just to touch her. She shook her head. "Oh, Bo don't make me cry, but I'm afraid the doctor can't fix this. My mother had bad headaches. So bad they made her go crazy. Don't tell anyone, Bo, about my mother." Tears dropped on to her lap and Bo's paw.

Samantha held her breath as she topped the last hill before descending the muddy road to the front of her house. The city's work crew had the entire road covered with dirt and rock. Which meant the sewer line was beside her property? The days of the commercial outhouse decorating her front porch were numbered.

But the trench across her yard was still there. She grabbed Bo, slid out of the Escalade and jumped the trench. "Bo, we need to hurry. Patterson will be here soon with our food."

They both hopped up the steps and into the house. Bo went over to his water dish and looked down it empty. Samantha filled it from the five-gallon container sitting on her cabinet. The container was half full, enough to last until she refilled it on Saturday.

Gravel crunched outside. Patterson had arrived and Samantha opened the door for him. A dull eyed Patterson stood in her doorway. He trudged into her house carrying a basket full of delicious smelling food. Garlic, ginger, and soy smells floated through and filled her home. She loved Chinese food almost as much as pizza. Bo jumped up and down. He put food on the small yellow table in the kitchen.

Patterson slowly looked around. "More furniture since I was here. Looks good. But, is there a Johnny-on-the-Spot on your porch? Why? New idea for the 'in' look in county living?"

"No, it isn't the new look for country living. My septic tank died then backed up in to my house. Now, I have to have all new plumbing to match the new sewer system the city is putting in along my property. I'm sorry." Her tears lurked.

He picked up Bo and put his arms around Samantha. "Why didn't you tell me?"

Samantha wondered what he was talking about she hadn't seen him in months. She was old school and had waited for the gentleman to call when he didn't she figured he wasn't interested in her. And now, he is all caring. What happened to stone man? Normally he was very reserved. She rested her head on his chest. Despite the starched fabric and the hard muscled body, she felt safe. Peace filled her. She leaned against him for a few minutes and felt like butter against warm toast, yum. Whoa, quickly she backed away her eyes wide open and her mouth ajar. *Compassion and caring, Patterson? Oh, me.* Awkward moment. Quickly Samantha started removing the various containers from the basket. The stranger who had taken over Patterson's body pointed with the chopsticks and explained what each one contained.

"This is like opening presents at Christmas time." Samantha scrunched up her shoulders in delight.

"What did you do with your day after your ordeal at my school?" Samantha wanted to know the real reason he had visited her school. Old robot man didn't do social calls. Especially to a workplace.

"Well, I after I got molested by your principal. I went to The Worthington's house. Disrupted a love-nest of potential home invaders there. Scared the superintendent's cleaning lady. Got to know Mrs. Steinem from the board office. Oh and my favorite. I stepped in baby poop in Janet Monroe's mother's yard."

"And how do you know that is was baby poop?" Fear seized Samantha's heart. Suppose he already had a family. Whoa, I need to focus on why all the visits relating to Superintendent Worthington?

"Well," He puffed out his chest and leaned back in the chair, with a smirk on his face - a dramatic pause. "When the Army deployed my sister's husband to Iraq. She and her two kids stayed with my mom. They thought it would be fun to teach me how to change diapers. Man, babies can really poop. The smell makes your Johnny-on-the-Spot smell like a rose garden."

His face twisted in disgust. He decided to change the subject. "Have you checked on things downstairs yet?"

"Not after I had the cleaning people come and clean up the Yuk. The plumbers have been working down there. So I stayed away." Dread filled Samantha.

Patterson jumped up and trooped down the steps. Samantha reluctantly followed him into the basement. The once clean, light grey painted floor and walls were now stained a light brown up to a foot high on the walls.

"Thanks to your help all of Pop's stuff was containers and should be safe down here. I had to hire the disaster clean-up crew to come out and clean up the basement before the plumbers would even look in it."

He stood back in awe at the devastation, all the pipes, copper ones, rusty brown ones were all cut off or dangling in the air like giant strings. The cement floor had the Grand Canyon chiseled across it. White dust covered everything. Through pressed lips words erupted. "I remember when we finished putting all of the Rubbermaid containers down here. You danced around and hugged me. Now this."

The word Records on one of the containers caught Patterson's eye. "May I look in there? I don't remember seeing this before."

Samantha took the opportunity to check out Pops' stuff to make sure it really was okay and to find out about Superintendent Worthington.

"Sure look in any of the containers. While we are here, I'm going to check on Pops' stuff, too. Speaking of checking on things has something happened to Superintendent Worthington? I mean you seem to be running around to places that involve her. She hasn't absconded with all of the tax payers' money. Has she?"

Patterson paused then ignored her question for the time being. She was a suspect. Was she pretending to not know what happened to Worthington? Or was she innocent? Tax payers' money what was that about? He continued to open the container. Much to his delight he discovered old records in their original cardboard sleeves. "Now, this is like Christmas. Kenny Rogers, Benny Goodman. Your grandfather had great taste. Oh, for a record player"

Samantha pointed up high on the shelf, "There's one up there. Go for it."

He removed the phonograph and headed to the stairs.

"Hey, please help me restack some of these containers. Then we will go upstairs, have some wine and listen to music. We can discuss your day some more. I hope the turntable works. Everything else seems to be okay." Samantha smiled. She still had Pops' stuff. As long as she had part of her grandfather around, she would be okay.

Patterson cleaned the turntable. Checked to see if it worked on a Lionel Richie record. It worked. An idea, no, his reoccurring dream, came to him. Stealthy he moved across the room, turned on the fireplace, dimmed the lights and started the song that was perfect for only Samantha. 'Lady'. Gently he seized her hand, pulled her into his arms and held her. Hardly breathing, they swayed to the lilting music. He mouthed the song into Samantha's hair. Samantha pressed against his chest and thought. *As in the song, he is like my knight in shining armor.* Both smiled and moved as one. His lips touched her ear. He whispered.

"About Superintendent Worthington, well. We have a case."

15

FIRST JOB ON THE NEW CASE

Life was wonderful. Six o'clock in the morning and Samantha was still in bed, unheard for a typical work day morning. She stretched and snuggled down into her cushy bed and pulled the duvet up over her head. She listened to birds singing and the breeze blowing through the trees outside through her opened bedroom window. Oh, the intoxicating earthy fall aroma as if Mother Earth opened her arms and hugged the world before hibernating. Samantha decided to add more delicious smells to the air by cooking eggs and making coffee.

While breakfast cooked she quickly washed her hair using the small plastic tub in the kitchen sink. She poured water again and again to get the soap out of her hair. She watered her few plants with the soapy water. Pioneering wasn't as much fun as she had thought it would be. Comfortably dressed in her skinny jeans she could finally fit into, and a soft yellow sweater with a scarf. She brushed her damp hair into a pony tail. On a whim, she pulled her high-heeled boots on. Finally, she packed Bo's blanket for his stay at Katherine's.

The crunching sound outdoors meant Patterson had pulled into the driveway. She watched him march toward her house dressed in his police uniform, shoes shined and talking on his phone. *Wow, he can talk and walk at the same time.* She envied that skill. She listened to the one-sided conversation as he made his way to her front door. Held the door open just a smidge so it wasn't too obvious that she was dipping on his conversation.

"What do you mean someone broke into the Board of Education building? Nothing was stolen? They only went into the superintendent's office? How do you know? Tape down, door unlocked and open. I see. All the other office doors were locked? Nothing missing elsewhere? What were they looking for? No I don't expect you know either. I want just you, Henry, Roger and Ramon in that building. What do you mean it's full of people? They had keys. Keys, who gives keys to idiots. That means any of them or all of them could be the guilty party. Finger print anyone who hasn't been fingerprinted. Video everyone then, kick them out. We will go over the video for abnormalities. You know who's there that shouldn't be. Or who's missing. Dust the damn office for prints - again. Has the superintendent's secretary shown up yet? Get Steinem to find out where she lives or lived. Janet what's her name could be dead, too. What about Henry? Oh, the Reyes' alibi was they were together with their little boy. Of course, that's an air tight alibi. Not! Damn..." He growled.

Patterson hung up but kept talking to himself. "Civilians are idiots. They run amuck. I should have stayed in the army. I had order and control there. How am I to find the killer when the idiots continue to contaminate the crime area? And no one has an alibi. They can't all be guilty. Or can they?"

He clicked his heels, "hum" and went into his military mode as he tapped on Samantha's door.

It opened. Samantha and Bo peeked around the door. "I'm sorry I was listening to your conversation. You need to go back to work. I can drive myself to the doctor's appointment. Go on. You're needed here."

"Nope, Jim can handle it. He's the assistant police chief. He can do this on his own. Bo, let's go, buddy." Patterson patted his leg and Bo jumped into his arms.

"We are ready. Forgot to tell you Bo goes to Katherine's. It's just a little out of the way. Sorry." Samantha could feel a headache starting. She was imposing on him. She hated imposing on anyone. Nervously, she smoothed her hair and discovered something that she could have gone a lifetime without finding. There was soapy glob located at the base of her head. Of course, it was today when someone would be looking at my head. What should I do? The tightening in her head started. No headache. Relax, ignore it and leave. She noticed that he was talking about something. She looked at him strangely.

"What did you say? I'm sorry I didn't hear you."

"Bo is going with us. I'm the chief of police. I can do this if I so choose." With his nose in the air, he daintily tripped his way to the police truck, nothing like blades of grass to cause a person to almost fall.

When the truck door shut, the engine roared to life. They were off. Patterson was the only person who could drive down a gravel road and not stir up a dust storm. Samantha had a ten o'clock morning appointment, not ten o'clock tonight. Her leg twitched uncontrollably. She wanted to reach over and gun the car. They needed to get going.

"Samantha, remember how you and your friends helped out on the Roth case?"

She nodded her head. Excitement filled her at the thought of crime fighting once again.

"Well, I have something I need for you to do for me. Can you three find the superintendent's secretary? No one knows her address. Apparently she's a loner. She's either a suspect or a victim. We need to find her." He drove intently down the road with his jaw jutted out. It was against police protocol for civilians to help on a case, but the school system protected its own. He felt at war with the civilians.

Samantha sent a text to Gin and Katherine. One or both would know where Janet lived. The three of them viewed Janet as a phoenix rising out of poverty with a crazy prostitute mother. Janet had raised herself. Samantha, Gin and Katherine would protect Janet if she needed it.

"I have named the three of you. Fitting I feel. The Good, the Bad and the Scary."

He blurted out and then went back to his military mode.

Samantha twisted her lips. That wasn't funny and he has gone military on me. Now, I can't get any info on what happened to Superintendent Worthington.

16

VETERINARIANS ARE DOCTORS

The City's traffic had increased since the last time Samantha had been there, of course it would. It had been years since Samantha had visited. She noted that the number of highways and the number of lanes hadn't changed. So, when Patterson putt-putted along on the packed four lane highway during rush hour he created the mass hysteria. Drivers dashed up beside them, honked their horns and waved obscene gestures at them and zipped on. Each one with hate in their eyes were vindicated once they expressed their anger. He ignored them and continued to amble down the road. Samantha worried. *Can't he get a ticket for driving too slowly? Maybe he's exempt because he's the police.*

Samantha focused on locating the hospital signs along the way. Finally, they drove into City General's parking garage and found a place close to the elevators. Thinking that would make it easier to find the truck later. The parking garage was a breeze to navigate; the inside of the hospital was a different story. It was maze with a zillion signs all pointing in some obscure direction. Plastered against the wall trying to locate a person to help them, fear in their eyes, Bo barked and sniffed the air. They followed the direction of the arrow and located the information desk. Manned by a woman with a smirk and donut crumbs on her purple polka dotted blouse. She checked her computer then handed

Samantha a yellow circle. "Follow the yellow circles, not the yellow triangle or square, just the circle." She pointed to their circle. "If you get lost follow the yellow circles back here and restart."

Out of earshot Samantha whispered. "This is crumby. What a zoo. Thanks Bo for your help, but no donuts."

"I feel like Dorothy in the Wizard of Oz." Samantha clicked her heels and clutched the yellow circle.

"Hum, I feel like a preschooler. Do they think we are idiots? They hand us a circle like we didn't know what a circle looked like." Patterson click his heels.

He carried Bo and marched down the hall following the yellow circle. Samantha walked close beside him. They weren't the usual nondescript couple. Bo's presence made them special. A hospital security guard walked towards them. He nodded and pointed to his badge and said, "Service dog"

The man went wild with whooping, "He's no service dog. It needs to leave. Go and wait in the car."

A man on a mission, Patterson walked on. Samantha felt the headache waiting for a chance to explode. It zapped her causing her to tremble. He leaned against her. "It's okay Samantha. I know what I am doing. Trust me, please."

Samantha remembered her ex-husband had expected her to trust him. *Look where that got me? Patterson hadn't expected me to trust him. He had asked and asked nicely.*

"I wish I had my pedometer. We must have walked three miles at least. If I had known, I was doing a marathon I wouldn't have worn high heel boots." Now she had pain both in her head and in her feet. Finally, they were in front of the door of Doctor Millard, neurologist. *Great, now he will confirm the fact I will go crazy, just like my mother.*

They entered the room. The receptionist took one look at Bo. She pointed at the door. Patterson pointed to his badge. Sternly she pointed to the door. "I don't care about your badge get that dog out of here. Now…"

He prepared for one on one combat – gritted his teeth. "Doctor Ackerman told me to bring Bo with us for medical reasons."

With scorn she responded. "Did he now? I'll check."

He whipped out his phone and raced her to get to Dr. Ackerman first. "Patterson here. There's a problem Doctor Ackerman."

He handed the phone to the receptionist. She spoke. "Oh, I see. Yes, sir. Fine!"

All eyes in the waiting room focused on the interaction. Patterson and the receptionist had locked virtual horns. Using only her finger tips with distain she handed the phone back to him. "The three of you need to sit and stay or no doggy treats for any of you."

The wait seemed to last for hours. Finally, nurse in blue scrubs with prints of brains all over her top lead them back into the unknown. She weighed Samantha, measured her height and checked her blood pressure. "The doctor will be right in," and she left the room.

Samantha had decided to question Patterson about Superintendent Worthington's case while they waited. Unfortunately, a tall, balding man with hunched shoulder, and a baggy white coat entered the room seconds after the nurse left. "I'm Doctor Millard. I'm the head of the head department. Inside joke. Head of the neurological department. Dr. Ackerman said this was an emergency. What seems to be the problem?" He directed his attention to Patterson.

Samantha cleared her throat and told him about the headaches. Explained how they were getting more frequent and more intense.

"Describe what you feel, see and hear when you get one of these headaches."

Samantha described the tightening sensation and then a volcano in her head. Every sound caused more pain, and then blindness.

He typed all this into his computer. "Any falls or accidents lately?"

"My car blew up and came down very close to me a few months ago. Doctor Evans said it caused a concussion."

"And who is this Doctor Evans?" Watery blue eyes studied Samantha.

"My dog's vet. . ." She looked lamely down at her hands.

"Why didn't you go to a human doctor? Then, maybe you wouldn't be here wasting my time."

"A vet is just as good or bad as a human doctor. The same amount of schooling." The ugly giant stirred in her head. Her scalp tightened and crawled. The bright light in the office made her eyes squint and water.

Samantha trembled and wanted out of there before it was too late and the monster would attack her head again.

Doctor Millard noticed Samantha's eye movement and her reaction to the lights. "Are you having a headache, now?"

"One just started."

So infuriated by the doctor's attitude Patterson piped in, "She and her dog were both shot. A vet will take care of a human, but a human doctor will NOT take care of a dog. So, I took them to the vet. Now, you need to take care of her and don't waste my time." He tapped his badge.

Doctor Millard looked Patterson up and down with contempt, but he continued. "Are you under more stress than usual?"

Samantha grimaced when shrugged her shoulders. "Don't know."

Patterson lost it. "Samantha. Emphatically, yes. She is under tons of stress. I'll tell you. Her home had just been completely remodeled. When her septic tank quit and backed up into her basement. All the pipes had to be replaced to attach to the new city sewer system. There isn't any plumbing in her home, no water, toilet, or shower. She has a Johnny-on-the-Spot on her front porch. She works for this hideous principal who molested my arm. And a student mooned her class. While she was teaching. Something else is bothering her. She won't tell me." Silence followed by a sense of demand in the air. He thought, *I want Samantha fixed, now. Wasting that doctor's time. Ha, that doctor has wasted my time.*

He just tapped his badge.

"Okay, I see. Any one of those things could cause migraines. I need to run some tests, a MRI and blood work first. It will take an hour to get all that done. Then come back here. We will discuss the results.

17

THE FINDINGS

The nurse escorted the three of them to the lab area. The starched figure at the lab looked at Bo and started to speak. Patterson just pointed to his badge. Samantha twisted her sweater. She wanted to hold Bo and she wanted him to stop pointing at his badge. Locked in her personal hell, she just twisted her sweater, unable to talk just like her mother had done.

Patterson jumped up and started to follow when they took Samantha to have the MRI. The nurse in the severely starch nurse's suit smirked and said while she pointed to her badge. "No Dogs or Police Chief, in with the patient during the MRI. We will take good care of her, sir."

Samantha paused at the door and glanced back at Bo and Patterson. She slowly entered into an epic nightmare. First, they gave her a hospital gown with indecent exposure then they took her clothes and showed her a room out of a sci-fi horror movie. She laid on the sliding table and slowly entered into a small tight space with flashing lights and a heart monitor sound. The pounding in her head intensified and nausea nestled in the back of her throat. She had to face this unknown alone. Knowing Patterson would take Bo when she became crazy made her feel better. The machine pounding caused pounding in her head to match beat for beat. Fear had its ugly grip on her. Focus on anything, like dancing to *Lady* with Patterson. She prayed.

His brown eyes were dark blanks and his lips straight and tight. He had entered into his lock-down mode, no emotions – just focus. Patterson sit, stayed and held Bo tight. His phone rang, at first, it startled him. "What?"

"Sheila your dispatcher. Got information about Nick Chase's alibi. The Sage County Sheriff called. Wednesday night, when Superintendent Worthington was killed, Nick was in jail. Nick had been arrested at eleven o'clock in the morning at their local bar for fighting. They released him Thursday about five in the afternoon. So, he didn't kill Worthington."

"Released him on Thursday. You said. What about his milk-jug girlfriend? Where was she? Sheila, I need you to have her tell you her alibi. Then check it out. If it is okay. Call the police department in Sage County. Tell them to come and get her." Patterson mindlessly clicked off the phone and entered his military trance. Where he felt in control.

Numbly Samantha entered into Dr. Millard's office prepared to handle the worst. The nurse retrieved Bo and Patterson from the lounge and brought them to Dr. Millard's office. The three waited all were lost in fear. Bo shook.

Dr. Millard lumbered in and plopped down. "Well, Mrs. Grant, judging from your MRI. Dr. Ue, the radiologist, and I saw that you have two bruises. One bruise is a recent bruise and its sizable bruise. We are curious about an old scar it's from a very serious injury. Everything else looks fine. I don't have your blood results yet; I don't foresee any problems. If there is something, then we will call you. Right now, I'm putting you on a low dose of blood thinner. No activity where you can get hurt. No jumping or anything that will jar your brain for month. I want you back in a month. Then we will do another MRI. You need to have your blood tested every other week to make sure we aren't thinning your blood too much or not thinning it enough. Before you leave. I need to know for the record, where and when did you have a serious accident?"

"How serious do you mean?"

"Life threating serious." Dr. Milliard frowned at her.

"I don't know. I was in a car wreck when I was younger about nineteen years ago. But, that was a long time ago. Is that what you mean?"

Dr. Millard looked down at an image and scrunched up his face. "There's sizable scar tissue from a deep bruise. What did the doctors do for you after you were in the wreck?"

"I don't think anything. They made my mother and me go to the hospital for a few days. That was it. I need to ask a question." Samantha hung her head and spoke to her hands. She didn't wait for him to respond. She had to know. "My mother, after the car wreck, had very bad headaches where she couldn't see, move or do anything but scream. Just like the ones I'm starting to have. She just stopped doing anything and went, ah, crazy. Is that going to happen to me?" A tear rolled down her cheek.

Patterson and Dr. Millard stared at her, open mouthed, not believing what she had asked. He tensed his body, showed no emotion or feelings. He had to let her speak. Had to let her get it all out. His body shook. He wanted to hold her and make it all better.

Dr. Millard looked away, then answered very cautiously, "What was your mother's behavior before the car wreak?"

"She had been happy, full of life and our lives were wonderful. Then after the car wreck, that killed my father and sister, she changed. It banged us up, especially my mother. They took us to the hospital. We stayed a day or two. I don't remember. We took a taxi to our apartment. That was the last thing my mother did to take care of me. Finally, I called my grandfather to come and get us. We moved in with my grandparents."

"I don't have her medical records in front of me. Odds are she had a more complicated concussion than you. You were younger and kids heal quicker and better. For an adult a concussion left untreated can cause a person to shut down. Plus, you throw in depression. She wasn't crazy, but to a kid she probably seemed that way. No, you aren't going crazy, not from this anyway." Dr. Millard leaned back and thought for a minute.

"Do you know where you lived at the time of the accident? Or where you were when the accident happened?"

"No, I don't know the answer to either question. I tried to remember, but I can't. I was eleven years old. I should know where I lived and went school. But I don't. I just know Pops, my grandfather came and got us. He knew where we were. He's gone now."

Samantha covered her face and cried. *I'm not going crazy. Why didn't I ask Pops questions?*

Patterson couldn't take it anymore he bent down beside her. "Oh, Sam, how long have you been worried?" He placed Bo in her arms and held them.

Dr. Millard nodded to the nurse. "Please give her a month worth of Warfarin pills, one-month worth of pain medication. The list of foods not to eat or drink. She needs a follow-up appointment with me in one month."

Then he turned to Patterson. "What's this about the dog and your badge?"

"Dr. Ackerman told me to take Bo for her. If anyone tried to stop us just point to my badge. That way everyone would leave us alone. It worked." He smiled at Dr. Millard and pointed to his badge.

Dr. Millard smirked, "They need to fire the old coot for the things he says and does. But, he's too damn good."

Patterson did not hear one word. Joy filled him. *Samantha's problem was fixable. Thought she had brain tumor like my father. He died from it.* A smile cracked across his normally stoic face.

As they walked miles through the hospital back to his truck, he causally asked. "Hey, Samantha, are you hungry? Want some lunch? Want to sleuth? What do you say?"

18

A Person Can Learn Things if They Read

Patterson drove the police truck to the first fast food drive-thru restaurant he came to. The three ate in the truck because no matter how many times he pointed to his badge no one would let Bo into a restaurant. He planned to update Samantha on their case. And he wanted to persuade her and Bo to help. In his usual sophisticated way, he said, "Ah, Samantha, I need you to impersonate a Worthington. So we can check out the Worthington's condo."

"Sorry what just happened? One minute we were peacefully eating our tacos and the next you want me to impersonate a Worthington. Then unlawfully break-in to the Worthington's condo. Can't you get a search warrant or something? I mean you are the-." She pointed to his badge and laughed.

"Well, no, there was a crime, but they didn't do it. I hope not anyway. Something isn't right. I told you about the nephew, Nick Chase. He said he was their house sitter. I can't prove if he is telling the truth or not. I've tried to call them in Europe. No one will give them a message. Or give me their phone number. I mean it's as if they are hiding from something. Or they could be dead. I thought you like to investigate. But, if you don't want to…" He turned his head so she couldn't see his smile.

They finished their meals and Patterson cautiously drove back onto the four lane highway. The sound of honking horns greeted them as he drove the minimum speed limit to the west side of the city. He exited on to Scenic Drive Road and followed it to the off-set area with classic rock pillars with a scroll ironwork arch with Hathaway Manor written in the arch. A No Trespassing sign was tastefully placed beside the driveway. The elegantly manicured landscape added to the ambiance of wealth. On the left side of the drive was an English cottage with a wood sign identifying it as the Game Keeper Office. On right side of the cottage a heavy iron gate with an entry card machine blocked the drive.

Patterson reminded Samantha of the specific details of his plan. "You need to take Bo with you. He is a beautiful Shih Tzu. Makes you look all rich. That will add to you appearing to be a Worthington."

Police Chief Patterson marched up to the desk area, dinged the bell for service and waited. Samantha wandered over to a display table and picked up the high-end brochure and read. According to the brochure the condos were nestled in a woodland vista that over-looked the river. The professional photographs of the mansions' exterior filled the sleek magazine-like brochure. Eloquently worded inserts provided in-depth details of each mansion and the number and sizes of the condos inside the mansion.

Samantha read part of it to Patterson while he paced. "Location, location, location and the Worthington's had the location. The condos were remodeled mansions built in the last century. Since no two mansions were alike, no two condos are alike. They came in different sizes. The smallest has two bedrooms, two and a half baths and other amenities up to the 'Grande' size which consisted of four plus bedrooms and six bathrooms with an in-laws' suite."

A gentleman with slicked back dark hair, a thin mustache and piercing blue eyes dressed in an English Groundskeeper suit greeted them. He nodded at Police Chief's badge and asked, "May I help you?" Smoothly the Groundskeeper moved over to Samantha touched her elbow and slowly maneuvered them toward the door they had just entered.

Patterson stopped at the door, turned, put a hand on his gun, he clicked his heels, and that ended the maneuvering. With straight lips he spat the words out. "This is Samantha Worthington, a niece to Timmons and Lana Worthington. I need to notify them that their daughter has been murdered. Their niece has tried to help us find them. They are supposedly vacationing in Europe, but they haven't returned any of her calls or the police department's."

He tapped his badge. "She is frantic about them. As this county's police chief I have a right to check their home and make sure they are alright."

The Ground's Keeper's lip lifted on the left side only when he spoke just said "No. The grounds are private property. You don't have a Search Warrant. So, I won't let you on the grounds. Plus, I took them to the airport. They are fine. Sorry to hear about their daughter. But you will have to wait to notify them when they get back."

"Their daughter was murdered. I legally have to notify them. Now!" Patterson clicked his heels and stood at ease.

While the two men engaged in the war of wills. Samantha put Bo on the floor. He nosed around and stopped in front of a large architectural rendering that hung nicely on the wall for everyone to see. It identified the locations of the condos and the amenities. In the side-bar it showed T. Worthington with a bunny beside his name to mark his home. On the map the bunny sign showed the Worthington condo located on the back section of the newly redesigned mansion facing the river. It was located just down the road from the groundskeeper's office. Their condo was on the back side the mansion facing the river. The other two condos in the mansion faced the road. By all appearances the Worthington's had the very best location.

Samantha quietly placed her hand on his arm. "It is fine, Police Chief Patterson. After, I talk with Uncle Tim this person will be looking for another job." Snootiness oozed out of her. She whispered. "Good job." Into Bo's ears as she passed through the door.

Patterson sputtered. "But, this man has to give me the information I need. I am the law." He patted his badge.

"It is okay, Police Chief, come on I can't take any more of this." Samantha patted his arm and led him out the door.

Forlornly Samantha walked to the truck. Patterson opened the door for her and helped her. He trotted around and hopped in and off they went at a slow, dignified speed. Outside the gate, Samantha squealed. "Turn left and take the first street that goes to the river. Hurry."

"Where are we going?" Patterson asked.

"To the Worthington's isn't that the reason we're here?" Samantha and Bo had their heads in her purse and were digging around. "Great, we found it." She held up the tool for breaking into locked places. "This is a beautiful day. I found out I'm not going crazy like my mother and I get to legally break into a house. Well, sort of legally."

Patterson said. "We don't know where they live. We can't break into every condo."

"I read the map on the wall that showed where they live. It faces the river. It's the third mansion inside the compound we just left. According to the map we can drive along the old abandoned railroad rails, climb the cliff to their house and break-in. Easy-peasy, right Bo?"

"Okay, time to put this truck into four-wheel drive. Let's see if it works. Good practice for winter." A smile spread across his face as he pushed the gas pedal.

"WEEE-E you are going over ten miles per hour." Samantha laughed.

19

A Bouncing Good Time

The road disappeared in front of them. The truck ricocheted like a ping pong ball down the hill on the abandon road. Samantha shook her head and tapped Patterson on the arm. "I'm getting out of here and walking. I don't think this ride is what the doctor ordered."

The police truck hydroplaned through the air, landed hard, and bounced at least a dozen times. Patterson's death grip on the steering wheel started to slip. He hung on for dear life as they slid to a stop. A moment passed before they checked the location of their teeth.

Samantha and Bo climbed out of the truck. She watched Patterson flip and flop around with his arms stiff and straight. His body movements reminded her of the Tin Man in the *Wizard of Oz*. *I wonder if he has a heart or is he the real Tin Man. He would be very upset if he knew I about peed watching him drive down the road.*

"Sputter, squawk" His police radio paged him. "Pat –, Patter –n, –I'm here. Yes…" Followed by silence, Patterson stopped the bouncing truck and grimaced. *Wonder if they heard me scream like a little girl.*

He clicked on the 'speak' button, "Patterson here, what's up?"

"It's Jim, not much, still no purse, no phone and no Janet Monroe. Remember Superintendent Worthington's secretary. I caught Mickey Sims sneaking into the superintendent's office. He tried to step through the yellow tape and not disturb it. Had one leg up and over one strip then he got tangled up in the next one. I took a picture of him in his compromising situation. Sims told me he needed a file out of Worthington's office. It was his personal file. He demanded that he be allowed to get it. Oh, how's Samantha. Have you found the Worthington's yet?"

"Nope, no Worthington's. Have Mrs. Steinem go through Superintendent Worthington's office with you. Have her examine the room for anything that might be missing or out of place. Also, check Superintendent Worthington's office for any personal files. You need to stay with Mrs. Steinem the entire time she is in Worthington's office. Keep an eye on her every move. Don't trust her."

"Will do."

Samantha jogged, impressed with herself for jogging in heels. She heard Jim talking, even though she was fifty feet away, about the recent police activities. She looked down the road and saw a gate blocking the road. She had fond memories of similar areas as this one. This road was a dirt biker's dream - full of ruts, hilly and a slimy layer of water pooled over gravel. She remembered the summer before high school her grandfather Pops found a used blue dirt bike. She started off riding through the pasture on their property. She loved the wind whipping through her long, curly, out of control hair. Oh, to have that bike I would be over that gate in seconds.

Bo ran beside her, his short legs made bunny hops. A six-foot-high chain link fence ran down the sharp incline across the road and into the river. A gate wrapped with a heavy gauge rusted chain and lock blocked the entrance into the estate's grounds. She looked for cameras or other monitoring devices. There were none. She watched Bo for a reaction. He hadn't whined or moved his head due to hearing a high pitched squeal from the movement of a camera or the hum of a monitor. He saw a rabbit and wanted to chase it, but nothing else. The only strange sound was Patterson's truck coming up the road.

"Well, what do you see?" He asked, his eyebrows close together and his eyes dark. He was elsewhere mentally.

Samantha knew from listening to Patterson's side of the conversation that something wasn't right at the School District Board Office. Something was missing, she wondered what and could it prove her innocent of this crime?

"Just this big gate blocking our way to the grounds and a steep incline up to the top of the grounds. It's not being monitored I checked. I'm ready to break-in. Are you?"

She didn't wait for his answer. She fiddled with the lock and within minutes the rusty old lock rested in her grimy hands. She motioned for him to drive through and park by a small grove of cottonwood trees. She thought about what she heard of Jim's part of the conversation since she couldn't hear Patterson. *What have I missed? Were there more clues. Will he share?*

Patterson hopped out of the truck ready to climb the steep face of the bluff. Samantha stood still and listened. "It is too quiet something not right. Get your gun out. Watch where you step. Don't talk." Samantha whispered as she picked up Bo.

He got his gun out and started the climb. "Why?"

20

SILENCE

The clouds moved slowly like curtains shutting out the sun. The ancient trees stood close together as soldiers protecting each other and the castle on the hill. The helmet of dank air held everything prisoner. Whispering wind sent secrets out to the unknown. The wildlife hid from some kind of danger. Silence was an unwelcome sound.

Their walking caused a soft rustling which disturbed the silence. Despite the appearance of calm, an unseen energy ran through the woods caused Samantha to shiver. Patterson side-stepped up the steep incline using the trees as poles to propel him up the hill. Samantha, right behind him, grabbed saplings on the outcrop of rocks to hoist herself up. Her long, athletic legs made it look easy, but her ridiculous heeled boots made each step treacherous. She teetered on a ledge and listened, straining to hear the slightest change. She peeked down the neck of her sweater at Bo, – no growling, and no hissing. Okay, but she still felt something was wrong. Like some invisible person was watching them and ready to attack.

Halfway up the hill the vegetation changed. Long ropelike vines twisted and dangled through the trees. They weren't poison ivy or trumpet vine. Whatever they were they weren't indigenous to the Midwest. Patterson found two sticks just right for walking and handed one to Samantha. He whispered. "Test the ground before you step down. Your right. Something's not right."

Samantha whispered back, "I have goose bumps."

"Yep me too. That only happened when my men were in serious danger. Where the terrain was dotted with land mines. We were careful. Still, too many got hurt. I feel like there are land mines here. But why here. This is Kansas?"

Patterson tested the ground with his stick and stepped forward. He felt a snap under his foot. He inhaled and flew through the air with the greatest of ease so quick that he didn't have time to utter a sound. When his body started to lose momentum then the bouncing and erratic swinging started. "How in the hell do I get down from here?"

Samantha stared, her mouth opened, unable to close it. Giggling she replied. "Oh, my, I'm sorry, but wow. I have never seen anything like that before."

A few minutes passed while she assessed the situation. *Patterson's head was about a foot above me, plus he hung over a deep hole. A rope like vine looped around his ankles and held his feet tightly together. What can I climb on that will be strong enough to hold the two of us? On the ledge above an old tree grew out of the rocks. What would Pops have me do? He would tell me to scale the ledge, then climb the tree and cut the vine.*

Simple "Got a knife on you?" she asked.

He slid his hand up into his pocket and found his old faithful Swiss army knife. He tossed it over to her. If he could swing over she could catch him and cut the vine.

"Can you swing over to that old tree?" She pointed in the direction he needed to go.

"Swing? No, but, will today."

"Practice while I climb up and get situated." Samantha used the end of her stick to make sure there weren't any booby traps. She placed Bo on the ground with the strict order not to move. Next, she shimmied half way up the tree, wedged her body on top of the bent part, and tied one of the strange vines around her body using a nonslip knot just like Pops had taught her. *So much for my manicure. Oh well.*

Patterson had turned green and looked like he was ready to heave his tacos. That could complicate things.

"Okay. Sorry, but you have to focus. Swing hard towards me. I will grab you and cut you down. You will fall, so be prepared. There aren't any traps over here."

His dark eyes locked into hers. He swung. She reached out to grab him and missed. He swung, again, still locked on her eyes. She was his lifeline. His lips were pressed together so tightly they had disappeared. "One more swing, I'll get you this time. Push harder if you can." Samantha braced herself and checked the rope. It was secure enough for her to reach out further.

With determination, he bent his legs and sprang into the air and pushed with his shoulders. She clutched him around the knees.

She pulled him to her held his legs with one arm as she stretched to cut the loop around his feet. She sawed and sawed. "The vines are tough little darlings."

She had almost cut through the vine. *Now what to do, think.* "I want you to trust me. I think this will work. Patterson, you need to inhale, exhale, inhale, and reach. Wrap your arms around the tree's trunk. I will hold your legs. So you can pull your feet apart and break the threads of the loop. When your feet are free I want you to tuck your head up toward your body. Keep your arms around the tree until I can slowly let you down. Focus on what you need to do. Okay, I have your legs. Grab the tree."

The vine snapped. He was free. Dirt, leaves, moss and other unknown nature's gifts dumped down on Samantha, but she kept her grip around his legs. Slowly he pulled his head in and she lowered him down the tree's trunk. When his head was a foot from the ground she gave him his last instruction.

"Now let go of the tree, put your hands down on the ground. Do a head-stand."

He put his hand down then did a forward roll and landed on his knees. Bo jumped on top of him and gave him puppy kisses. Patterson looked up at Samantha her long curly hair was covered with dirt and green stuff. Mud was smeared on her face and clothing. Her green eyes sparkled. He had never noticed how beautiful she was, no denying it. She was lovely and probably Worthington's killer.

Samantha smiled down at him. "Now let's carefully going up the hill. You can tell me how Worthington was murdered."

"Don't know. Dr. Ackerman hasn't said. Plus, can't tell you. You're a suspect."

21

DAMSEL IN DISTRESS

At the top, the landscape turned from forest to a golf course. Worthington's mansion, a granite edifice of Gothic tradition, stood like a castle in Europe. In the flower bed beside the massive wooden front door was the bunny. An exquisite brass bunny statue, it welcomed guests to the Worthington's humble home. Patterson and Samantha went separate directions to search for an alarm. He bird whistled to Samantha and motioned for her to move to his area. He pointed to the alarm box with the wires cut at the ground level. By all appearances, the Worthington's had a connected alarm. Had the Worthingtons wanted everyone to think there was a system, but didn't have one? Or had someone cut the wires to easy access to their home.

Samantha pulled her lock pick out of her pocket and headed for the front door. The massive door reminded her of something out of King Arthur's court with a crest carved deep into the wood panels. She pushed, twisted and clicked. The door sprang open as if it weighed nothing. *Odd*. She thought.

"The door is fake wood. Oh my, a cheap door on an expensive home. Don't get it." She studied the door before opening it fully. Both stood still with their mouths open. The foyer's walls were made of the same granite as the exterior. The floor was cream colored marble. It opened up into a living room with a massive fireplace of polished stone in a deep grey. A long mantle made of the same stone covered the entire front of the fireplace. The only thing on the mantle was a painting of Mr. and Mrs. Worthington. Mr. Worthington appeared to be a tall slender man with peppered grey hair. Apparently, he thought of himself as an outdoorsman based on his wool tweed shooting outfit. A large polished shot-gun resting on his left arm. His right arm wrapped around Mrs. Worthington, another one of his possessions. His tanned aristocratic face was long, slender and life-worn. The deep-set grey eyes were humorless. Apparently he was serious about everything including the portrait painting. The petite Mrs. Worthington was dressed in a tennis outfit. Her jet black hair styled in a short bouncy bob. Unlike her husband, her face was oval, ageless, and porcelain color. Her large blue eyes looked up lovingly at her husband. Her skin color was similar to that of her beautiful daughter. It was startling. Bunny Worthington represented a blend of the two, tall and slender like her father with his grey eyes and had her mother's coloring. It equaled perfection. Patterson did a double take on Mrs. Worthington's smile.

"Hey, Samantha do you know the Vice Superintendent's secretary? Isn't Mrs. Worthington's smile just like hers? How odd. They could sisters. She didn't mention being related to Superintendent Worthington." He wrote in his notebook. *Check Mrs. Steinem's family tree.*

Samantha placed Bo on the floor and told him to behave. He wilted to the floor and tried to look up at her. He moaned softly unnoticed.

"I'm going upstairs and check to see if anything is missing or has been disturbed. You take a quick look around the main floor." Patterson raced up the stairs, not giving Samantha a chance to say anything.

Samantha knew his real reason for the race to the second floor, the restroom. His flying through the air must have really scared him. It would anyone. On the main floor, Samantha nosed around the living room which was scantily furnished. An enormous open living space had been decorated with only two gold brocade antique looking sofas with simple, elongated, slender black tables behind each sofa and a small cluster of decorative tables between the two facing sofas. They were placed perfectly symmetrical on a Kashan oriental rug. The octagon shaped dining room had a massive rectangular table with four small chairs making it impossible to comfortably pass food to each other. Why only four chairs? The table had enough space for at least twelve chairs to fit easily around it. Samantha moved into the kitchen with its beautiful cabinets, marble floor, and expensive appliances. She looked in the cabinets – no food, only paper plates and plastic glasses and silverware. No coffee maker or cups, or pans of any kind, Samantha wasn't a Suzy Homemaker, but she had some pans and even an espresso machine. A small laundry room was off the kitchen which opened into the garage. Nothing in either one – just plumbing for the laundry appliances. The condo resembled a poorly staged model home, but not a place where people lived.

Samantha noticed white tags sticking out of the sofa beside Bo. She examined it. The tag showed the sofa was from the city's major furniture store. The tag had a big red X across it and listed the price as six hundred and sixty dollars for the two sofas. Oh my, that was certainly a bargain. Not far from the tag she noticed Bo had thrown up on the floor. Now, he just laid there with his head on his front paws panting hard.

Bo started gagging again. Samantha picked him up and ran outside just seconds before the next explosion. Had he eaten poison hidden someplace or what? Was it lunch? She held his trembling body close to her and checked his nose. It was dry and warm. Not good. She had started to yell for Patterson. Then she saw the groundskeeper's truck speeding down the hill. He was less than five minutes away. Samantha yelled, "Patterson come quick."

He tripped down the steps, but kept his cool as he slid down on his backside. Breathlessly he asked, "What's wrong?"

She pointed to the vomit, Bo and then to the groundskeeper's truck racing along the road. "I think Bo ate some poison. I didn't see anything." Terrified, Samantha held Bo.

He looked at the vomit. "Looks like poison. Did the ground have poison on it?" He raced towards the truck. He ran full force, waved his arms and whistled a long, loud high pitched sound. The truck sped up and came to a slamming stop inches in front of Patterson.

"What are you doing trespassing on this property?" The Groundskeeper jumped out of the truck shook with anger, his arm moved back ready to punch him.

Patterson grabbed the man's coat. "What poisons did you put out on the grounds and don't tell me nothing."

"I put a rodenticide out for the river rats and other pesky varmints. Why? Your little mutt must have got some on his feet and then licked them. I picked the kind that makes them want to lick their feet. Then they die." A smirk crossed the Groundskeeper's face.

Patterson grabbed harder, pulled and dragged him to Samantha. Patterson clicked his phone on and hit number three. "I need Dr. Evans. This is an emergency, I'm Police Chief Patterson."

A few seconds passed Dr. Evans asked. "What's wrong Patterson?"

"Bo has been poisoned from a rodenticide. What can we do?"

"What brand rodenticide was used and where?" Doctor Evans asked. "Here is the Grounds Keeper guy. He'll tell you." Patterson gritted out. "Tell him the kind."

"It's RoddX, keeps the rats and other varmints out of the houses. I put it only on the hillside between the Condos and the river. If they hadn't been nosing around, their little mutt wouldn't be sick." The man whined into the phone.

Patterson grabbed the phone away from him. "Well?"

"Get some hydrogen peroxide and pour it down his throat until he vomits."

"But he has vomited already." Patterson yelled.

Calmly Doctor Evans spoke to him. "Okay, okay, just do what I said. Call me in an hour."

Patterson's face was just inches away from the Groundskeeper face. "Got peroxide?"

"Yup, got it in my office, let's go." The Groundskeeper knew he had to help or end up in jail. Things worked that way, for him. "I keep peroxide around because of the poison. I have reminded the residents that rodenticides are controversial. Due to secondary poisoning, like what happened to your dog. But, they don't care they don't want rats around their home."

All of them sped off to his office. The Grounds Keeper ran to his desk, opened a desk drawer with the peroxide, slid everything to the floor and made space for Bo. Patterson and Samantha administered the peroxide. Minutes passed before Bo tried to stand up. He wobbled, puked a large gunk of white foamy stuff and flopped down.

"Samantha, call Dr. Evans and ask him if we need to come by or what."

Patterson motioned to the Groundskeeper. The men hopped into the Grounds Keeper's truck. Off they went to retrieve Patterson's truck. Patterson exploded. "Did you set up the jungle warfare in the woods?"

"Yes, I did. The Home Owner Associate pay for my military expertise. I used to set up training obstacles in the army."

"You did a good job on the human snare. What do you know about the Worthingtons? They have no furniture or anything. Do they really live here? Look, I told you. I'm working on a murder case. Their daughter's murder case. I need your help or I'm arresting you for obstruction of the law.

Patterson's whole body became a large grey rubber band taut and ready to snap the Groundskeeper in half. He waited intently for the answers he needed.

"Hey, the Associate just pays me to keep people out. The poison makes intruders sick and kills animals. A two for oner. The Worthingtons are, well, different. They're loners. I heard they have money problems. The gossip says it's because of their daughter."

"So you really don't know how to get in touch with them?"

"Nope" The Groundskeeper pulled up beside Patterson's truck and reached inside his big game hunting jacket and pulled out a business card. "Here, let me know if I can help. I'll keep my eyes open. Hope the little guy will be okay."

Patterson pulled out a business card and handed it to him. "It has all my information on it. The little guy better be okay. Let me know if you hear from the Worthingtons."

He read the groundskeeper's card. "So, your name is Kip Kipling."

"Yelp and don't ask."

22

A Shower,
a Pizza and a Fib

As they neared River Bend, Samantha started squirming in her seat. She itched from head to toe, and thought poison ivy. She had never had problems with it before when she and Pops roamed the wild, but that had been a few years ago.

She just needed to think about something other than itchiness. She watched Patterson as he drove with serious intent. His strong blunt hands were at three o'clock and nine o'clock on the steering wheel. He checked mirrors and stayed at the speed limit. She guessed it wouldn't look good for the Chief of Police to get pulled over for speeding. The late afternoon sun played in His silver hair; causing sparkles to dance here and there. When he relaxed to a non-robot state, he was drop-dead gorgeous.

Samantha couldn't stand it anymore. "Patterson I need a big favor from you. I really need to stop at your house and take a shower. Sorry, I know that's inconvenient for you. But, I can't go to Katherine's. Her husband Johnny Jones will be home soon. The school is locked. I feel itchy all over, like poison ivy itchy."

He did a quick look at her and shook his head. He had forgotten about her plumbing problem. Man that would literally stink not to have plumbing. "Of course, we can order pizza. Want to watch a game on TV? Plus, if Bo needs Doctor Evans. My place is closer."

"That would be wonderful. But, sorry, I can't stay that long. It'll be too late drive back I won't be able to see the trenches they put in the road. Just the shower and pizza, okay? I'm buying and thank you this will be nice." Samantha thought. *It would be so awesome to have a meal with someone else besides Bo.*

"Sure," Patterson was disappointed. *At least, I won't be eating alone. Again.*

Samantha's pink phone dinged a text message bell. She picked it up and read it to Patterson. *"Keep eye on Bo, need to stay n town 2nite, doc evans.* I guess I need to impose on you more. May we spend the night?"

"Fine. I have a spare bedroom." His outside appearance stayed chiseled. But the left side of his mouth smiled.

"Thank you." She looked down when her phone dinged a text message again. She saw it was from Gin. Better read first, before sharing.

"Found Janet m – something wrong very sic – I hate texting" Samantha read a different message to Patterson. She read Gin says, "I'm sick going home"

Samantha texted Gin. "Ask her where she was Wednesday night?"

"Won't talk- tired - sick."

"I'll see you tomorrow," Samantha messaged back.

Samantha started her mental list for tomorrow's activities. *Do errands. Meet up with Gin and Janet. And get ready to go to Robert's to baby-sit. The neurologist said I wasn't crazy. He had to be wrong. Only a crazy person would baby-sit for their ex-husband.*

23

PLEASANT TO DANGEROUS

The evening went peacefully. Patterson ordered pizza and salad while Samantha fed Bo and got the beer out of the refrigerator. Samantha noticed that his refrigerator only had protein bars, beer and a new, unopened can of dog food. *Surely, the dog food was for Bo, Samantha* reasoned. The area between the kitchen and living room became their ballroom. They floated in and out of the space not touching yet an embrace hovered between them.

While rubbing his legs to ease some of the damage caused from the flying through the air Patterson commented, "You know, when I was in the Army I didn't have to go out and climb mountains to tell parents their child has been killed. We had a department that handled that for us. I always appreciated that department. Now I have to do that job. I feel so inept. Superintendent Timmons Worthington was an only child. Her parents don't even know that she's dead. That's so wrong."

Talking or sharing had relaxed Patterson. As he sat on his couch wearing a freshly ironed t-shirt and jogging pants, his silver hair glistened, every muscle taunt. Closing his eyes, he inhaled the atmosphere of sweetly scented soap and freshly ironed clothing. The clean smell contrasted with all the stinkiness of this case. Samantha sat on the floor cross-legged with Bo in her lap. The hum of their combined breathing was the only other sound in his house. Slowly he opened his eyes and looked down at Samantha. The tears in her eyes told him she understood his pain and she understood sharing was not easy for him. Feelings were dangerous things. They made him vulnerable not a good thing. He trusted her despite the fact she was a suspect. One of the top on the list suspects. The victim had written Samantha's name on a sticky note and placed it under her computer. Maybe the killer had interrupted Worthington before she finished her 'remember to do' list. Maybe the note was for a positive reason. Somehow with Worthington, he doubted it. Worthington was the beauty and the beast all in one.

Samantha's hand slid down the pressed clothes and marveled. "You know Patterson the thought of ironing T-shirts and jogging pants has never crossed my mind. Do you do your own ironing or send it out?"

Indignantly he answered, "I do my own ironing."

"Good now I know where to send my stuff." She marveled at Patterson's house. Pressed clothes and lack of junk food said a lot about him. By all appearances, a person would assume Patterson was like his beige, nondescript couch or the sturdy built coffee table. In truth, that was all surface stuff. Under the bland sturdiness laid a vulnerable, interesting man. He had built the coffee table in eighth grade, out of four by fours. He valued things hand-made and things that had personal history. Samantha denied the need to hug him.

The big game of the season had started. The teams, Samantha's state team and their archrival were competing against each other tonight. Patterson started cheering for the opposing team with Samantha whooping and hollering for her college team. Samantha's team won. They prepared for the next game with another round of beer for him and coffee for her. A shrill ring from Patterson's phone stopped them.

Patterson answered. "Yes. . . What?"

Crackling sounds filled the air and disjointed words stumbled out. As Patterson listened his body moved to the edge of the couch and with his full attention to each word. He nodded and jumped up, headed to his bedroom. "Give me three minutes. Call Roger from maintenance. Tell him to get there immediately." Patterson grabbed a clean uniform, dressed in one and a half minutes. His record time. As he rushed to the front door, he collided with Samantha and Bo.

"What happened?" Her eyes were wide with excitement.

"Someone tried to break into the Board of Education building, again. I don't know anything more. Go to bed. I'll wake you when I get back and tell you all the wonderful gory details." He kissed her lightly on the forehead and ruffed Bo's hair. Then he sped off to the latest invasion at the school district's office building. More like he putt-putted off to save the day.

Samantha checked her phone for the time, expecting to see three or four in the morning, but the phone's clock showed eleven. Eleven at night was way too early to go to bed, and waiting wasn't one of her strong points. She pulled her crime notebook out of her purse and thought about the who's who in Worthington's world. Think. *Teacher's lounge talk and other rumors about her? Who would benefit from Worthington's death? Any family members who would benefit. What about faculty.* Her list revised, that chore done and now, it was fifteen after eleven.

A walk. She needed a short walk. It would help pass the time and burn off the calories from the beer and pizza. She turned off the television and the lights and walked out the door with the mighty Bo by her side. His little Shih Tzu chest puffed out and his long feathery tail, swished up on his back. A mighty warrior, indeed. The walk meant time to think on her way to her destination – River Bend's Board of Education building. She had to travel the distance of a mile or more. Just a jaunt. . . What could happen?

24

THE SHADOW SAW

Sorry, but I just can't sit here and wait. Maybe, I'll see something that Patterson won't. I'll be the hero. Ha-ha-ha-a. I'll just walk the Board Office, check out things and ride back with Patterson. "Hi, ho, Bo, off we go."

A lovely night for a walk, the moon appeared a sliver of a waxing moon. It played hide and seek in the clouds. The crisp air mixed with a slight breeze that carried a hint of the sanitation plant's scent along with the intoxicating scent of fall, all blended with the euphoric relief of the doctor's statement that she wasn't crazy. The doctor's warning of taking care was ignored as she and Bo walked along the abandon streets on a cloudy night. The chorus of howling dogs followed their progress. At the footbridge that linked the warehouse area to the business district, Samantha tripped on the lip of the step, fell, and slid across the old wood boards tearing Patterson's pressed jogging pants. It wasn't safe walking alone and without a light. *Undeniable, I am crazy.*

As Samantha neared the Board of Education building she decided to take the sidewalk located along the dark and ominous football stadium side of the building. She picked up Bo, they walked through the visitors' poorly lit parking lot. She tripped here and there on cracks in the pavement. Wasn't this area a part of the improvement bond? Samantha expected to see a television inspired vision of a crime scene. The scene would be vibrantly alive with screaming sirens, whirling lights on police vehicles and men with guns. Her expectation of a crime scene deflated when she saw it had only one police car with no sirens or lights on and two ordinary trucks. One had Police Chief on the side and the other Maintenance – no flashing lights or sirens. No drama. Samantha moved through the dark shadows to get a closer look. Something had shattered the glass of the front doors on the right side. She watched Patterson and Henry stand around an object on the foyer floor. They pointed, squatted and peered closely at it. *Probably a bomb. Oh, how exciting, that building needed to be blown up.*

A flash of light caught her attention. A cigarette had been lit. It revealed a heavy-set man smoking just inches from the No Smoking sign just around the corner from the front of the building. Samantha studied the man, just in case he needed to be pointed out in a police line-up. Oh my. It was only Roger, the head of the school district's maintenance department. Patterson must have called him to come down and check on things. Just as Samantha started to step forward, out of nowhere, a person jogged up to Roger. The jogger had emerged from the darkest part of the parking lot. Bo started to growl. She hushed him and moved deeper into the shadows.

She wondered who was crazy enough to be out jogging this late. Why was he here talking to Roger? She moved closer so she could try to listen to the conversation. Bo squirmed in her arms as she tiptoed through urine smelling puddles.

"Sh-h-h Bo, you are lucky I'm carrying you. That's not rain water that you hear me splashing through. Nasty!" Samantha moved close enough to hear part of their conversation.

Roger's voice moaned, "Why did you have to throw a rock through the door. The police are here again."

The jogger, dressed in black with a hood that concealed the details of his face, hissed at Roger. "I didn't do it. Remember I don't need a rock to get in. I came down as planned but the police were here. You were to turn off the alarm. Why didn't you? I could have been in there when whoever heaved whatever through the door. And the alarms would have gone off. I would have been arrested. We don't want me arrested, now do you?"

Roger whined. "I did turn it off. I bet Ramon and that nosey baby-faced cop turned it back on."

"Well, Roger, you have a mess to fix. Fix it or you will be going to jail." The vertical snake hissed as he sprinted back into the shadows. Skimming just inches from where Samantha and Bo were hidden.

Samantha prayed that the human snake hadn't seen her. That her grey outfit was like an invisibility cloak and blended with the grey brick. Or that the snake thought she was a hairy homeless person since Bo was pressed close to her face. Cautiously, Samantha back tracked her steps to the front of the building just in time to see Patterson trotting to his truck.

"Hey, Patterson. Please wait for us." She yelled and ran towards his truck.

Patterson screeched to a stop, pivoted around. "What are you two doing? Get in the truck."

"Sorry" Samantha said as she climbed in. *Should I tell him what I just heard? Nope.*

Patterson scanned the area to see if anyone saw her. Deep in his gut he knew it wasn't safe for Samantha to be seen here.

The shadow saw.

25

PIGGY BACKING FUN

"Why does it smell like an outhouse in here?" Patterson wrinkled his nose in disgust. "Why did you just show up? This is police business, not teacher business."

"Sorry." *Curiosity killed the cat and probably my almost relationship with Patterson.* Samantha stared at her shoes and analyzed the smell. *The feces were not animal excrement. It was human. Or at least I would bet it was if I remember my Forensic 101. Had to be human feces because it had a pieces of corn and lettuce mixed in it and the smell.*

Patterson sat brooding about the message Jshupodi written on the rock then thrown through the glass door. *A threat should make sense. When I was in the army, now and then one of my kids got drunk and would throw something through a window of an ex-girlfriend's or boss's window. He just threw, puked and passed out no message written on the projectile. This was more than anger. It was a promise to harm someone.*

"Are you up on the lingo of today's youth?" He asked staring at the windshield.

"Depends on what you are talking about?" Samantha was still focused on the feces.

"Don't know. The rock thrown through the front door had the letters '*Jshupodi*' written in red paint on it. The letter J was capitalized. Then next to it was the letters 'shhodi' done in lower case. It made my skin crawl. When, I saw it. Could it be a warning to someone?"

84

"Sounds like text messaging jargon. Gin hates to text but she is the texting queen. I will ask her if she knows what it means." Samantha sent a text with the letters to Gin and told her it had been on the rock thrown through the Board of Education's door.

"I have something to tell you. The smelly stuff on my shoe is human feces. I stepped in it by the front corner of the building. It could be your rock thrower's bodily excretion. You know, mad at the board for something. So, he or she took a dump by the building. A statement of their displeasure, but that didn't satisfy their intense anger, so they threw a rock with a message through the door."

Patterson slammed on the brakes. "You could be right. Take off your shoes. Now, let me bag them. I'll give them to Ackerman tomorrow. By the way. I'm mad at you. I took you to the doctor. He told you to take it easy. What do you do? Walk a mile in the dark. You could have fallen and hit your head."

He thought for a minute, and then asked, "How do you know about feces? How can you tell it's human?"

"When I started college I wanted to go into forensic science, so I took classes. One was about body excretion, you know, to find DNA. Now, I know poop. I had a grad student who must have gone door to door collecting various specimens." She giggled. Her phone told her she had a text message. She read it to Patterson. "Gin says Jshupodi means, J shut-up or die. Talk tomorrow don't bother me again tonight, or U will die."

When they pulled up to his house, Patterson jumped out the truck and whispered, "Stay and I'll get a bag." He ran into the house

He was back in seconds with a storage bag. He carefully pulled her shoes off and placed them in the bag, sealed it and placed it on the floor of his truck He grabbed Bo and tucked him close to his chest and turned around. Samantha felt like she was Cinderella with Patterson as Prince Charming and the shoe fit. Magic.

"Hop on, Bo and I will give you a piggy back ride."

Samantha wrapped her arms around Patterson's neck and hopped on his back. She could feel his muscles ripple as he moved. She knew he could feel her legs wobble as he carried her to his porch. She inhaled late night crisp apple smell and his light musky smell. *Oh my, he smelled sexy.*

Samantha took another shower. Paterson gave her another clean outfit to wear. Both snuggled in their separate bedrooms with smiles on their faces. One smiled because his hunch was correct. It had been a threat on the rock. The other one smiled because of the piggy back ride was just like when she was a little girl with her daddy.

"I had forgotten all about that. I barely remember anything about him or my sister. I need to write down my memories and figure at some things. For now, I need more information from Patterson about this case. Goodnight Bo."

26

SAMANTHA NEEDS A LIFE

Samantha had gone to sleep with a smile but woke up feeling guilty. She should have told Patterson about Roger and the snake last night. Did it have anything to do with Worthington's death, or the break-ins at the Board office? He told her that Worthington's death had been the act of a diabolical killer. One who planned and committed the perfect crime. On the drive to Patterson's he told her that everyone close to Worthington had denied any involvement in her death. Everyone loved Worthington. But, Worthington didn't have any close friends. Her social life was her work. In the interviews her staff denied having any reasons for wanting her dead. Samantha thought. *Logically everyone has enemies, especially the rich and famous. Worthington was rich and famous by River Bend's standard she was rich and famous.*

Outside, as Bo took care of business, she looked around, no Johnny —on— the spot anywhere. A faint memory of indoor plumbing and clean clothes in the laundry room reminded her never take modern conveniences for granted again. She needed to get moving, there were so many things to do before babysitting tonight. She did need a life. If she had a life, then she would have something to do besides baby-sit for her ex-husband.

"Hey, want to get some breakfast before I take you home?" Patterson looked at the floor and moved an imaginary ball with his toe while he waited for her answer.

Samantha mentally jump up and down and screamed 'yes', but instead said. "I've imposed enough." The word 'no' formed on her lips, but her heart said. "Yes, that would be wonderful."

"Would you like to go bowling or to the movies tonight? Bo could stay here. You can spend the night in the guest room, again. Tomorrow you could do the rest of your laundry here

"Oh, that sounds great, but I promised Robert, my ex, I would watch little Robbie tonight. He wants to take Vicki out with both of their parents. Robert went on and on about 'poor' Vicki never gets out because of the baby." The headache's roar had started. Samantha pulled the medicine out of her jean pocket, twisted up her face, took a pain pill, and then the blood thinner pill. She prayed the medicine would kill the monster in her head.

"Let's go eat. Your headache may be caused from thinking about babysitting tonight. Or you're just hungry or both." Patterson grabbed up Bo, turned and told her to hop on his back since she didn't have any shoes. They giggled as they hobbled to the truck.

Samantha made a mental note to do research about the blood thinner. The medicine bottles didn't say when to take them or if she should take them with or without food. She was glad for the research project. She needed something thought-provoking or she would continue to day-dream about Patterson, just like her seventh grade girls did with their crushes. She made a mental note to add leg exercises to tighten-up her legs in case she got another piggy back ride.

Breakfast at the local drive-through turned into a picnic at a nearby park. Samantha looked over at Patterson. His profile showed a dimple crease in his taunt skin and a smile. He had a smile on his normally emotionless face. He was a gorgeous man, showcased in a pressed white t-shirt and tight blue jeans. A crush, she had a crush. No - don't go down that road. It had to be the drugs messing with her mind.

He did a side glance at Samantha. Her coloring had returned to that golden blush. The yellow sweater brought out yellow specks in her eyes and made her green eyes sparkle. He wanted and needed to deny that she meant more to him than just a friend. Fear won out on this. No more one-sided relationships. She was just a friend. A friend who was still in love with her ex-husband. Or why else would she waste a Saturday night babysitting for him and his new wife?

Sitting still wasn't a Patterson trait so he stood and kicked at the bushes looking for something to throw like a forgotten toy. He found a ball and threw it to Bo. Bo got the ball and ran it back to him. He had always wanted a dog that played fetch with him. After several rounds of fetch both crashed on the ground. He rubbed Bo's tummy. Then, looked up at Samantha. She smiled down at them.

"I'm so glad you play with him. Bo always wanted Robert to play fetch, but Robert never had time for us, I mean him." Her lips tighten. Her eyes darted away.

Patterson thought, she still can't say 'no' to Robert. "What time do you have to be at Robert's?"

"Seven, they are scheduled back by ten, so Vicki can feed the baby." A pathetic look settled on her face.

"Well, why don't you bring Bo to my house while you baby sit? Spend the night. We'll do laundry tomorrow." His head nodded 'yes'. He added, "It will be so much fun. I have indoor plumbing."

Red faced and totally embarrassed she started shaking her head no. "Okay, it's a date.

I mean thank you that would be great."

Patterson focused on Bo, afraid to look into her eyes and see rejection. "I had hoped it would be a date or at least a date to have a date sometime."

"You hoped?" Samantha smiled and her eyes danced. "Me, too."

He cleared his throat. Slow down old fool or you will get your heart cut out. "Have you heard anything from your two friends about the superintendent's secretary?"

"Not from either one." Samantha lied. She needed to talk with Gin and Janet first before Patterson became involved. She had to protect Janet.

27

SILENCE IS GOLDEN

Silence was golden on the drive to Samantha's house. It allowed each to formulate their plans. Patterson's plan had two parts. The first plan involved a pleasant drive to the city and meeting Dr. Ackerman to hand over the box of new evidence. The odorous box that contained the feces from Samantha's tennis shoes. Hopefully, it was full of useable human DNA. Plus, the vile rock found at the scene at Board of Education with writing on it. Hopefully it had identifiable prints from the rock thrower's hand. Doctor Ackerman should know something from his examination of Superintendent Worthington by now. He had been on the case for two days. He still didn't have facts about how the victim died.

The second plan involved driving back to the Worthington's condo and getting their finger-prints and DNA if possible. Then, Patterson planned to check with Kipling to see if he had heard from the Worthington's. The man had to know more than he had shared yesterday.

Paterson drove slower than usual as he went over in his mind the information he had gathered so far. There was something about the case that didn't fit. For example, the victim's missing phones and purse. If it had been a robbery, the missing items would have been easy to explain. By all appearance, it hadn't been a robbery. Then why was the school board ransacked again? Robbers take what they see and move on. This robber searched for something specific. Maybe looking for the two phones and a purse, too. Were they gold plated? Why were they were so important? Patterson needed to talk to Mrs. Steinem. She knew something. Samantha's plan involved hitting the ground running. She sent a text to Gin, "Where r u and J?" She was desperate for a chance to talk to Janet before the police. The police, meaning Patterson, he would eventually discover Janet had a juvenile record. When they open it they would discover she had killed a man. It was self-defense. That didn't matter the police would think if she had killed once then why not again. The fact that the first time had involved a middle aged man, one of her mother's regulars. He had decided he wanted Janet, not her mom. He paid Janet's mother extra to have Janet. Unknowingly, Janet and her two little sisters were asleep in another room when he rammed their door. Drunk and aggressive, he flew at Janet and her sisters. Janet swung a baseball bat at him, hit him, and knocked him off balance. He fell, hit his head, and died. Janet was only fourteen.

River Bend's education community protectively circled Janet and her sisters. The younger siblings stayed with their teachers until they were able to find an appropriate grandparent to take them. Samantha's best friend, Katherine talked to the editor at the River Bend Journal and suggested the sensationalism wouldn't be good for River Bend's image. Gin had Janet live with her until the courts could find a suitable permanent home. The Benders, an elementary teacher and her husband, a school board member, became Janet's foster parents until she graduated from high school. Then Mr. Bender helped her get the job at the Board of Education office. She worked in the daytime and went to community college in the evening. He also found her a suitable place for her to live.

"Oh, my" Samantha remembered that the Benders knew where Janet lived. Thinking to herself, *I'll tell Patterson after I talk with Janet.* Her phone buzzed, a text from Gin. "My place, need 2 java – I buzz u n."

Patterson pulled up to Samantha's house. Samantha suddenly aware that she was home. They hadn't talked. She had questions that needed answered. "Thank you and I'm sorry about not talking and about inconveniencing you."

"No problem, see you tonight. Right?" Patterson realized he too had been lost in thought. He should have asked her some questions. After all she was a suspect. *Idiot.*

Samantha turned to ask. "What? To the mumbling she heard. He was gone. She watched the rock in his tire slowly moving over and over as it went down the road.

She dashed in and put her babysitting outfit on the bed. Bo nudged his food bowl across the floor towards her. "I'll open a can of your favorite food and then we are going to Gin's. Okay?"

Apparently not, Bo snarled up at her. He did not like Gin.

"Sorry, Bo. It will be okay. Janet will be there. She needs you to make her feel better. Then you're going to Patterson's to watch sports."

He ate his food, trotted to the door. His lip snarled, a growl sound continued as he walked across the room and the hair was his back bristled.

She picked him up, hugged him and ruffled his short gold and white fur. Outside, the air's warm fall perfume swirled around her gently. She walked to the Escalade through a whirlwind of rich multi-hued leaves. The mid-afternoon sunlight covered the earth in a russet glow. Samantha savored the deliciousness of the moment. A piece of paper dropped on the floor of the car - her list of ideas about who killed Worthington. She bent down to retrieve it and refocused. Who needed Worthington dead? Or who would benefit from her death? Or was it revenge? What if someone felt Worthington had gotten the job under the table, and they felt they deserved the position more? Or what about a rejected lover?

28

DEATH TO RUMORS

With a drink carrier full of hot coffee and a squirming dog balanced perfectly, Samantha pushed on Gin's bell next to her gorgeous glossy ebony door.

The doorbell buzzed. Gin yelled. "Come in, Janet is upstairs on the deck."

At first Samantha thought the darkness was just her eyes adjusting from sunlight to the interior light. But, Gin's living space was dark like the inside of a cave. *Maybe Gin is a vampire or just an ordinary bat.* Fearful she would fall over something unseen thing, like one of Gin's old lovers, Samantha shuffled toward the slivers of light beamed down the stairs that led up to the roof's deck. Sadly, since Gin started dating Detective Jim Murphy, there hadn't been a leftover lover left on the floor for several months. The romance has caused a death to school rumors. Now, teachers didn't have anyone to gossip about Or did they? Maybe the Superintendent? Samantha smiled an evil smile. Wonder if I will find the murderer before Patterson, again. Maybe, my beloved principal, Devora Moore did the dastardly deed. Now, that was just hopeful wishing.

Samantha teetered on the top step blinded by the sunlight trying not to spill the coffee. She saw Janet Moore a few feet away loving Bo. He made everyone happy, except Gin. Gin called him a rug rat. Not like a child *rug rat*, but a real rat that lived in rugs.

"Janet, it's me, Samantha, I'm here with coffee. I hope they're still hot. Is Bo bothering you?" Samantha spoke in fast forward. She was anxious to talk to Janet without Gin around. Janet looked up through red-rimmed swollen eyes. Trembling like a leaf in the breeze. Samantha knew that something was terribly wrong with Janet.

"It has been a long time since I last saw you. How are you?" The moment the words hit the air and stumbled into Janet's ears Samantha knew she had messed up. Cold grey eyes bored through Samantha.

Janet spit out. "I'm just fine."

"Janet, I'm sorry, but I need to talk to you." Samantha knew gentle worked better with Janet, but she had to get answers, now, in order to protect Janet.

"Has Gin talked to you about Superintendent Worthington?"

The girl's coloring went from pale to deathly white, and she started shaking. "No"

"I'm sorry, but someone murdered Worthington Wednesday night between six and nine o'clock. When you didn't show up at work on Thursday, and you didn't call in sick. You became the primary suspect. Did you fill out a leave form and forget to turn it into the office?"

"Yes, I forgot all about the leave forms. I'll fill them out Monday. You see, I got very sick Wednesday night and slept all day Thursday and Friday. I was too sick to think about anything." Janet grumbled. Hoping that would stop Samantha's questions. Nervously, Janet added, "I'm not answering any more questions. And who can I thank for murdering Worthington?"

Samantha watched Janet's large grey eyes changed from frightened to angry. "Janet, the Police Chief needs to talk to you. It would be better for you if you call and talk to him."

"No, I won't talk to him. I didn't – do – anything." Janet picked up Bo and held him so tight his little round eyes almost popped out.

"I'm arranging a meeting for you tomorrow. I'll be there to help you and so will Gin. You know that. Don't you?" Samantha bent and removed Janet's hair from her wet face and loosened her hold on Bo. "Janet, it's a different Police Chief. Police Chief Patterson will help you. I promise."

No answer just a small nod from Janet. Bo tried to clean up Janet's tears. Out of nowhere in a strange little girl's voice, Janet asked. "Did Gin tell you what she's been up to?"

Samantha was shocked by Janet's voice and the thought that Janet thought that Gin confided in her. "No, not a thing. What has she been up to?"

In a conspiring voice, Janet told Samantha all about it. "You know, she has a boyfriend. They have a date here tonight. She told him to bring a friend for me. He asked a guy named JR something or the other. I remember JR from high school. He was a senior. Do you think he will remember me and all the bad things?"

"No, Janet, he won't. He has had his own problems. He is a wonderful person. You will enjoy talking with him." Samantha gently remover Janet's vise grip from her hand.

"I told her no date. I do not date. Please tell her she won't listen to me." Janet started shaking again.

"Okay I'll talk to Gin. Sorry"

"Yes, Sam, we all know you're sorry. But, what are you sorry about this time?" Gin jogged up the stairs and on to the deck wearing jeans and a state university sweatshirt. She never dressed like that. She looked cute with no make-up and her real ash blonde hair color. Without contacts, her eyes were a sparkling hazel. Underneath the bling Gin was a real person after all.

"Janet is afraid that you are setting her up tonight on a date. She doesn't date." Samantha brushed a piece of imaginary lint from her shirt, raised an eyebrow and gave her best imitation of Katherine's stern teacher look.

"I can't wait to tell Katherine you tried to give me one of her 'looks'. You know she practices her looks every night until they are perfect. You are in trou-b-le. Change of plans, it was going to be a date like thing. Jim just called. He has to bring his kids. So, there isn't a date for either of us, Janet. So no problem, right? But, I need you to help me come up with things to do. I want his kids to like me. Just having you around will help. Everyone likes you." Gin gave Janet her best 'please' look. Gin needed practice on her please 'look' because it appeared to be a constipation look.

"I'll help you but don't leave me alone with any man. Please promise me." Janet pleaded.

"No problem. Now for ideas." Gin rubbed her hands together and smiled. "I have soda pop. We'll order pizza and…I'm surprised that I really want them here and to like me. This is my chance for a real family. I never thought I would have one or even wanted one for that matter. But, I do."

Samantha, shocked by Gin's revelation, stayed focused. "I hate to break in, but Gin, your coffee is right there. Janet has agreed to meet and answer Patterson s questions tomorrow. When and where would it be good for the two of you to meet with him?" Samantha waited firm in her resolution to solve Janet's problem.

"What about Katherine's at five o'clock? He can join us for our Sunday pizza time. Then we can make fun of him when he leaves. Oh, yeah, I forgot. You're in love with him. You want him to kiss you!" Giggling Gin gave Samantha the gotcha look.

"I'm not in love with him. I just know it's a good time for him to meet - with us." Samantha picked up Bo and her cup of coffee and started to bolt.

"Well, refute all you want. He's in love with you, my darling. I can prove it. Want me to prove it?" Gin hugged herself and asked very innocently, "Oh, by the way how do you know it will be fine for him to meet us tomorrow at five. Did you get an ESP message from him? I didn't see you text him. I didn't hear you call him. Hum-m-m. Tell us Samantha, how do you know he will be available?"

"Magic, I know by way of magic." Red faced Samantha hurried down the stairs into total darkness. "Where's your damn light switch?"

"On the wall at the end of the stairs, about shoulder height. . ."

With the lights on Samantha ran out of Gin's condo. The echo of Gin's laughter followed her all the way to the Escalade. Muttering to Bo as she dashed to the car. "Gin is prettier since she's in love, but not nicer. Maybe she killed the superintendent? No, she couldn't, but that's interesting point. Everyone in our education community has access to the Board of Education building and to the superintendent's office. No one even asked why. They just figured the person had a meeting with someone. Great! That makes the number of suspects – oh my – hundreds of people.

29

PATTERSON, A KNIGHT IN ORDINARY ARMOR

"Double, double, toil and trouble, Fire burn and caldron bubble," whispered Victoria. She had loved the witches from *Macbeth*. Robert had talked her into having Samantha, his ex-wife, babysit their baby. Samantha was everywhere Victoria looked. All of the furniture had been Samantha's. The bed in their bedroom where Robert had gotten her pregnant had been Samantha's and Robert's bed. Robert refused to buy new furniture. He told her, he personally, not Samantha, had selected each piece or had it designed for the house. Victoria wanted Samantha and her stuff gone from her life.

Victoria stood in front of the mirror. "Who's the fairest of them all? Me." She smiled. Tonight was hers. She smoothed the tight dress over her flat stomach, lowered the neckline a touch, powdered her breast with glittered powder and fluffed her luxurious dark hair. More than anything, she wanted Robert to notice her. Notice and desire her young and voluptuous body. Then let him compare it to skinny old Samantha's body. Victory for Victoria. Step one in her obliteration of Samantha.

The night's breeze swirled menacingly. Samantha pulled her jacket collar closer. An ominous feeling seeped in. Just nerves, she tried to convince herself as she pushed the doorbell to her old house.

The door swung open. Victoria was silhouetted by the bright interior lights. When the wind caught her hair and turned it into a Medusa like snake hair. It was perfect for an opening scene to a Halloween movie.

"You're fifteen minutes early. Did you know that?" Victoria's brown eyes blazed at Samantha.

The word *sorry* slipped out, but Samantha wasn't sorry. The whole witch scene with a bad attitude added to babysitting for her ex's baby was too much. Samantha turned to leave, but the sound of Robert calling her name stopped her short.

"Great, you're here. Thanks." Robert slid to a stop with baby Robbie held away from his body. "Robbie has an upset tummy, doesn't hims? This is my third shirt in less than twenty minutes." Robert held the baby high in the air and kissing the baby's pink little toes.

Still standing by the door Victoria unrolled her scroll of 'how to take care of my baby'. Samantha was reminded of the movie, <u>Ten Commandments</u>. *Oh, Moses would have been proud.*

"At seven o'clock, play with baby. At seven fifteen change diaper. Seven-thirty feed the baby..." Victoria droned.

Over of the top of her scroll Victoria watched as Robert placed his hand on Samantha's back. He guided her to all of baby Robbie's areas of the house. He smiled down at Samantha and for a brief second time stood still. Victoria stopped reading. Samantha and Robert stood together with Robbie, as it should have been - instead of Robert with her. At that moment Victoria promised herself to get rid of Samantha. The ringing of the door broke her trance.

Victoria opened the door. The gusty late October wind blew in the two unexpected guests. A knight, dressed in ordinary clothing with his furry squire. She turned on her charm. "Oh, look Robert. It's your jogging buddy. Oh, it is so good to see you again."

Robert smiled affectionately at his wife. "Hey, Patterson. What brings you out here? I hope it's no business reasons."

Patterson stood there with a pizza in one hand and Bo in the other. His appearance reminded the two women of a Boy Scout. The creased jeans and freshly pressed blue chambray shirt added to the total scout look. Victoria ogled him like a *Thin Mint*. One bite would not be enough for her.

Unaware that he had any effect on women, Patterson stood frozen. He saw Robert with his hand near Samantha's back like it belonged there. While Samantha held Robert's baby in her arms like it belonged there, too. The tension gathered in the house, thick and dark as witch's brew. At that second, Robert had become his archenemy. Patterson instinctively clicked his heels and turned into military mode, his safe place for personal control. For a brief second, his mind had ridden an emotional whirlwind roller coaster. Anger and pain, stuck in his mind like a wet piece of toilet paper. Then, he remembered. Just a minute ago, when he showed up. Samantha looked up at him like he was her knight in shining armor. Remember. . .

"Hi. I came to help Samantha with the baby."

Irrationally Robert questioned him. "Do you have experience with babies?"

"Yes, I helped my sister with her two kids. When the Army deployed her husband, she moved back home with my mother."

Patterson put Bo down on the floor, irritated that he had to explain himself to Mr. Perfect and Mrs. Slut Next Door. Bo started the hunt for his familiar spots.

Victoria started sputtering, "No dogs in my house."

Patterson pivoted on one foot, took one step toward the door with the pizza in hand. In a commanding voice said. "Bo and Samantha come on. We're leaving! We aren't wanted here."

Robert came unglued, "No, please, no don't leave. Victoria, Bo lived here before you. Remember? They are staying. I'm getting dressed. You need to give the sheet of instructions to the Police Chief and finish dressing."

Robert tried to pivot like Patterson, but tripped. He did kiss the baby with sliding lips as he ran to the bedroom. "Victoria, come on!"

"Oh, my," echoed Samantha and Patterson in unison. They felt like they were center ring at the fights. Bo nonchalantly continued his investigation. Samantha drifted to the sofa to play with the baby. Patterson put the pizza in the oven and moved next to Samantha. He eased down and examined the baby.

"So this is little Robbie? Cute, looks like Robert thank goodness." He whispered to Samantha. Then he started to read the scroll. "Wow, we have a lot of work to do. Don't *we?*"

Samantha asked, "Why are you here? Shouldn't you be out solving crimes?"

Patterson's eyes met hers. So many emotions escaped from him in that fleeting moment. "I didn't want you here alone and afraid. Watching your ex-husband's baby has to be emotionally hard. Has to be. This whole evening was setting you up for a migraine and issues. You know Victoria will find something wrong and blame you. So, I'm your witness."

With perfect timing, Patterson ended his sentence as Victoria and Robert waltzed into the room. Robert busily adjusted his gold cufflinks. Victoria adjusted her bulging breasts inside a new fur jacket with the price tag conspicuously hanging on it. She smoothed the jacket and found the tag.

"This would be tacky for everyone to see how much Robert paid for my jacket. Just a mere two thousand dollars for this little old thing. Ridiculous isn't it." Smugly she looked at Samantha old worn out barn jacket hanging on the chair.

Victoria stared out of the car's window as they backed down the drive-way and obsessed about Samantha. She thought about ways to destroy Samantha Grant, then both men would be hers. Victoria whispered, "I have nothing but a baby. All I have is Samantha's used husband, Samantha used furniture, Samantha's used car and Samantha's used house. I can't do anything because I have that baby. I have nothing. I deserve more. Something new besides a baby."

30

CONFESSION TIME

The smell of pizza filled the room. Patterson and Bo watched sports and ate pizza. Samantha watched the baby in wonder. She never allowed herself to realize how much she had wanted a one. Babysitting for Robert and Victoria felt like a burning knife stabbed through her. She had blanked out the dream that she had about having a baby with Robert and of them being the perfect family. Apparently, dreams were hard to kill.

At nine o'clock sharp little Robbie went to sleep just like it said on the scroll. Samantha and Patterson carried him into his bedroom and placed him gently in his DIY nightmare bed. The intense color and smell of the freshly painted room overwhelmed them. He opened the window as a safety precaution, afraid the fumes would harm little Robbie. The ornately decorated room had been painted Peacock Blue – the furniture, walls, the ceiling and possibly the floor. The decorator's designer can of paint had been left on the shelf with a yellow sticky note 'buy more'.

The minute they reentered the great room, Samantha blurted out her confession.

"Patterson, I need to tell you what I found out. I knew Janet's location yesterday. I know I should have told you. But I needed to talk to Janet first before I told you anything. I got her to agree to meet with you tomorrow five o'clock at Katherine's."

She told him everything about Janet's juvenile police record for killing a man. Samantha explained the circumstances surrounding the incident. "Janet refused to tell me or Gin where she lived. I asked her. Then I remembered that Mr. Bender, a school board member and a real estate magnate, knows where Janet lives. He will tell you because you are the police chief. Sorry."

"Are you finished? Is there anything else I should have been told?" Hurt showed in his eyes.

"We have taken care of Janet for years. I'm sorry." Samantha lowered her head tears flowed, she had never intended to hurt him.

Patterson became stone once again. He couldn't believe that Samantha had withheld information from him. They had spent days together. He had taken her to the doctor. He felt like arresting her for withholding information pertinent to solving a crime. Now he had to interrogate her about the sticky note found at the scene of the crime with her name on it. She had to be involved in Worthington's death. Up until now he had decided to ignore the note. He had wanted to protect her. *Well, no more mentally playing house with her. Yet, it had felt so right.* He had to deny his feelings. He knew better than to trust a woman.

Patterson thought. *Think only facts. Facts - he needed Samantha for the meeting with Janet. He needed Samantha to provide equipment for investigating. My small town police budget didn't cover anything he needed for investing. Major fact: I need Samantha. Hope she not the superintendent's killer.*

31

THE FINER POINTS ON HOW TO OBSTRUCT JUSTICE

Sunday, the day of reckoning had arrived. Patterson planned to metaphorically part the river of lies and -half-truths. Katherine, Gin and Samantha, the scary, the bad and he had trusted them. They had helped him on the last case. Now, they had aided and abetted a person who could have meticulously and cold bloodily killed the Superintendent of River Bend's school district. Patterson, in robot mode, sat at Katherine's table and considered each woman. What part did they play in the murder of Superintendent Worthington? Patterson viewed Katherine as scary. Katherine, the organizing one of the three, probably planned the whole thing. Tonight, disarmingly, she catered to his every need. Samantha, the good, knew how to cover up the evidence. Maybe, she used her scientific knowledge for evil instead of good. Samantha fidgeted with Bo's collar. Bo was probably the lookout for all of them. Gin, the bad, had a wild side to her. She may have brazenly assisted Janet in the murder just for fun. Gin's attire tonight created a wholesome look, like Sandra Dee in the *Gidget* movies. Another ploy.

Katherine introduced Patterson to Janet Monroe, the missing secretary. He focused on the striking willowy young woman with thick long dark hair tied back in a ponytail. Her deep grey eyes reminded him of her boss, Bunny Worthington. He pondered. *Did the three women help her look this ill to disarm me? I should be alone when I interrogated Janet Monroe. The privacy act demanded it. She was my prime suspect. But, no, they circled Janet and had her back. I don't understand the code of women. These women were law abiding citizens, yet, they have purposely obstructed my investigation. Without any civilian protocol or procedure, I'm lost. Was this typical of small town police work? Questioning a prime suspect anywhere. In the army there was procedures for everything.*

"Janet, I need some answers about Wednesday night. So I can find the person responsible for your employer's death. For the timeline where were you Wednesday after six?" He waited. Janet twisted her fingers and glanced away with tears ready to fall.

"I went home."

"Can anyone verify that you were there? And did you stay home all evening?" Patterson poised over his notebook, ready to write her information down.

"No, to both…" Her lips tightly gripped holding back words.

Gin jumped in, "Janet has nothing to do with murder. She took some private time. She's allowed, isn't she? She didn't know Worthington was going to pick that night to get killed."

The room fell silent as if it held its breath. The women waited all eyes on Patterson.

"Listen, Janet, I can't help you if, you don't help me. I need to check everyone related to this murder whereabouts. Do you understand?" Patterson persisted.

Katherine started brushing off imagined particles from her clothes. Gin winked at Janet and sipped sparingly at her wine. The women encircled Janet with their presence, including Samantha.

Janet whispered "I went home at five, but left my house before seven that evening."

Patterson backed up, "Were you the last person to leave the office or was Worthington still there?"

"I left at five. Mrs. Steinem and several of the teachers were still there Worthington had a meeting with them. When I left, Worthington still had teachers to interview."

A quick scribble to the notebook, he circled around and hoped to snag more information.

"What was the meeting about? Was it one-on-one or as a group?"

"The meeting involved about fifteen teachers, but she met with them, one-on-one. I don't know why. Worthington called each one and set up the appointments herself, all very hush-hush. One of them said something about a <u>Teacher of the Year</u> nomination. I don't know anything more than that."

Janet faced him, eyes blanked, lips pressed tightly, and hands gripped. She had given him all the information about that night for now. Gin and Katherine smiled at her and patted her.

"You said you left your home that evening around seven. Where did you go? Anyone I could talk to about seeing you?"

Nothing. She just stared at him.

He moved on to another question. "I need your address."

He already knew how to get her address, but it would be better if she told him. He prepared to write the information. He wasn't prepared for the blatant refusal from very ill young woman.

"Unless you have grounds to arrest me, I don't have to tell you where I live. It is not for public knowledge." Janet leaned toward him and placed her statuesque arms on the smooth granite surface. Her hands reached out for the handcuffs ready for him to arrest her.

Katherine's and Gin's mouths dropped opened, but, they nodded in agreement. Gin gave her a thumbs up. Katherine smiled at Janet.

Patterson aggravated by the blatant obstruction by everyone except for Bo. He looked over at Bo. Bo's round eyes were filled with tears. Patterson raised his hands in defeat, but continued with more questions. "Maybe you could tell me where Superintendent Worthington kept her phone and her purse. We didn't find any personal items with her or in her office."

"Good question. I know she had a safe or some professionally made hiding place in her office, but I wasn't privy to it. She had two phones. One was the school districts, and it should have been on her desk or in her jacket pocket. The other one she always stored in her favorite purse of the week."

"Do you know anyone who knows where she hid things? How can I get in touch with her parents? Does Nick Chase really live in the Worthington's house?" He waited, pencil itching to write something down.

"The only one who might know where she hid her purse would be Mrs. Steinem. She was the only one Worthington talked to when she had a problem. Mrs. Steinem could march into Worthington's office when the rest of us were afraid to. That is all I can tell you." Janet's coloring had paled the area around her lips had turned purplish.

Patterson watched as Janet leaned limply on to the side of the chair; her grey eyes turned a deeper grey. Her eyes were just like Superintendent Worthington's. She was a younger version, but with russet colored hair and not as tall but just as thin. Maybe he just had Superintendent Worthington on his mind. He re-read his notes. Well, at least, he had some direction. Tomorrow a visit to the Board Office was in order. One last thing he needed to ask. "Will you be at work tomorrow?"

"Yes. May I leave now? I mean, may Gin and I leave now? I'm not feeling well." Her long slender fingers touched the base of her neck and tapped. Beautiful hands like her dead boss, long and graceful.

"Yes, you may. I need to leave also." Patterson stood up and marched to the front door. No one saw the tears in his eyes or heard the moan that escaped his soul. They had broken him. *The government needed to hire women to terrorize any of our opposing countries' leaders.*

Then he remembered something Samantha had said, 'Pops always said, listen to what was not said. Watch what people do – actions speak louder than words.' Or something like that. Samantha had helped him just by not talking. Bo hadn't turned on him, either. Bo teary eyes showed he was sorry.

The clues from what wasn't said. He wiped away a tear and thought. *Janet hid everything from everyone. She didn't try to defend herself or point the blame at anyone. Strange, most guilty people do. She didn't say she was afraid, but her eyes showed fear, but not of him. Something was physically wrong with the girl. Maybe she killed Worthington in self-defense and got hurt in the process.* He wrote down; need to double check for signs of a struggle. *Great, that means I have to revisit the inferno. What was Janet's relationship with Superintendent Worthington?*

Patterson denied his pain and denied that it was caused by Samantha. He focused instead on his anger. *Thanks to the Good, the Bad and the Scary, Janet Monroe may get by with committing the perfect crime.*

32

THE PLAN

Katherine and Samantha stood at the door and waved goodbye to Gin, Janet and Patterson. Tears slipped down Samantha's cheek as she watched Patterson leave. She had betrayed him by not demanding Janet to answer his questions. What they did was wrong and hurtful to him. He trusted all of them, especially her. Katherine put her hand on Samantha's arm and walked her back into the kitchen.

"Samantha, get plates and wine glasses for us, please."

"I'm sorry, I forgot to get the pizza. For once it would have been super easy to get it. It would have been super easy because I stayed in town for the last two nights at Patterson's. I could have picked up anything you wanted." She waited for Katherine to respond to her revelation about staying Patterson's. Katherine smiled, hummed and even did a little waltz movement. Katherine never waltzed – just not her style.

They dined on lovely veggie and fruit plates with a bottle of wine. Katherine had classical music playing in the background. The silent guest, the cheesy garlic smell of pizza was missed. Samantha looked over at Katherine, "Why no pizza tonight? It's our tradition. Tonight's meal reminds me of my recent observation - that the entire faculty at our school have turned into diet freaks with bad attitudes. At first I blamed the bad attitude on Principal Moore. Now, I think it's the dieting, plus

Moore. Katherine, who isn't dieting? Why are we doing it? I'm dieting, also."

"Your observation is correct. Everyone is trying to lose weight. Why? It's based on the rumor that our jobs depend on our appearances, that's why. Want some ice cream?"

Samantha watched Katherine glide over to the freezer. Katherine glowed. Samantha analyzed Katherine's appearance. *I bet she has another hair-brain idea. Like the idea to break into the accountant's office a few months ago. She glows while Gin and I executed her break-in. A man was killed beside the desk where I was hiding. But, Katherine glowed.*

Samantha asked. "So, what's your plan?"

"Well, now that you asked. In your Pops' stuff did he have a metal detector?"

"Yes, I think so. Why?" Samantha shook with excitement. She couldn't help it. She was an adrenaline-rush junky, too.

"Well, get it out and clean it up. We need it by tomorrow night." Katherine danced back to the table.

"Sure… Where am I breaking into this time? Let me guess – the district's Board office right?"

"Yes, tomorrow night. I have the keys and the code for the alarm. We are looking for Superintendent Worthington's phones and purse. She always kept them with her." Katherine daintily pattered her lips with the linen napkin removing her imagined ice cream mustache.

"Sorry, but I don't think so. Patterson has his men in the area waiting for another break-in there. If I get caught, he will arrest me and throw away the key. Sorry can't do it." Samantha shook her head sadly. "But on the other hand he did have me break into the Worthington's condo in the City. Maybe if the timing was right, we could get in and out unobserved and not arrested."

"Oh and what did you two find at the Worthington's?" Katherine's arched eyebrow lifted into her hairline.

"It was strange. The condo was beautiful. An architect divided the old mansion into huge condos. They used top end finishes absolutely beautiful like what you see in a Designer magazines. The Worthington's' condo's decor was bargain-basement chic. It looked okay to the average person, like me, but I saw price tags still on the furniture and checked them out. Cheap prices. After knowing their daughter, I just can't see them as bargain furniture people or people who left price tags on their furniture."

Katherine listened with a perplexed look on her face. "Me either, I've been on committees with Lana Worthington. She's a snob with excellent taste defiantly not bargain-basement taste. We need to talk to Gin about them. She knows Mr. Timmons Worthington intimately."

"You mean Gin and Mr. Worthington were lovers. Sorry. I never took Gin for being stupid. My code of conduct, rule one is never date the boss's parent. Don't you think Gin has changed since she met Detective Jim Murphy?"

Katherine ignored Samantha's question. "Sam, my plan is - no one cleans the office on Mondays. But the police don't know that. They'll think cleaning people are normal. So we will dress in cleaning people's clothing. I'll get an old truck for you to drive. This is important for you and others. I think that Worthington has a safe in her nightmare of an office. In that safe she has stuff on everyone, bad stuff. You have to go into Worthington's office for two reasons: you know how to use the metal detector and her office makes me sick. I always get vertigo in that room."

"Lucky me. What do you mean every time you've gone into Worthington's office? I have never been in her office. Why have you been in her office?"

"For curriculum meetings, Worthington had a few of them in her office." Nervously Katherine brushed invisible lint for her slacks. She avoided eye contact with Samantha. No need telling Samantha she had been there selling her soul to that female devil just to keep Samantha employed.

Samantha noticed the change in her best friend's behavior and wondered what it meant. She ignored it for the moment and pressed on about the break-in plans. "Okay, let's hear more of your plan. Janet mentioned a safe or hiding place. Either one could be encased in metal. I don't know how to open a safe. Do you? Oh, silly me, of course you do."

"Sort of, wait right here. . ." Katherine dashed off. She returned with an expensive looking stethoscope. "This belonged to my father. You put this against the safe, turn the dial and listen for the tumblers to drop. We'll practice on my safe. Okay?"

Samantha held her hands up as if reading a newspaper. "The headlines in every newspaper will read *No safe is safe from the Kat.*"

Katherine glared at her. "This is a teaching moment, Samantha. Now focus."

"You do know, Katherine this is insane."

"Yes, but Worthington is dead. Judging from all the break-ins the identity of the killer is on one of her phones. Apparently, several people had reasons to want Worthington dead. Right now everyone is a suspect including you, Samantha Grant. So, we *have a* situation."

"Sorry, back to work. We can't have any mistakes. I feel we need to hide our identity. I might try to paint my face to look more masculine. Plus, I think putting cardboard in my shirt would hide my femininity. Doesn't the Board office get cleaned by men?" Samantha's hands had fluttered here and there illustrating the different disguises. She paused. "And, I may… What do you mean by *have a situation?*"

"Well, I didn't want to tell you, but there was a sticky note on Worthington's desk. Let me explain. She wrote names of her 'not good visuals' on sticky notes then call them in to fire them. She wanted you gone. She told me you didn't dress professional enough for her school. She had incriminating evidence to prove you were Not River Bend teacher material. I think the real reason she wanted you gone was the fact you questioned her about the way money was spent for the bond issue."

Shocked and hurt Samantha asked. "I knew about the note. Patterson showed me. What do you mean she had incriminating evidence against me? Like what? Still, I didn't kill her."

Katherine's voice imitated a cynical lawyer's tone. "Where were you on the night in question?"

"Ah- I was at home doing school work as usual." A wave of where this was going crossed Samantha's delicate sculptured face. She picked up Bo.

"Do you have a witness that can verify that?"

"Yes, Bo… Patterson is going to arrest me, isn't he?"

"Not if you find Worthington's stuff first. Then, we will accidentally destroy anything that pertains to you. You know how bad I am with technology. I'll tell Patterson I was simply trying to help him."

"He won't believe either one of us." Samantha hugged Bo. "At least I look good in orange."

33

THE SHADOW SAW

On Monday, before the sun had shown its face, Mrs. Steinem was dressed and heading to work. Her mission was to locate the missing phones and purse before the police. Her plans after the items were found was to remove all embarrassing items off the phones and place them back into Worthington's purse. Then innocently give all items to the police so everything seemed on the up and up. It was all about appearance.

A shadow watched from the grove of trees across the street from the Board of Education's office. A soft laugh echoed in the brisk fall air. Sneaking through the dark recesses of the parking lot, he moved toward the main entrance. Armed with the key and code, the shadow planned to find evidence of his unlawful activities. They were hidden in Worthington's office. There was enough information to put him away for a very long time. The shadow crossed the parking lot and prepared to enter the building when headlights bounced around the side of the building. The shadow quickly hid.

Eyes watched Mrs. Steinem's every move the moment she pulled in and parked in her usual space. Watched her smoothed her skirt and touched her hair. Watched as she checked that everything was in place before she hoisted a large satchel onto her shoulder. Watched her walk briskly to the front office door, unlocked it and pressed in the code to the alarm. Mrs. Steinem scanned the terrain for witnesses. She saw no one, then she entered the Board of Education building.

The shadow listened to Mrs. Steinem nervously talks to herself. "Every day when I open the door this building it smells like a kindergarten classroom. A curious smell for a school district's board office, but Bunny demanded that hundreds of boxes of crayons stored in the building. My niece loved the smell of crayons. She was a strange girl."

The shadow watched. The moment Mrs. Steinem entered the interior part of the building, he slithered in and unlocked the door with his own key, put the code in and slipped into the building unobserved. Hidden from view the shadow observe Mrs. Steinem moved quickly to the superintendent's office. Slinking on the floor to get a closer look without being detected, the shadow watched as Mrs. Steinem's arm reached through the tape and unlocked the door. He silently laughed as she wedged her mature body between the stripes of yellow tape. Mrs. Steinem entered the room and stealthily moved to the chrome wall in front of the desk. She pressed a button under the center desk drawer. When she pressed it a chrome panel, in the lower part of the wall, popped open. The shadow watched.

Mrs. Steinem held her breath as she looked down on the shelf. "On the shelf just like Bunny left it. Let's look inside her purse. A phone, but which phone. There is nothing else, no keys to her car, office or home, no money – nothing, Bunny always had her keys with her. Did the killer know about Bunny's hiding place and steal everything else? But, why?"

Hearing just snippets of what Mrs. Steinem said, the shadow did a snake slide across the carpet to get closer. Mrs. Steinem got down on her hands and knees and dug through the lower file drawer. It was empty. Something alerted her to his movements. The shadow paused and watched as she paused and listened. Then Mrs. Steinem shook her head as if she had dismissed the feeling that something wasn't right. She continued her search, but, she cautiously raised her eyes and glanced at the chrome panel. Their eyes met, his eyes showed fear and her eyes narrowed in anger. Mrs. Steinem lips tightened into a grimace, she lowered her head as she sprung to her feet. The shadow was surprised by Mrs. Steinem's agility and even more surprised when she stood in attack mode. Face to face and armed with only Worthington's small purse, Mrs. Steinem lunged and bashed him repeatedly. With one arm protecting his face. The shadow swung a bony fist up and sucker punched her in the jaw. The one and only thing he remembered from a grade school boxing classes. It had knocked Mrs. Steinem out, hopefully it would be long enough to find the evidence against the shadow.

Grabbing the purse, he yanked, but, Mrs. Steinem had a death grip on it. Nothing happened. He pulled again. This time one end of the strap snapped. He pried her fingers from the front of the purse. She had gripped the purse so hard that it left an imprint of the pyramid shape in the palm of her hand. The shadow dumped the contents out. One and only one item fell onto the thick black carpet, a phone. But, which phone was it? His thumb moved swiftly across the keys. The phone was the school district issued phone, damn it. The shadow checked the photo area for incriminating pictures. Nothing just pictures of different school events. He checked the messages – nothing but business contacts for legally conducted school business as far as he could determine. The phone vanished into his pocket.

Mrs. Steinem stirred. The shadow panicked. Using the purse's broken strap, he straddled her body. Mrs. Steinem frantically twisted. The shadow slipped from his perch smashing the strap down tight across her throat. The shadow whispered. "Whoops" after he heard a snapping sound. Then, a gasp escaped from Mrs. Steinem's lips. The shadow slithered out of the superintendent's office, slinked out the front door, and slipped into the dark early morning.

34

A Monday to kill for . . .

A sunless late October morning greeted Janet as she left for work. She was focused on one thing: finding Worthington's purse and two phones just like the Police Chief asked her to do. First, she had to remove the blackmail videos of her from Worthington's phone. No one needed to know what Worthington had done to her. If the police found the evidence, they would have the motive needed to charge and convict her with the killing of Superintendent Worthington. Janet drove into her usual parking spot and heaved a heavy sigh when she saw that she was not the first one there. "Oh, no. Mrs. Steinem's car. Don't panic, I have been absent, so I have logical reasons for being in Worthington's office."

Janet put her key into the front door, but found it was unlocked. It was not like Mrs. Steinem to leave it unlocked this early. She was probably upset about Worthington's death and forgot. Janet punched in the code, and the alarm squealed and buzzed loudly. She heard the alarm dial 911. She tried to hush it. She put a sweater over the buzzer, pushed in old codes and finally banged it repeatedly with the heel of her shoe. Janet had no choice now. She had to wait for the police. If she entered, she would be blamed if something had happened inside. If everything was okay and she had gone in, then she would have been in trouble for breaking security rules.

Sirens screamed, and tires screeched. The police arrived. Patterson marched up to the door, nodded and asked, "Did you go in already?"

"No, it's against the district's security rules. We are to wait for the police."

Patterson entered with his gun out, just in case. A piece of yellow tape from Superintendent Worthington's office waved at him. He moved to the side of the door frame and pushed open the unlocked door peering in the void. No blinding lights just total darkness. He listened and heard only silence. He sniffed the air and smelled the scent of death. Patterson felt for the light switch and flicked on the lights. He clicked a number into his phone to the local coroner. On the first ring, Flanigan answered in a slurred voice said, "Wha – t –s you want . . .?"

"Patterson here, I have another dead body. I'll have to call Dr. Ackerman to take care of it. Flanigan get help. I can't help you anymore." And hung up before Flanigan could protest.

He called Dr. Ackerman. "Patterson here, I have a dead body in the Superintendent's office. I haven't gone in yet. I don't know who, yet. Don't want to compromise the area, so I'm waiting for you. Keep it to two speeding tickets this time."

Ignoring the grumbling sounds Patterson ended the call then called his assistant, Jim Murphy. "Hey Jim, I'm at the Board of Education's office. We have another body. I'm waiting for Doctor Ackerman and you before I enter the office."

Absentminded he said, "I'll interview Janet Monroe, while I wait."

"Got it, Boss?" Jim smiled. *This case just gets better every day.*

What to do now? Patterson's plan had fallen apart. His plan had involved asking Janet Monroe and Mrs. Steinem about who had keys to the office building as far as they knew. Who knew the alarm code besides them? Had there been threats or problems that Worthington might have had with other people? He needed both women, together, to go through Worthington office and hunt for the missing items. Now, he had to take care of another dead body before he had a chance to have Janet and Mrs. Steinem search Worthington's office.

Seated in a chair by the front door, Janet waited. When Patterson approached her she bombarded him with questions. "Where is Mrs.

Steinem? Why is her car here? Normally she would have beaten the police to the front door. Did she fall or something?"

Patterson ignored her questions he had his own. He took out his notebook and asked, "Did you notice anything unusual when you arrived or when you opened the door?"

"No. Mrs. Steinem's car was parked in her usual spot. She doesn't usually show-up until around seven-thirty. I haven't seen her yet. Normally, she would have charged the front door and stopped the alarm before it called the police. She would have taken a bullet before she would let the police be called." Janet strained to look around Patterson. *Where was Mrs. Steinem? Something is wrong. Maybe she dead, too. Oh, great, now, I'll be blamed for her death too.*

Jim drove up. Patterson ended his interview with Janet Monroe. He and Jim both drew their weapons and slowly walked through the Superintendent's door. They had checked all of the other office doors and found them locked. Patterson reached through the yellow tape and turned on the lights, again. The light deflected off the polished surfaces and blinded them. When their eyes adjusted to the blinding lights they saw a body lying on the floor. They recognized the body of Mrs. Steinem in a fetal positioned. They saw a black thing jammed in her neck.

The smell from the room drifted to Jim and Patterson. "Time for new carpeting." They commented at the same time as they moved closer to examine the body.

"Looks like a purse strap or handle. I bet Gin could tell if it was a designer strap and the designer's name in seconds at fifteen feet away." Jim smiled proudly at the thought.

"Well, Samantha couldn't." Patterson smiled and puffed out his chest proudly at that thought.

Jim grinned, "Samantha is your perfect woman."

Patterson's jaw muscles rippled as he denied it. "No one is perfect for me."

Jim took pictures of the scene. They searched as they stood between the door and the body. Dr. Ackerman didn't like to have things contaminated. Where had the purse been hidden? The strap came from a purse, but definitely not Mrs. Steinem's since her bulky wide strap purse lay beside her.

"Why was she even in this office? It had been taped off."

"Bet she came early to find Superintendent Worthington's purse and phones." Patterson absentmindedly commented.

"So she could give it to us like you asked her to do?" Jim asked.

"Bet not. She was here on her own agenda."

Minutes later Dr. Ackerman entered with his entourage. "Who's this?"

Patterson gave the doctor an update on the victim and what he knew about her. Dr. Ackerman sent his people to check finger prints on the alarm, door and the office. He creaked as he folded his tall lean body down to examine the body.

"Beautiful woman. She reminds me of the other one that died in this room last week. Is this place where River Bend's lookers come to die?" He snorted a laugh.

35

QUICK SAND

Patterson moved out of the nauseating room while Dr. Ackerman and his team collected evidence. Frustrated about the blatant lies he had told. His potential suspects answered in what seemed like honest answers. Their responses had proven to be deliberate lies. Mrs. Steinem had sounded honest. She wasn't. It cost her, her life. He needed to get the truth from Janet. Could or should he scare the truth out of her. She knew something important about the case. The secret could kill her, too. His hands in tight fists as he quietly walked over to her desk. She looked up from the computer.

Her grey eyes filled with fear. "Is there a problem?"

"Yes, Janet there is a problem in Superintendent Worthington's office. We found Mrs. Steinem's body. She apparently found Superintendent Worthington's missing purse. Her killer has it now and the phones too." Patterson waited for Janet to tell all.

Involuntarily her hand flew to her lips, an inaudible scream escaped, then she crumbled to the floor.

Jim had stepped out of the superintendent's office and saw the scene between Patterson and Janet Monroe. "Well, did you scare her to death?"

Patterson said, "Get Ackerman. Hurry"

He felt he had sunk deeper into the *civilian no- procedure* quicksand. *I had never fully appreciated the military with the protocol, straight answers*

*and no fainting. Or was the problem I am dealing with women? Crazy.
All of them.*

Dr. Ackerman stood beside him, rubbed his stubble chin and looked down at the young woman. Innocently he asked, "How many rooms do they have in this building?"

Patterson's granite face turned and looked at the old coroner in disbelief. "What are you talking about?"

"Just trying to finger out the number of bodies I'll be hauling back to the City." Ackerman chuckled at his cleverness.

"This one isn't dead, is she?" Patterson threw his hands up and moved out of the way.

The old doctor knelt beside the deathly pale young woman and did the usual; check the heart, blood pressure and then he sniffed the air. A knowing look crossed his rugged features. "She's not dead. She does need to go to the hospital. I'll take care of it. You keep people out of the superintendent's office this time. No maintenance people and no children."

Dr. Ackerman paused before continuing. "One thing, Patterson, you need to know that woman in the office was a fighter. The killer broke her jaw and crushed her neck. I felt broken ribs on both sides. It looked like he straddled her body while he crushed her neck. He was taller but more slender built than her, judging from the angle of the strap's pressure the killer made on her neck. I'll send you the report when my people and I have thoroughly examined her."

36

THE EPIDEMIC

Dr. Ackerman scanned his phone for a number and made a call. Within minutes, an ambulance showed up and whisked Janet Monroe away. All that Patterson heard of Ackerman's conversation was. "Isolate her and she needs blood." The word *isolate* scared the Police Chief. All he needed was an epidemic. He already had an epidemic of women being murdered in School District's superintendent's office. What kind of infectious disease could that young woman have contracted? He sorted through the most common types of epidemics. And decided how to handle each one of them. Detective Jim Murphy yelled at him, but he had been so deep in thought he hadn't heard Jim. Jim walked over to Patterson and touched his arm.

Patterson flinched and stared at Jim as if confused.

Jim asked, "You okay?"

He considered telling Jim about a possible epidemic. Then, decided to talk to Ackerman first. Before he told Jim, because Jim would tell his mother, and then it would snowball. River Bend would PANIC.

"Hey, you need to come outside. I have something to show you. This case gets better and better." Jim led Patterson out the door and over to a corner of the entrance's offset and pointed to the ground. "I took a sample of it. I think its cocaine, don't you?"

Patterson bent down, wet his finger, picked up a few particle of the white substance and tasted it. "Yep, it's cocaine. Were there any footprints here before everyone stomped all over the place? Have you checked for more spills of this stuff? Look everywhere; look for things that don't belong on this property. Anything might tell us to who killed Mrs. Steinem."

"Well, I think today's case was a robbery for drug money. When Mrs. Steinem came to work to find the missing purse and phones, this druggy broke in, killed her, and stole the purse. Thinking there was money in it." Jim waited for Patterson to agree to his brilliant solution to the latest murder.

Patterson looked at Jim, turned, walked to the door, opened it and studied the dusted print on the lock's turn knob. Then he examined the outside lock's opening. He smiled. "Do you now. How about putting a wager on your theory?"

"Fine." Jim nodded, "How about I take your night shift for a week. And you, Patterson, you can just admit that I'm a better detective than you." They shook hands. Jim had a smug smile on his face and Patterson's lips curved up on one-side.

"Well, Detective Murphy, the clearest prints are those of a woman, a small thumb print. Plus there are no traces of white powder on the inside of the door or in the building. There should have been some powder on the door because snorting coke takes two hands. And, judging from the spill outside whoever used it here had shaky hands. Look at the front lock. No scratches. I bet Mrs. Steinem unlocked the door let herself in and then relocked the door. She was a stickler about doing things the right way. Whoever followed her in used their personal key. Mrs. Steinem locked the door and the killer unlocked it. The only way to open a locked door and not leave scratches is with a_?" Patterson twirled his hand forcing Jim to finish the sentence.

Jim answered the end of the sentence. "Is with a – key. . ."

"That's my prediction, someone used their key. We need a complete list of who has keys to this place. That's your job. Have the powder checked by Ackerman's group. Let's see what shows up. Check the perimeter for more spills." Patterson paused, clicked his heels and spoke through clinched teeth. "Jim, you were right, drugs were involved somehow. Also, you are right there was a robbery. Not for money, but for Worthington's phones."

Dr. Ackerman waited as Police Chief Patterson finished his talk with Jim. Ackerman grumbled. "Hey Patterson, I need to talk to you a minute."

"I need to talk to you, too. Me first. What does Janet have that could cause an epidemic? Just so I'm prepared to protect River Bend."

Ackerman's head rolled back, and his Adam's apple bobbed up and down. He looked like the cartoon characterization of Ichabod Crane.

"Patterson, you were dipping into my conversation. I put Janet Monroe in isolation because you need to have a guard with her. I thought you would realize that she could be the next victim. She knows something. Or at least, the killer could think she knows something. Have someone watch her to see who visits or loiters around her room. I can't discuss with you the details of her personal problem. She needs to be in the hospital for a day or so. Then, she will be fine. No disease epidemic, but, you have an epidemic, alright. An epidemic is good looking women being murdered in the superintendent's office. A weird serial killer like epidemic."

Doctor Ackerman paused, rubbed his chin and tried to remember what he needed to ask Patterson. "My question is. I need to leave one of my technicians here to finish collecting DNA samples. Can someone give her a ride back to the city?"

Patterson nodded. "Need to throw an idea at you. Jim found cocaine spills outside the building. Suppose the killer snorted after he left the building. Nervous about killing someone."

Doctor Ackerman interrupted Patterson. "Yup. He might have snorted and then ran off. You need to check and see if there are more spills. If there are - they could point to the direction the killer went. That could help you catch the killer. And don't forget your street camera's footage."

"Street cams in River Bend, you have to be kidding. Yes, on your tech and one of my men will drive them back to your hospital." Patterson snarled at Dr. Ackerman. The big city coroner left the building, but the timbre of his laugh stayed.

"Jim, I'm sending someone down here to help you." Patterson started to walk toward the door prepared to leave. Paused as he wrote in his notebook. *Need to search Janet Monroe's and Mrs. Steinem's homes — hiding something. But what? Samantha said that Mr. Bender, a realtor, knew where Janet lived.*

Over his shoulder he gave another order. "Jim, get Mrs. Steinem's address from the employee's file. Text it to me. Thanks."

37

RUMOR HAS IT

Out of the corner of his eye Patterson saw movement. He turned. People were entering the building contaminating the scene. He marched towards the door stood straight, an imposing figure in his uniform, and in his best military mode - barked at them. "Get out of here. Now. STOP! Wait and stay."

Jim came up beside him and spoke, "Of course, the personnel would show up early. Someone must have activated the phone tree and spread the rumor that someone else had died in the superintendent's office again."

"But, this time we know how to handle the masses. I'll stay until our other officers come to help. We will detain everyone outside. Non-employees will be told to come back tomorrow."

Patterson marched out of the building and asked the crowd, "Who handles the personnel information?"

A fluttering waved as a bird - like women raised her arm. The wind caused her coat sleeves to flap as she swooped towards Patterson. "I'm Louisa Meeks, the district's Human Resource person. How may I help you, sir?"

"Please, step into the board office. Attention people. We need your DNA sample. To help eliminate you as a suspect. When you finish, go back to your office and work. Before entering the building, you need to understand. No one goes in the superintendent's office. No excuses… My men will shoot you." He added, "Then arrest you."

Louisa Meeks followed behind Patterson into the building. Between her body shaking and the wind flapping her coat, she appeared to be a bird in flight.

Jim and Henry directed the staff into the reception area. Their instructions were simple, stay in the reception area and wait to get swabbed. A pretty young secretary sashayed up to Jim and insisted the police were violating her rights. She wouldn't allow them to take her DNA. She looked over her shoulder to make sure her friend was recording her fifteen seconds of fame. In her mind, it would go viral. Jim smiled nodded, and then clicked his radio.

"Sheila, send someone to the Board Office I need assistance. I need to arrest a young woman. Need to have someone take her back to the police station and book her for me."

The young woman backed away and replied she would be more than happy to assist the police. She no longer looked at Jim like a yummy piece of cake that needed eaten. Humbly she edged back into the crowd. Jim canceled his request.

Patterson was amused by the scene and satisfied with Jim's response. Jim smoothly ended any potential problems, efficiently. Now, he needed information from Louisa Meeks. Patterson refocused on the needed information. "Louisa, I need the address for Mrs. Steinem and to read her personnel file."

Louisa turned, her arms flapped as she took short running steps towards her office. In seconds, she returned with a file under her arm and a piece of paper in her hand. *She's a bird* thought Patterson. He clicked his heels. *Why did I retire from the army? Civilians were strange creatures.*

"You need to sign this before I let you see her file. It's a privacy form. You have to sign it." She held her ground. She was very much like Mrs. Steinem, a stickler for procedures.

With Mrs. Steinem's file in his hands, he quickly read through it. It contained little information. Steinem had lived in Chicago, divorced, and lived in an apartment located in one of the mansions in River Bend. Patterson thought, *she must know someone here or how did she find an apartment in that area.* Only an ex-husband and his phone number were listed under family information. He wrote her phone number and current address down. He handed the folder back to Ms. Meeks.

"You can put the file back, now. Thank you for your help and don't forget we need your DNA sample."

Patterson wrote down more notes. Then told Jim. "You're in charge. I'm serious, if anyone tries to enter the superintendent's office. Shoot them in the foot, and then arrest them. That's my orders. I need to ask your opinion, Jim. Do you think that Sheila would be willing to guard Janet Monroe at the hospital?"

Jim leaned closer to Patterson his baby face twisted in confusion, "Sir, our Sheila, our dispatcher isn't a policeman. We can't give a gun or at least a gun with bullets to her."

Jim informed Patterson of something he didn't know. "The world will not be safe, especially for you, Patterson, if she had a police gun with bullets. She would shoot you first and claim it was an accident. I bet she does target practice in hopes of one day we'll give her a gun. And, I bet the target has your face on it."

"I'm calling her and ordering her to do this. Then, I'll call the hospital and warn them." He squared his shoulders and called Sheila. "Sheila, Patterson here. I need you to step in and help us with a police problem. You need to guard a young lady at River Bend General for the next few days. Do you have a problem with doing that?"

"Nope no problem. But, I'll need a gun to do this, right. I'll just get one from the safe."

Patterson visualized Sheila standing there picking through her gray scouring pad hair. Her red lips all scrunched up, her paper thin body in an S-shape. He responded: "No gun! The young lady is Janet Monroe. According to Dr. Ackerman she's not contagious. We just fear for Janet's safety"

"So, I do need a gun to protect this Janet person. I'll just get one out of the safe."

Patterson closed his eyes, clinched his teeth and said. "NO GUN!"

"Okay. What time do you need me there? Who will do my job? Get one of the boys to do it. Anyone just not you." Sheila started to explain in great detail – why not him.

"I'll call the hospital and warn them that you will be with Janet fulltime until her release." He clicked off.

38

EDWARD WOOTEN'S CHANCE

Ah - Monday, Samantha did toe touches before she reached into the back of the Escalade for the heavy box full of today's experiment. Movement close to the building caught her eye. It was a small boy. She started towards the child to make sure he was okay. Edward Wooten stepped out of the cafeteria service doors. He handed the child a breakfast roll, helped him put it inside his jacket and then placed his hand protectively on the small child's shoulder. They headed toward the elementary school a block away. Samantha watched. Edward never took a bite of food. She noticed for the first time that Edward was very thin for his age and pale very pale.

Samantha walked back to the Escalade, pulled out the back-breaking box and lugged it to the teachers' entrance door. Thank goodness Bob Douglass and Louis Henderson saw her and rushed to her aid. Both pushing the other one to be first to help Samantha. Louis won. He grabbed the box and swaggered off.

"Bob, you need to play golf with me every night. Then, you would be carrying this box." Louis scoffed as he staggered up the steps.

"With Worthington dead, I don't have to worry about losing weight or my job. Judging from the way you're waddling up the steps, golf hasn't helped you. Want to put a fiver on our tonight's game." Bob laughed.

Louis huffed. "Sure the easiest money I'll ever make."

Samantha walked behind the men and thought *they both needed a wife. What exactly did Bob mean by losing weight or his job? Bob's weight loss comment sounded like the comment Katherine made about our job security and a person's appearance. Had Superintendent Worthington talked to Bob about his weight? Need to find out. This was a clue. But Bob a killer – no, not sweet old Bob.*

In her classroom, she placed a shoe box with weights and magnets on each lab table. This was her brain-child, so she was nervous about the experiment working. The experiment was designed to have the students' line the ball shaped weights (planets) and then figure out how many magnets were needed to keep the weights or planets independent from each other and the sun.

She watched her students try to place the metal magnet balls with the right number of magnets, so they couldn't be pulled into the sun, or other planets. When they found out the planets closer to the sun had more difficulty staying independent, they turned their attention to the distant planets. The visual of the battle clicked in Samantha's head. *The planets closer to the sun had more problems than the distant planets with the sun and its power. The intense struggle of the closer planets to remain independent was parallel to the intense power struggle at the District's office. Superintendent Worthington ruled her universe just like the sun ruled its universe. The observation provided interesting facts concerning who may have killed Worthington. Whoever killed Worthington hadn't broken into the building. They had used their key and knew the alarm code. Plus, Worthington trusted them or they wouldn't have gotten close enough to stab her in the neck. No one lets an unknown person up close and personal like that. Plus, the police hadn't found any signs of a struggle. Or at least Patterson hadn't said anything about a struggle. Stabbing, usually related to a crime of passion and passion evolved from love, hate, or fear. Had one of the planets had enough of the Sun (Worthington)? Were there any love or hate issues in Worthington's life? Need to talk to Gin, the queen of gossip...*

During her planning time, Samantha ran to get her lunch out of the car. Ahead of her, Edward Wooten walked quickly toward the service entrance. Bet, he planned to leave the school building. She intended to foil his idea. He ducked into the cafeteria, then zipped out and passed her. His thin jacket puffed out. She followed him down the hallway to his locker, watched him opened his locker and placed fruits and sandwiches in it. He stood up, looked around and sauntered off. Her first instinct said this time I have him. Principal Moore can't save him from the stealing school food. Then Samantha had a flashback to when she stole food from school. Her mother had stopped buying food and taking care of all other household jobs. They were starving. A teacher had caught her, listened to her story and helped her.

She jogged to her car and seized her lunch and raced back to her classroom. The pounding of a headache had started its cruel journey. Samantha popped a pain pill, the first one she had taken in three days. She waited in the quiet of her classroom as the pill began to work.

Today's experiment had been beneficial to her metaphorically. It related to life's struggles. She analyzed the question. Do life's struggles create enough passion to cause a person to kill? On that note, she needed to prepare for Edward Wooten.

Samantha waited in the hall for Edward Wooten. She had a plan. She planned to face her worse nightmare, Edward Wooten. She planned to offer him an option. She watched him as he crashed into students on the way to her class. It was insane to give him a chance. She lined up the class and told them they would enter into classroom and to keep their hands off the items on the table. Edward's eyes lit up and the cliché 'chopping at the bit' crossed her mind. Fear of mass destruction stirred up the angry monster in her head, again.

"Edward, I need to talk to you before you go in."

Edward stepped up to her. She waited for the class to enter before she started, "I want you to participate in this experiment. You are to follow every step, or I will send you to the P.E. teacher, Mr. Henderson. If you follow every step and try, then I will send you to Principal Moore for candy."

She waited for his response. He peeked again at the shoe boxes on the tables. Then he looked at her. A deep sadness filled his eyes.

Edward squared his shoulders, "I will do the dumb experiment, but I want a table by myself."

She walked in and pointed to a table in the back of the room with three students. Eliza May was one of the three. "Tom and George, please move. Eliza May, Edward will join you."

Edward glared at Samantha. Instructions were given and the students enjoyed the challenge. Tears welded in Samantha's eyes, as tiny dark haired Eliza May and copper hair Edward Wooten bent over the table, intent on the experiment.

"You know your stuff. It's been good working with you." Eliza May nodded her head contentedly.

Edward puffed his thin chest out. "Thanks." And turned back to their work.

Samantha, locked in the ivy tower of education, had no knowledge of the second murder at the District's Board Office. If she had known about the second murder, would she have changed her mind about breaking–in, probably? But, then again her curiosity would have driven her to find out what was in that room that caused the deaths of two people. Plus, Katherine needed an adrenalin rush. It cured her asthma. This was a matter of breaking and entering - for medical necessity.

Plus, any excuse involved with not going home and using her outdoor toilet pleased her. Samantha trembled at the memory of how her day started. When, the alarm clock screeched its cockle doodle-do. That had startled her. She sprinted to the front door, slid into the Johnny-on-the–Spot, and flung open the door with her one eye open. She scanned for snakes before she sat down. Unseen by the one eye was a layer of frost that covered the toilet seat. Rushed in; her bottom touched the icy seat, she slipped and ricocheted out. Zoom...The momentum propelled her out of the Johnny-on-the-spot, kaboom- onto the porch. The only good thing was that the workers hadn't shown up yet. Semi-naked, urinated on and cold, she stood and screamed.

So the thought of going to jail and having indoor plumbing was almost appealing.

39

POLICE CHIEF
PATTERSON'S WAR PATH

A feather floated down toward Patterson, a large golden brown feather. He raced over and picked it out of the air. He examined it closer, probably a hawk's feather, was it a sign? His mother named him Winding Path Charles Patterson. She was part Cherokee and grew-up on a reservation. His mother used her heritage at strange times like when she named her two children, Winding Path and Little Song Bird Patterson. He returned to his roots and went on a war path.

Patterson sat in his truck and read through his notebook, and then speed-dialed Jim. "Jim, what all have you collected from today's crime scene?"

"A couple of cigarette butts, an end of a joint, and a used condom. I have picked and bagged all said items. What do you want me to do with them?"

"First, who can we hire to replace Sheila? Secondly, you need to hand deliver your items to Dr. Ackerman in the City. Third, who's guarding the superintendent's office?"

"Henry can stay here at the Board office and talk with Ramon. Hopefully, Henry will get Ramon talking and he'll share work gossip. Oh, my mom worked at the police station before Sheila. She could help us out. I'll head to the city after I call my mom and find out if she would step in. Call you back in a minute. See, ya', Boss." Jim saluted the phone.

Patterson tapped a beat on his chest and remembered the inner vibration of the drums at the tribal powwows. How powerful he felt back them. He placed the feather behind one ear and channeled his Native American spirit. To find food, he looked for animal tracks and to find, a killer he needed to look for human tracks. List of Suspects, he titled a clean page in his notebook. Which one smoked? Nick Chase smoked and did drugs, two strikes and we already have his DNA from his cigarette butts. He left them when he spent time in their jail. Patterson wondered if Nick Chase's DNA matched the poop sample.

Who had the opportunity to kill Steinem? Janet could have killed both people. No, Janet wasn't well enough to have killed Steinem today. Who knew about the purse and phones? Probably, Nick Chase, more strikes against him. Janet, Mrs. Steinem, and the Vice Superintendent, all knew the victim's habits. Needed to call Judge Tomas Sloan and have him sign the search warrants for the school district's personnel files, Janet Monroe's place and the older Worthington's home. He wanted to see what Nick had hidden at the Worthington residence. Don't forget to call the Worthington's, again. His last note, 'call Samantha and check on her'.

The next call came from Jim, "Patterson, my mom said 'yes' as she ran to the car. She said to tell you thanks. She will be there in five minutes. She's beyond excited. . ."

"Good, thanks Jim. . ."

Tires squealed as Patterson sped off to find out Janet Monroe's address with the search warrant. He called ahead to the Bender and Hicks Real Estate Office and made sure that Mr. Sterling Bender expected him. Patterson remembered the social connections of Sterling Bender. He was friends with the Worthington's and their crowd and had been friends with Al Roth. Al had been his mentor and his first civilian murder case. That was all he knew about Bender, he appeared to be a decent man. After all he and his wife fostered Janet Monroe when she was a teenager.

Bender and Hicks Real Estate office was nestled in the warehouse district of a fabulously renovated building. They had a corner office with easy access for people going north or south or east or west. Patterson pulled up to the building and strode to the door and swung it opened. The door hadn't completed the full swing open before Sterling Bender pounced on him with his hand out, all smiles with perfect very bright white teeth. He reminded Patterson of a sleek jaguar dressed in black pants and a white casual shirt. His name tag dangling off his shirt added a touch of humanness to him. Sterling Bender flicked his arm motioning Patterson to follow him. The movements like the tail of an irritated cat.

Patterson tapped his chest and re-centered, 'follow the tail, no, he meant trail' get the address to Janet Monroe. Focus. . . Something about Bender stirred a memory. Samantha talked about a thin, agile man she heard talking with Roger, the maintenance man. They had been outside the district office the night of the rock incident. Bender was definitely agile. The trails lead to Bender. What would a sprayed-tan arrogant man like Sterling Bender have to do with a robust, rotund man like Roger, an irrelevant maintenance man? Patterson opened his notebook. He wrote Bender/Beauty and Roger/Beast a connection (?).

"Mr. Bender, we haven't met. I'm the new police chief Path Patterson. I'm here on official business. I understand that you know Janet Monroe's address."

"Yes, I do." An arrogant smile slithered across his face. "But I don't have to give it to you unless you have a warrant."

Patterson pulled the search warrants out his back pocket. One of the search warrants indicated a search of Janet Monroe's home for evidence involved with Worthington's death. He held it out for Sterling Bender to see.

"I need the address or I will arrest you for obstruction of justice." Patterson released his handcuffs.

"Now Patterson, ease up, I'm just seeing if you understand the law and you do. She lives in the carriage house behind Timm and Lana Worthington's house. You just take the driveway that goes straight to the left of the big house." Bender smiled his much practiced innocent look he used when lying to his wife about his affairs. Now, he used it on everyone to get his way.

Patterson puts the warrant away and started writing in his notebook. "How well do you know the Worthington's and their daughter?"

Patterson studied the man in front of him. Focused on listening to what wasn't said. He wrote it down in his notebook as he formed a total dislike for this man. Bender oozed a thin layer of 'wicked' grease. Patterson had dealt with men like Bender in the army. They, like Sterling Bender, were word men; they spoke hollow words and lied just for the sake of lying.

"Old Worthington, I met him when I started as his caddie. Then, I married my wife, now I play golf with him. We play every chance we can at the club. I have known the Worthington family for years. Bunny Worthington, their daughter, was like our own child."

"Bunny, I thought her name was Timmons like her father." The name Bunny only added more dislike to Patterson's Anti- Superintendent Worthington fire. Game players, too much time and money, so they played mind games. Bunnies were soft and sweet – stupid name.

"Bunny is Ms. Timmons Worthington. When she was little, she called herself, Bunny. When her mother called her Timmie she wouldn't answer, only answered to Bunny. She was a pistol even when she was little." Bender smiled at the fond memories of an exciting person.

"Thanks I'll be getting back to you." Patterson darted towards the door; he had to get out of there and back on the trail. In his truck, he added Janet's address to the Worthington's and to Mrs. Judith Steinem. The addresses were in the same area Janet's address 333 Mockingbird Lane, Worthington's 334 Mockingbird Land and Mrs. Steinem's 334 B Mockingbird Lane. He couldn't believe it, three birds with one stone. Search Worthington's, Steinem's and Janet Monroe's at one stop searching experience.

Could this be a neighborhood serial killer?

40

NICK LEFT HANGING

"J.T. and Alex, please answer." Patterson spoke to the air after he called on his police radio. He needed help on the searches and someone to keep an eye on Nick Chase. In case, Nick was at the Worthington's house sitting.

"Yup, boss. . ." J.T. Brown's deep good-natured voice answered his call.

"I need you and Alex to meet me at the Worthington's house. I mean mansion in the old section of town with the big estates. Know which one I'm talking about?"

"Yup, boss, didn't go to school with any of them but used to drive through there on Friday nights looking for a party. Someone always had one going on. . ." J.T. snorted.

"Bet that was fun." Patterson rolled his eyes. He had grown up in a larger city than River Bend, with recreation centers as the place to hang out on Friday nights.

They met outside of the Worthington's mansion. Patterson and Officer J.T. Brown prepared to search the Worthington's house. Officer Alex Wilkes drove off to search Janet Monroe's carriage house. Nick Chase answered the door of the Worthington's house, tried to slam the door on Patterson and J.T. They pushed the door open and handcuffed Nick to the large door knocker on the front of it. This allowed both of them to search and not worry about Nick getting lost.

Patterson found Nick's bedroom and dug through the trash, closet, under and over every piece of furniture. He found tennis shoes with a brownish substance on them like the substance on Samantha's shoes. He photographed and bagged the shoes. In the bathroom closest to Nick's room, he found old powdered toothpaste can full of a white powdery substance in it. He tasted it, and it tasted like mint flavored cocaine. He photographed it, bagged it up and put it with the shoes. Both men checked all the closets in the house and under all the furniture and in every possible hiding place for the purse and phones. In one closet in what they thought had been one of the master bedrooms there were shelves of bags containing purses, hundreds of purses with the name Kate Spade on all of them. Who is Kate Spade, Patterson wondered, and who needed all those purses?

Mid-search Patterson received a call from Alex. "Patterson, you need to come down to Janet Monroe's. Someone tossed it."

"Guard the place. Shoot anyone who gets near it, except me. . . We will be down when we finish our search up here."

J.T. and Patterson found a door marked 334 B on the side of the mansion towards the back. They entered the door to Mrs. Steinem's apartment. Apparently at one time it had been the house keeper's quarters since it was attached to Worthington's kitchen. It was plain room with a twin bed covered with just sheets and a blanket, a love seat, a table and chair and on the wall above the table was the television. A small closet had held all her of clothes and shoe, but everything had been thrown on the floor. The twin bed and loveseat had been ripped open and dumped on the floor. In her bathroom, everything thrown into the tub and smashed into small pieces. Patterson had J.T. finish the photographing and fingerprinting of every surface. While he drove around to the carriage house that was Janet's leaving Nick Chase handcuffed to the front door.

"Okay, Alex, have you collected evidence?" Patterson nodded; impressed with Alex's professional skills and glad he had hired him.

Alex picked up a paper bag full of small plastic bags, which were full of different items and handed it to Patterson. "I photographed and fingerprinted the entire place. I looked for her computer, phone and any and all electronic devices, I found nothing. In fact, she apparently doesn't even own a television. She does have a few items of clothing, minimum of everything. Furniture is old. She has lived here for some time because of the size of her Boston fern."

Patterson looked at Alex bewildered. "What?"

"You can't move a Boston fern around especially one the size of hers. They die. You buy them smallish about nine inch pot or so, plant them in a larger pot and leave them alone. You water and feed them sparingly. Her fern is at least thirty inches or more and hasn't been moved. She has plants, good books and wine, not a lot of wine, but what she has is excellent. What she owns is of good quality and expensive, but she doesn't own much." Alex smiled, "I liked this woman's style."

"Good job, now we'll go in and look again. This time we're looking for a black purse, smallish." Patterson made a square shape of the purse about the size. All of them went in and came out empty-handed.

They looked in the attached garages - still nothing. Patterson told Alex and J.T. put all of the evidence into their police car. Then, stop, pick-up Nick and tell him he had another twenty-four-hour vacation at the local jail free of charge.

Patterson's last instructions were to place Nick in lock-up, write their report and to itemize all of the bags of evidence. The film needed to be taken to Click's Photo Shop and processed, only one of them needed to handle that. Whoever stayed at the station needed to help Jim Murphy's mother.

Just on a hunch Patterson raced out to Pretty Prairie. He needed to check on the victim's house. When he looked through the window, he knew he needed help. It had been trashed, too.

"Jim, how close are you to Pretty Prairie?"

"I'm just leaving Ackerman's office with the results, so about an hour away."

"I need back-up I'm out at Worthington's, the victim's house. Someone has trashed and torn the place up. Someone had a serious need to find something. But what?"

What good would a one strap or no strap purse be to anyone, or cell phones? What was on the cell phone that they needed or wanted so badly? Jim had talked Patterson into using Gin to hack the phone records. Patterson had all of Superintendent Worthington's cell phone records for both of her phones. Nothing jumped out at him. He had ordered the release of her financials, nothing out of the ordinary. She made a lot of money, more than he did. She drove an older car but more expensive than he did. Her house payments were less than his payments, but her house was five times larger. He thought, *how did she do that – strange. All of it was strange.*

Henry showed up to help him. Neither talked they just dusted, photographed and examined every common place for safes to be placed in a home. They found nothing.

"Police Chief Patterson, sir, I got an idea. Why don't we have Angela come out here and have her look at things? She would recognize if something was missing and maybe she knows where Superintendent Worthington hid her safe."

"Great idea, Henry, call Ramon. If he can't drive, then offer to go get them and their little boy. Do it tomorrow after school. I want Samantha Grant and her metal detector to help us." He wrote in his notebook and called Doctor Ackerman and updated him on the latest situation.

Then, he turned his attention back to Henry. "So Henry, what did you learn today at the Board of Education?"

"Well, sir. . ." Henry smiled and told Patterson the information that Ramon had told him.

Patterson placed the feather behind his ear and wrote. . . men are more efficient than women at gossiping.

41

A NIGHT TO REMEMBER

Samantha and Katherine prepared a light evening meal. Neither talked, both were lost in thought about the mission they planned for tonight. Samantha took Bo for a walk around the block avoiding her ex-husband's house. She remembered the nightmare she had of Victoria and Principal Moore as they chased her on their brooms into the river. Probably, just the effects of the Halloween season. . . Samantha checked the clock they still had an hour before they needed to leave.

"Katherine may I use your computer? I need to look up something."

Reading her magazine, Katherine didn't look at Samantha, just nodded her head and pointed to the computer on her desk.

Finally, time to check out something that had concerned her. The side effects of blood thinners, she typed in the question and waited for the response. Blood Thinner Medication – Side Effects: Nausea, diarrhea, loss of appetite, or stomach/ may occur. If any of these effects persist tell your doctor promptly. Severe side effects: medication can cause serious bleeding – it affects your blood clotting proteins – unusually high INR lab results – if there are any signs of serious bleeding / bruising – tell your doctor immediately... The worst case scenario she could lose weight easier. Maybe Superintendent Worthington used blood thinner to stay so thin. Did Worthington even have a blood problem? Something to check out . . .

The sun finally settled below the horizon. The moonless night covered the earth like a down-filled quilt on a cold winter's evening. Football practice had been over for an hour, and all of the tardy parents had picked up their children. Adventure time . . . Samantha checked for the last time: metal detector – worked, pin light flashlight – worked, gloves – in her pocket, stethoscope – around her neck, and lock pick – in her pocket. She looked at Katherine and nodded her head. Katherine shimmered with the thought of an adventure and Samantha turned ashen with fear of being arrested. But it had to be done. Both dressed in their black exercise outfits which this time included black stocking caps. Thank goodness it had turned cooler.

"Katherine, I don't think we should really do this I have a bad feeling about it." Samantha scrunched down in her seat.

"You have to – Worthington said she had incriminating stuff on you. We have to find it before the police and destroy it. Or you will hang for her murder." Katherine brushed imagined lint off her outfit.

"I haven't done anything for her to have as incriminating evidence."

Katherine looked away. "Samantha, our superintendent was an evil woman. If she said she had incriminating evidence she had it. Even if she faked it."

"Okay, let's do this." Samantha hugged Bo tighter.

Katherine circled the district's building like a bobcat on the hunt. Slowly, they prowled toward the target. The parking lot lights were on and lit random areas of the lot. An abyss covered the main entrance as if the architects had designed it for undetectable, easy, and illegal entry. Katherine parked her car in the darkest area of the lot. They scampered up to the entrance. Katherine unlocked the door and darted to the alarm keypad, her perfectly manicured nails clicking on the keys. They heard a ding. A green light flashed, and Katherine and Samantha glowed green. Katherine unlocked that door and moved aside allowing room for Samantha and the metal detector to enter in the building. Once in Samantha lowered her night vision goggles into place. She acclimated herself to the building's sub-lights from computers and areas of total darkness.

Katherine backed up, relocked the door, reset the alarm, relocked the entrance door and stealthily scampered across the lot to her car. Bo waited nervously for her and pawed at the window while he witnessed their break-in. Katherine used her keys to unlock the door so there would not be a beep sound. She had removed the interior light bulbs earlier, absolutely no sign she and Bo were there. Bo and Katherine barely breathed as they watched the board office. Their job involved warning Samantha of any unexpected guests so she could exit the building before anyone caught her in there.

Samantha walked to the door with yellow tape across it. Thankful she had worn the night vision goggles, without the moon to shed some light into the interior of the building it became hazardous. Waste baskets, cords, and desk floor mats innocent in daylight, but at night they were traps, just waiting to trip a person. Samantha thought of it as a power trip for the unappreciated inanimate objects of the world.

Inside Superintendent Worthington's office, the reflective surfaces created a nightmare effect. Samantha looked around and saw her zombie like body multiplied a thousand fold. Every movement caused a ripple across the surfaces. Nauseating. . . She turned on the metal detector a rhythmic clicking started, its normal sound. Where did Worthington hide the safe in this ominous office? The walls were covered with chrome, glass panels and mirrors. How do you check that? She held the detector in front of her and walked slowly around the office. The metal detector clicking quickened when she neared the desk. Slowly she scanned the walls, the clicking increased as she lowered it towards the desk.

While Katherine and Bo intently watched the front of the building an intruder crept along the back of the Board of Education office building toward the service entrance. The night, a perfect moonless night, was cool enough that no one thought anything odd about his bulky vest as he jogged along the streets. The only thing visible was a light fog from his breath. By all appearance, he didn't exist, just a shadow on the move. The service ramp, encased in total darkness, provided a perfect cover for the Shadow's activity. Excitement electrified the Shadow as he released the M4 strap and reached back and slid the M4 down and around. He had purchased the gun just this morning after being embarrassed by an old lady overpowering him. Mrs. Steinem's strength had surprised him. He lovingly patted the gun, the magazine full and ready to go. It came already loaded as part of the process of teaching him how to load and unload the gun safely. Each magazine held thirty shots, so he had a total of sixty bullets. Ready to party. . . There shouldn't be a reason to use this bad boy, but had it just in case someone got in his way. Bam! A moment spent relieving himself and then back to his mission.

Bo noticed the bobbing light and growled. Katherine looked and saw a faint light bobbing sporadically along the office windows located along the front of the building. Katherine tried to call Samantha. No answer . . .

Samantha focused on finding the safe as quick as possible. She moved the metal detector quickly over the area most logical to hide a safe. In the area under Superintendent Worthington desk the clicking increased and became louder. The increased noise from the detector made it impossible for Samantha to hear her phone. Finally, she heard it and tried to answer it, but her phone had died. Unable to check caller ID, Samantha assumed a phone call meant someone was near. She reasoned. *Probably the police patrolling of the area looking for intruders. Well, I need to hurry – I'll cut the carpet and come back tomorrow night and investigate.*

Katherine knew whoever wandered inside the building had not gone in the front entrance door. Right now it didn't matter how they got in Katherine had to warn Samantha. She knew one way to warn Samantha. She needed to enter the building and scare the bad guy or the maintenance man and cause them to run out of the building causing the alarm to go off. Then Samantha could run out too and they would speed away for the scene. For some insane reason she decided to crawl out the window of her car so she could surprise the intruder. She rolled out the window and fell to the ground. It was at that moment, when she hit the dirt, Katherine remembered she had removed the lights inside her car. Oh, well, she dusted herself off and scuttled to the entrance door. She unlocked the door, clicked the alarm pad, waited impatiently for the green light to flash. She opened the second door and turned on the lights.

Katherine put her phone to her ear and announced in a loud angry voice, "I'll be home in a minute I forgot my briefcase. I have a project due tomorrow. Damn it, you like the money I make. Watch the television, until I get back."

The Shadow froze. Samantha froze. Katherine walked and hummed her way to the superintendent's door the yellow tape was in disarray. Katherine brushed the imagined lint off her black outfit and stylishly adjusted her stocking cap.

The Shadow panicked. Power surged through him, he placed the M4 butt against his shoulder, and he looked in the sight, aimed at the lights, pulled the trigger long and hard. *Exhilarating, whoever is in the building is in my way. They deserved to die just like Mrs. Steinem.* He needed the blackmail videos, photos and copies of the fraudulent contracts with the school district. His life and career were at stake. This was self-defense just like it was this morning. He fired down the hall with intent to kill. The bullets hit walls and zoomed through them. The bullets hit metal doors and crashed through them as if they were made of cardboard. The more he shot the better his aim became. He blasted the fluorescent lights. The lights sparked and smoked, and then total blackness. Blink bang blink, and then he fired again in another direction and hoped to kill or at least scare the other intruder.

Katherine shrieked, "Samantha get out of here now."

The Shadow almost cried. Someone else was in the building. He whined. "Were they holding a convention or something in the building tonight? The police had told the school board staff not to schedule any night meetings until the murder investigation was over. Well, these people didn't belong in the building. I just protecting the building from intruders, he rationalized."

Empowered by his new toy and the fact they could execute him only once, he fired into the darkened area. A big smile spread under his mask - his radiant white teeth glowed in the dark like a jack-o-lantern.

Wearing her night vision goggles, Samantha opened the door of the superintendent's office and peered out. Surprised that Katherine was just inches away. She turned her head and saw a purplish zombie-like slender body erratically danced down the hall towards her with the sparks flying from his gun. His teeth glowed through the mouth opening of a mask. She shined her light in his direction. She aimed for his eyes and hoped she had blinded the intruder enough for herself and Katherine to escape.

He stopped briefly and involuntarily shielded his eyes. Quickly he regrouped and fired off more bullets.

In that second Samantha commanded, "Katherine, run to the door – run."

"Okay –I have my key ready for us."

"No. . . . Just flip the lock, go and don't touch the alarm." Samantha turned off her light and used her night vision goggles to locate Katherine and the door. Crouching and dragging the metal detector she ran towards the door and Katherine.

The damn women plan to set off the alarm. No they won't . . . The Shadow moved swiftly in the direction of the superintendent's office pulled and held the trigger so bullets flew in every direction. Thirty bullets dispersed in what seemed like seconds. The Shadow had swung his arm and randomly aimed at what he hoped were people. The adrenaline-rush was like nothing he had ever experienced. It felt good, better than sex – good.

A scream erupted. A fog of plaster dust from the bullets shot through the walls saturated the area. The old fiberglass insulation combined with plaster dust irritated the hunter's and the prey's eyes. Time stopped.

"Katherine, are you are right?"

"No, I've been hit. Run, Samantha and get help." Katherine ordered.

The Shadow's gun ran out of bullets. He pushed the release button and the used magazine hit the floor. He pulled out another magazine, banged it hard on the cement floor and inserted it into the gun. Just like they did on TV.

Samantha heard the click of the magazine going into place, but, she didn't hear the click of the trigger connect in the fire position. She heard nothing. The gun had jammed or something. Confirmation came when she heard the man cursing. She whispered. "Yes"

For a few seconds, the bullets stopped. Now, they had a small chance for survival. Samantha raced to Katherine and wrapped her arms around her friend, "The gun has malfunctioned. We have seconds to get out. Run – now."

A few choice words flew out of the Shadow's mouth. He pressed once more and held the trigger. Bullets sped out erratically. The shock of it almost knocked him down. Zing – zing. When Samantha heard the zinging, she thought they were doomed. Menacingly they zinged and blinged, a laser light show of bullets flying.

The shadow had lost control. The gun had taken on a life of its own and turned against him. The shooter panicked, but his finger was frozen on the trigger. Finally, his last bullet spent, only the echo of his cursing lingered, and the air cloaked in the blinding dust – time for him to disappear. The Shadow backed against the wall and retraced his steps to the safety of the warehouse. And - he vanished.

Katherine held her finger on her phone just one key so it automatically called 911. Samantha glanced at their reflection Katherine's good arm draped around her neck. Katherine looked pale but lovely in her black turtle neck ensemble. She, on the other hand, looked like an alien with the night vision goggle still on and her black outfit decorated with cobwebs, plaster dust and insulation fiber. The hair, it had to be the hair, Katherine's hair, every single strand still in place. If she removed her stocking cap, her hair would look like a rope mop that could clean the cement floor. Samantha shook her head and reached out flipped the door lock. They sprinted past the alarm and unlocked the front entrance door. Alarms blared, lights flashed, and the police sirens screamed.

"Yes!" Both women shouted.

"Let me take you to the vet." Samantha half carried Katherine to the car.

"No, Patterson is on his way." Katherine leaned against her car and made sure that her blood didn't get on the flawless exterior.

"So, if he wasn't coming, then you would have gone to the vet?"

Katherine gave Samantha the raised perfect arched eyebrow followed with a teacher frown. The sounds from the police sirens grew louder and the flashing lights illuminating the sky.

"Did you see that?" Katherine pointed in the general location of the football field.

Samantha turned and saw only total darkness. "I didn't see anything. Sorry. . . If it was the shooter, at least, he isn't using us for target practice, anymore."

Patterson pulled up, looked at Katherine, then looked at Samantha, and finally at the building, with wisps of dust drifting out of it. Alarms blared. He touched his feather. *Stay – Calm*

"Okay, the ambulance and fire department are coming. While we wait, want to tell me what happened?"

"I went in to find the safe." Samantha answered. She looked him in the eyes. She was not sorry, and she wasn't going to say 'sorry' either.

"Okay, did you find it?"

"I think so, I have the general location where the meter went nuts, but Katherine called and the shooting interrupted my search. Want to go inside and search with me?" A look of hope crossed her face.

"Sure, after they fix Katherine up." Patterson knew it was wrong. He shouldn't let a civilian get involve. But, he wasn't in the army any more this was a small size town with a tiny budget. A fancy contraption like a metal detector wasn't in his budget. In order to find out what everyone wanted in that damn office he needed a metal detector. Samantha had one. He should deputize her. At least make her a consultant like on TV.

"Just sit in the truck for a minute. I need to check out the building." Patterson marched back towards the Board of Education building.

Samantha and Bo climbed into his truck and Katherine climbed into the ambulance. While, Patterson turned off the alarm and checked out the building. The service entrance interested him the most.

First, he went into the interior of the warehouse, the door before the alarm pad and the exit door were both unlocked. Someone had left the door unlocked. *Wait,* he thought. *The alarm - the outside door had to be locked or the alarm would have gone off when the intruder entered. The intruder had a key and knew the code.* He re-examined the two exit doors, the one on the outside was a heavy metal door and the exit door on the inside was light weight door. More importantly different locks with two deadbolts meant two different keys. Patterson ran outside and looked for forced entry signs. Nothing. It was an inside job someone had purposefully left the inside exit door open. First, he thought Roger did it, because Samantha had noticed Roger talking to a mysterious man outside of the building when police were here investigating the rock incident. In truth, it could have been anyone. Anyone could have flipped the locks open or had been given a key. His heart sank.

42

A Phone has Many Uses

Forty seconds later, the adrenalin rush had left Samantha edgy and bored. Bored meant the kiss of death for Samantha. Every single time she got bored trouble happened. Well, she thought why change at this time in my life.

Scattered all over the floor of Patterson's truck were files, they looked important, official-like; marked with Dr. Ackerman's, the medical examiner, stamp on them. Patterson paid for Ackerman's expertise out of his own pocket. He thought he needed valid facts when dealing with any case. To end the boredom, she started picking up the files, in order to make sure she placed the papers in the right file, she read each piece of paper at least scan it. Her excuse, she needed to help Patterson, but in truth, she was investigating to prove her innocence.

She noticed some of the pages had tabs and yellow highlights – notes to Patterson, the most relevant information. She did a quick glance to make sure no one was around. Then, she pulled her phone out and photographed the tabbed pages. All she had to do was download, print, and read, ta-da. Speaking of phones – maybe, Worthington photographed or downloaded things on her phones that were worth killing her for, like secrets or incriminating things. What kind of secret information would a superintendent of the public school system have on a phone or any other technical devices?

Samantha needed to talk to the queen of rumors, Gin, who had the inside information on everyone especially the country club crowd. Plus, Janet Monroe, the superintendent's secretary was staying with Gin. Maybe she could share information about Worthington.

Samantha started to call Gin, but Patterson pushed through the Board of Education's door. Carefully she put her phone away and slipped out of his truck. Katherine lumbered out of the ambulance and staggered towards her car. Samantha and Bo raced to Katherine and helped her into the passenger's side. They waited for Patterson to give them their orders.

The stone wall marched towards them. "Samantha, bring your metal detector along we are examining Worthington's office, now."

Patterson pivoted and marched back into the building. Samantha and Bo ran after him dragging the metal detector. She wondered, *how did I get Katherine and the detector out at the same time?*

The interior of the building's air was clearing up from all the plaster and insulation that had filtered down after the shooting frenzy. Patterson put floodlights out so he could see and assess the damages. Small bullet holes splattered over everything including the light fixtures and made it hard to see in the dark. The new style, the pegboard-look covered the walls.

"Well, the building needed updated." He commented.

The cleaning fluid and sulfur smell hung in the damp air. The combination of the two odors wouldn't be the next "in" smell for a new perfume line. The Board of Education building had always had a strange odor from the previous owners – River Stones Laundry and Cleaners. It had been a large commercial operation in the mid-1900. Tonight's activities hadn't helped the normal unpleasant odor of the building. Now, it needed a professional remodeling and cleaning before they could us it again.

They stepped into superintendent's office it was untouched by the wild gunfire.

Great maybe we can still find the missing phones, thought Patterson. Samantha walked toward the desk area where she had been when things turned scary. She placed the machine on the thick black carpet.

"The carpet's density makes it hard to get a strong reading, but under the desk I got stronger and quicker beeps." She explained to Patterson.

"I imagine the blood and other body fluids don't help with the reading either." He added his explanation.

"Thanks for the information – TMI and too late."

The meter's reading arm moved some and the clicking sound remained consistent. Nothing excited it, yet. As Samantha moved closer to the desk the detector responded with an increased clicking. Way in back - under the desk it clicking increased and the reading arm bounced to the right and beyond. Bo dashed over sniffed and started digging. Samantha crawled under the desk and felt around for the edge of the safe or the loose edge of the carpet. It seemed reasonable to assume if the Superintendent used the safe daily it would have easy access. With Bo's help, Samantha found the edge, lifted, and removed a heavy fifteen by fifteen square of thick carpet and nestled nicely in its hiding place was the safe. She removed the stethoscope from around her neck placed it on the safe at the location Katherine had shown her. Slowly she turned the knob and listened. The first tumble dropped.

"Twelve" She looked up at Patterson he just stood there smiled and down at her. Irritated she said. "Write the numbers down, as I give them to you. Twelve"

"Now – One"

"Eight"

Slowly she listened as she right turned, again. Hopefully she had all of the numbers, but she checked for more. One more tumbler dropped.

"Three" She tried the handle – click. Excitement filled them and hoped for answers. Samantha lifted the door of the safe and peered inside. Nothing . . .

Patterson got down on his knees peered in, felt around inside the safe and found. Nothing. "I guess Mrs. Steinem had removed everything before someone killed her. But, she was killed by that mirrored panel in the wall."

Samantha reasoned. "Maybe, she opened this, found part of what she needed then put everything back nice and neat just like Mrs. Steinem. Then, she checked Worthington's other hiding place. Could that have happened?"

"Whatever she found the killed has all the information. We need to find the killer before what is on the phone is destroyed. What in the world could be on a phone that was worth killing for?" Patterson muttered.

"Mrs. Steinem was killed?" Samantha looked at Patterson in disbelief. "Another death in this room in less than a week."

"Janet Monroe found the building compromised. The alarm sounded, and we came. Jim and I went in and found the office opened. We found Mrs. Steinem strangled with a purse strap." He showed Samantha the photo on his phone.

A thought joined the fact about what could be on Superintendent Worthington's phone file in her mind. *Could it be pictures taken of illegal activities and people who didn't want it known? Like what? Like the incriminating stuff about me, someone else may have the same type of thing on Worthington's phones, too.*

They stood up. Patterson photographed the safe and the surrounding areas with his phone.

Then he called J.T. and Alex on his police radio.

"Hey, I need you two down at the Board office and you're spending the night."

"Sure, but, we're watching the rest of the game down there. We'll be there in a few minutes." J.T. and Alex were at Alex's parent's watching the game with Alex's brothers. They had been drinking beer. So, Alex's mom made a thermos of coffee for them and packed lots of food. They were ready now. J.T. brought his computer so they could watch their game from anywhere. Life was good for both young men. They had joined the police force together after Alex's college and military stint and J.T.'s plumbing school training fiasco. They liked and respected Police Chief Path Patterson and enjoyed the excitement of police life. Life was good.

Time to take care of his women, Patterson gently told Samantha. "I need you to take Katherine home. Stay at Katherine's tonight. I know it breaks your heart not to have your outhouse. Just pee in the yard with Bo. That will make you feel at home."

He walked her to the car and made sure she drove off. Then he called the Vice Superintendent of the district, Mickey Sims.

"Mr. Sims, this is Police Chief Patterson. We had another incident down here at the Board of Education tonight. I'll tell you more about it tomorrow, o-eight-hundred. Be here. Tonight I need you to contact every single person who works here at the Board. Tell them to stay home tomorrow. Tomorrow we will assess who, what and where for everyone."

"What happened now? I deserve to know, that is my building. I'm in charge not you." Panic rose in Mickey Sims. He needed someone in his office to figure out how to cover up his problems. He had tried to fix it, but couldn't. He needed to talk to old Steinem after the meeting tomorrow. She knew how to hide or find things better than anyone he knew.

"Sir, I said we will meet tomorrow. We will figure this out together. I'm here to help you. I have two murders and multiple break-ins. We need to figure out why. Just call everyone. See you tomorrow."

"Wait, please." Mickey Sims blurted. "Who else was killed in the Board Office?"

"Mrs. Steinem, so have a damn good alibi for today."

"Oh, no…" Sims phone went dead.

Patterson phoned Jim. "Jim, where are you?"

"Sir. . ." Jim's usual upbeat voice sound strained.

"Jim, I need you and Henry at the Board of Education building tomorrow at eight. Can you do that?"

"Yes. . . Do you want my mother back at the police station?" Jim's voiced dragged.

"If possible. . . What's going on?" Patterson knew he needed to cut the boy some slack. Jim worked hard. Plus, he knew everyone and that helped him.

"Well, my dad forgot to pick up my kids. My mom called him and reminded him, but he went back to sleep. No one showed up to get the kids. They became scared. So, they called my dad, then, my mother and finally, me. With everyone calling him, he finally woke up. He went to get them. Now you need to understand. He has never picked up my kids or anybody's kid from school before. They gave him a ticket for going the wrong way in the pick-up area. He blew up at the teachers on duty. They gave him another ticket and threatened to ban him from the pick-up area. The kids are home and fine, but starving. My mom can't wait to go back to work, I can see why."

"Okay. Tell your mother to take care of the kids first. Tomorrow she can take time off to get them and take them home after school. I'm sending pizza out to you guys. Okay?"

"Thanks, but too late I ordered one made my dad go get it. He's mad and – so – am – I. Gin has offered to pick up and take care of the kids until Mom gets off work. Isn't that sweet?" Love oozed out of every word when he talked about Gin. If anyone asked him if he loved Gin. He would deny it.

Next, Patterson called Henry asked him to come straight to the Board of Education building in the morning. Told him coffee, and donuts would be there. While he waited for J.T. and Alex in the superintendent's office he checked the office's wall thermostat it read 90 degrees. *What reason would someone have for keeping it so darn hot in here?*

43

WHO PLAYED WITH GUNS

Alex and J.T. wandered into the District's Board of Education building. Immediately Alex put his hand on his gun – ready. Resting in one of the secretary's chair Patterson stood up, walked over to his men and waited to see what they had to say about that battle field.

J.T. chortled. "Who did the Board tick-off this time? Does this mean the entire town is a suspect?"

That response wasn't appreciated, Patterson knew he had too many suspects without someone telling him. Encouraged as he watched Police Officer Alex Wilkes measure, probe and extract one bullet and bag it. Slowly, Alex moved around the reception area and into the hall area. Using his phone, he photographed close shots of the walls and door frames.

After Alex examined the holes and studied his photos, he reported his observation to Patterson. "Only one shooter used a M4 or M16, not a professional. The person's height ranges between five foot-ten inches and six foot tall. Also, the shooter watches too much TV because he or she banged the magazine on the cement floor like they do on TV and jammed the magazine. Bullets went through sheetrock, insulation, and wood framing. Also, whoever remodeled this place used cheap stuff. Usually the bullets just start to go through and don't tear up much. But, the walls disintegrated. Is there much damage in the other rooms? What do you need for us to do?"

Patterson smiled for the first time in hours. "Alex thought you were an officer in the army. How do you know so much?"

"I guided my men into areas where this was the norm in decorating. My young men, who watched too many movies banged their magazine on their helmet. Damages the crap out of the magazines and causes them to misfire. That's how I know about the wild bullets. Sir. . ." Alex stood at ease and waited to be told what to do next.

"Great job, pick up the bullets and bag them, dust for fingerprints in the service entrance area. It's too dark to look for footprints in that area. The door wasn't forced open, so whoever did this had a key or keys. Figure out, how many new locks are needed to secure this place, got it. Now follow me out and lock the doors." Patterson headed to the glass entrance doors which were still intact the only good news about the Board's office building. Patterson wondered, *who, in my increasingly long list of suspects, plays with guns?*

44

MR. POTATO HEAD DID IT

Samantha slowly drove Katherine home. Once there, they moved like zombies securing the garage and house against an unknown enemy. Then, poured a large much needed glass of wine for each of them. Samantha held Bo until both of them stopped shaking.

Katherine went to bed with her pain pills given by the paramedics. Samantha checked on her a few minutes later to make sure she was asleep.

"Katherine may I use your computer."

A snore passed for a *yes* to Samantha. She slid down the banister. On the computer, she downloaded her photos of the files from Patterson's truck. She read the first one: picture/page *T*. Worthington's medical records – no drugs or alcohol in the system, appeared healthy. As she read further it became more interesting for personal reasons. Worthington's blood workup shows her INR was at 9.5 with her PT 18.3; it should have been INR 2.0 to 3.0 and the PT should have been 11 to 13 seconds.

A childhood illness furthered damaged the already genetically affected heart valve. T. Worthington had been on blood thinner since age eight; last known blood test was in _. *Oh me.* Thought Samantha, *that was twelve years ago.*

From her brief encounter with blood thinners, she knew a person should be tested at least once a month. Other findings showed

Worthington was malnourished, and intestines showed stress from constant diarrhea. Who knew that intestines had stress issue? Stress from constant diarrhea, Yuk! So, did Superintendent Worthington use a Warfarin- like medication as a way to stay thin? How sad. . . Samantha wondered if the strain of being on top may have added to her health issues and eating disorder.

She scanned the information until she found the autopsy report. 'A forced sharp trauma to the jugular vein . . . small blade .4 cm in length…used to stab the victim . . . angle – downward in the left side of the neck at left to right angle. Victim seated at the time of the attack. . . Rigor Mortis –sitting position-

Samantha went to the refrigerator removed two small oval potatoes four sticks of butter. She remembered how her grandmother got angry when she and Pops worked theories out with potatoes. She put tooth picks as arms in one potato and moved it to the spoon or the door of the Superintendent Worthington's office. In the second potato, she placed a toothpick through the butter and into the bottom of the potato. Stacking two butter stick as the superintendent's desk, and one stood up as the mirror like panels in front of the desk. The first potato waddled up to the second potato. The second potato looked in the butter/mirror to see who was behind her.

Samantha re-read the report. Used her hand as the legs for the potato, she waddled the Killer potato closer to the Worthington potato. She moved Killer potato behind Worthington potato and tried to stab it. She used the right arm of her potato on the Worthington potato's left side. She closed her eyes and visualized Worthington at her desk. Worthington had acute hearing so any sound would have caused her to look into her mirror. Did Worthington just sit there and watch someone come up behind her. Then moved, so it would be easier to stab the left side of her neck. No one, especially Worthington, stayed in one position while someone tried to harm them.

Samantha stopped, and then restructured the scenario. Worthington seated at her desk watched a person she knew and trusted, move closer. The person stood slightly to the right of Worthington, maybe talking. Using the left hand, they stabbed Worthington in the neck on the left side. For some reason, Worthington hadn't moved until Ramon touched her. Then, she fell over in a sitting position. They weren't facing each other because there wasn't enough room between the body and the desk. It had to be a left handed person. . . Worthington and the killer watched each other in the mirror. Worthington never dreamed this person would hurt her. Who in the world did Worthington trust that much?

What else did the killer see besides Worthington at the desk? The computer, Worthington's computer – what did the police find on and around the computer? Like – everyone, Worthington saved everything she worked onto a USB flash drive or some other backup device. They killed her at the computer. The police should have found a USB flash drive by the computer. Need to ask Patterson about that.

Time to try this theory with the potatoes she thought. Mirrors. . . People talked to each other as they looked in the mirror. Like when a person has to sit in the back seat, but they needed to talk to the driver of the car. They both look into the mirror and talked. But, a person would notice if someone moved behind them and had a sharp object, like in the movie *Psycho*. Worthington hadn't noticed the left hand as it moved closer to her neck. Because why? Worthington was seated, and the killer stood beside her. Maybe Worthington couldn't see the hand moving because it didn't show in the mirror. If the person was tall, then Worthington's body hid the knife or, would the person have to be short? *Need to check that out at Worthington's desk.* What about if they were arguing? Then, Worthington's attention would have been focused on the mirror. Stabbing is a crime of passion, whoever stabbed Worthington was emotionally upset and without a thought stabbed her with a –. Samantha needed more visual information before she had any ideas about that.

She had her theory on how Superintendent Worthington died. Next, she needed to figure out the reason someone killed her. What had upset a person so much that they killed in the heat of the moment?

The phones, the answer to that had been on the phones. Samantha thought, *what did Worthington have on her phones that made them so significant that a person had killed for them, at least twice? Worthington had stuff about me on the phones or on something, but where?* The experience of being the duck in a shooting gallery had left her wired. Katherine had taken a sedative and was not able to talk now. That left Gin. Gin knew all the dirt on everyone. Secrets, Truths and Lies. . .

45

HEARD IT ON THE GRAPEVINE

"Gin got a minute to talk? Is Detective Jim there?"

"No, Detective Jim has problems at home since his mother has gone back to work. Their house has fallen apart without little mama there to take care of them. I'm taking the kids tomorrow after school to help out. I hope I don't screw up."

"You won't, you're good with the kids at school. I'll be brief. Katherine got shot in the arm tonight. We broke into the board office and an intruder broke in while I was in Worthington's office. Both of us were looking for phones and a safe. Katherine came in to warn me. The guy started shooting all crazy-like and winged Katherine. We caused the alarm to go off on purpose. Now, the board office looks like a scene from the *OK Corral*. The dust was so thick I could barely see even with wearing my night goggles. I got a look at the guy, and he got a look at me. Well, he sort of got a look, I had on my knitted hat and my goggles. What do you know about our superintendent? What could she have on people that caused someone to kill? What do you know about her parents?"

"Wow, is Katherine okay? Yes, I miss Jim not being here, I love him, but he doesn't me."

"She will be fine. Are you sure about the one way thing?" Samantha knew Gin had denied Jim's feelings for her. Apparently, it had been on Gin's mind since she added that to their conversation.

"Well, as you probably already know I had a fling with Worthington's father. Just a country club affair, nothing more. He's a nice enough man. Lonely, tired of trying to cover up that he was almost bankrupt because of his daughter's spending. He said on more than one occasion 'Bunny will bankrupt me first and then kill us with her stunts. He asked me what to do. I told him to sell everything of value, put cheap imitation stuff in and down size. Tell his wife and let her help on the downsizing and hiding the money. You know Lana Worthington has it all, she is bright, beautiful and a bombshell. The Worthington's, Timm and Lana love each other, but Timm is a sexually healthy male and Lana has health problems, her heart or something like that. So, he has affairs, and she ignores them. Lately, they have spent more time in the city away from their daughter. In fact, Timm told me they had followed my advice. Now, they were going to Europe to hide from Bunny and their nephew Nick Chase. It will kill them when they find out she's dead. Oh, I almost forgot there's one rumor that Worthington has fathered several children from Janet Monroe's mom to the past mayor's wife. If you see anyone with deep-set dark grey eyes they're related to him, closely related. He is a beautiful man; smart, hardworking went from being worth zero to millions. He sold a lot of land to the school district and made a bundle. He kept making more bundles of money. Then, Bunny grew up and drained the bundles. Anything else?"

"What about Bunny Worthington, hard to think of Superintendent Worthington as Bunny. Again, why would someone kill her? Oh, Mrs. Steinem was killed early this morning in the same place – the superintendent's office. Janet arrived just after it happened, but got locked between the entrance doors by the alarm."

"Poor Mrs. Steinem, why was she in Worthington's office? About Bunny Worthington, it's just a rumor but it has been said by more than one person. She took bribes, if she had you on her 'remove/fire' list. You could pay her some exorbitant amount of money, and your job was safe. I heard you were on her list, were you?" Gin asked.

"Yes, I was and I don't know why. Now back to the problem, Mrs. Steinem went to Worthington's office to find the missing phones and purse. Instead, she found a killer. Why did Bunny Worthington need money? I mean she made a ton of money compared to us."

"I don't know I stayed clear of her. She knew about her father and me. It didn't make her happy. She was vindictive."

"I'll let you go, now. We need to be fresh for tomorrow. Hey, are you going to the club's dance on Friday?" Samantha asked.

"I think so, I want to, Jim's not a country clubber. But, he said that you and Patterson were going and Katherine and Johnny Jones. Why doesn't Katherine leave that creep of a husband, Johnny Jones?"

"Katherine adores Johnny Jones, the creep. Keep your ears open for any more gossip and tell me."

Samantha put her phone on the charger. She let Bo out to do his business. He stood still and growled at the shadows. *Must be the wind,* she thought as she picked Bo up and took him inside.

The shadow had waited and followed them from school board's office to Pretty Prairie. Now, he knew where they lived.

46

HAPPY DANCE

Patterson jumped out of bed. Today had only one bright spot, Nick Chase's court appearance to be sentenced on possession of illegal drugs. Too bad, it was not for murder. Unfortunately, Nick had not been the one who killed Mrs. Steinem. It was not Janet either. So, who did it?

Today, he needed time with the Vice Superintendent, Mickey Sims. The man knew something. He was never at the Board Office unless specifically asked. Plus, he had broken into Worthington's office when he had been told not to go in the room? Vice Superintendent Sims risked being arrested just to find the hidden item in Worthington's office. Also, I need to talk to Mrs. Judith Steinem's ex-husband. Need to try and contact Worthington's parents again. Patterson knew their number by heart, but not his own.

Slowly, Patterson opened the door to the police station nervous about the state of the office since Sheila wasn't there to boss people around. He heard the hum of voices, the smell of coffee, and a brisk sweet voice answering the phone. Peaceful, he entered and there at Sheila's desk sat a short, thin, freckled face woman with dyed bright red hair, orange lipstick and black horn rimmed glasses. She talked on the phone as she wrote down things with one hand and typed with the other. He had a Mrs. Steinem, the iconic secretary, Jim's mother was the perfect dispatcher/secretary. He smiled life was good.

"Mrs. Murphy, welcome to River Bend's police department, I'm Path Patterson, the chief of police. It is a pleasure to meet you, again."

The tiny woman's freckled face smiled up at him and handed him a handful of messages. "Thank you, these are yours. Update - Nick Chase's lawyer wants to talk to you. Something about suing you and the city of River Bend. . ."

"Okay, first I need to speak to our Mr. Chase." He turned to go to the jail section of the police department.

"Oh, he is gone. Left yesterday, the lawyer came in and handed me this."

"Who is Chase's lawyer?"

"That Sean Watts, the old fart playboy lawyer, you know." Mrs. Murphy looked at Patterson her penciled-in arched eyebrow, orange lips pinched together and a disapproving look on her face.

She handed Patterson a release signed by Judge Tomas Sloan.

"The Idiot", Patterson clenched his fist. Oh, he needed to swear, but, not in front of, Mrs. Murphy. Rigidly he marched to his office and read the bench release, again. Timeline he needed a timeline Nick Chase booked 9:30 A.M. and bench release signed at 11:32 A.M... Patterson stopped short in his office.

Perhaps, an answer to a prayer, then he asked, "What time did Nick Chase get released yesterday?"

"Around noon. . . Oh, another thing, Sheila called, they are letting Janet out today, said she would stay with Janet today but will be back here tomorrow. . ."

"Mrs. Murphy, if you want a part-time job let me know." Patterson leaned out of his office. Just in time, to see tears roll down her thin, freckled face. That only tightened the already hard knot in his gut. Civilian life had made him soft. Patterson wrote out his timeline, then opened his desk drawer and pulled out a recorder and turned it on, tested it, and recorded his thoughts.

"Have to go backwards to see if we can match Nick with the times of the crimes."

Patterson inhaled deeply. "So – Nick Chase, at 9:05 cuffed to the door of the Worthington's house. He said he had been home all night and early morning. No alibi, no witnesses, no reason to be out on bond. Nick could have killed Mrs. Steinem before nine in the morning and broke into Janet's, Mrs. Steinem's and his cousin Bunny Worthington's homes. Looking for something. Janet and Steinem lived on the same estate as he did, plus, the estate was just minutes from the school board's office building. He could have spent the night at Superintendent Worthington's searching if that happened then exact when and where was not necessary. What is important? He had the opportunity and motive. Then, we released him at noon on Monday. Gave him the free to go forth and kill card, again."

Patterson faced the recorder pushed the start button, again and said, "I, Police Chief Path Patterson need to substantiate the exact time of Nick's events. Then I will destroy Nick's alibi and prove he killed Mrs. Steinem. He could have done the damage at the Board of Education, also."

Patterson revisited his notes then continued. "At 7:30 PM last night, the first visitors, Samantha Grant and Katherine Jones, entered the Board of Education office building through the front door. A second visitor entered the same building through the service entrance at around 7:35 PM. The second visitor used his own keys. He knew the code. Suspect Nick Chase had access to the board office's keys. Either Superintendent Worthington gave him keys. Or he stole them from her. The alarm's code had been obtained from Superintendent Worthington or stolen from her. Monday evening: Nick planned to find what he had missed that morning when Mrs. Steinem interrupted his search or, did he interrupt her search? He killed Mrs. Steinem and went home. We knocked on his door at nine o'clock Monday morning and apparently woke him. Another question, did Nick know that the board had canceled all evening meetings? Yes, it had been in the newspaper, radio and even on the television. He knew no one had any business at the board office last night. I'm assuming that Nick must have parked his car somewhere close to the board office, but not in the parking lots. Then, he walked there, opened the service entrance door, plugged in the code and entered the building. He walked through the warehouse area and on towards the superintendent's office. Katherine and Bo saw the light from his flashlight. Katherine entered the building in order to warn Samantha. The two women had interrupted his search, again.

Angry, frustrated and high – he started shooting with intent to kill whoever got in his way."

Patterson stopped the recorder then began again. "Nick hadn't found the phones on that trip either. He found the purse earlier. He had the purse because the strap of Worthington's purse was only thing left at the scene. He probably had thrown the purse away. No, maybe not, Samantha said Nick was lazy. Would a lazy person stand up and walk out the door with the purse still in his hand. Probably did not even realize he still had it. Like, he hadn't planned to kill Mrs. Steinem. He just wanted the purse and – well, things happened. Patterson had his men searched Nick's premises for the purse and phones. Remember that entire room of purses. I saw hundreds of purses and ignored them. Did Nick hide the purse in plain sight? He wasn't the sharpest tool in the shed. Maybe, when he realized he had it. He went to the purse room and threw it in with the rest. Nick figured no one would notice it there. He had been right."

Patterson wrote in bold print find Nick, arrest Nick and Nick cannot use a phone. He has lost his right to call anyone. In Fred Astaire fashion, Patterson did a happy dance.

47

PATTERSON

"We need a professional hacker. Or IT person on staff or as a consultant at the police department." Patterson spoke into his recorder. "Drive to Board Office – get the bird woman Meeks to give him information from her records. Meet with Vice- superintendent Sims. Give men their assignments."

Patterson wrote a note on his calendar to approach the River Bend's lawyer about being able to do legal digital searches. He did not care if the old Police Chief never used it. He ran River Bend's police department in this century, not late eighteen hundreds. He gathered up his things. As he started to leave, he remembered to stop and tell Mrs. Murphy if they brought Nick Chase in, do not let Nick touch a phone. Patterson exited left the station and drove to the Board Office.

When he pulled up to the board office his men, Ramon and Vice Superintendent Mickey Sims were side to side in a crowd control situation. The crowd was getting ugly. Patterson asked. "What is the problem here?"

Alex stood at-ease and summarized. "Basically, they're nosey and want to see what happened inside. Vice Superintendent Sims explained to them there had been an accident here, no one was injured, but for safety reasons the building is closed. Very simple and to the point, that seemed to anger them more. Attitude is how dare, we say 'no' to them, Sir."

Patterson paused, "Sims got a megaphone? Get it."

"Sure…"

Using the megaphone, he spoke to the gathering of about twenty roguish adults. "I'm Police Chief Patterson. Mr. Sims and my men have informed you the building is closed today. They explained that it is a crime scene. Now, unless, you want to be arrested. I suggest you leave quietly."

He stood at ease. The crowd disappeared except for Sterling Bender and a Mrs. Goddard.

"I'm a board member, and I have a right to enter the building. I need to see what happened. It is my duty as an elected official to keep abreast of all activities that affect the school district and its buildings." Sterling Bender paced in front of Patterson like a bull ready to charge.

Calmly, Patterson kept his eyes on Sterling Bender's aristocratic face with his blazing white teeth. "J.T. escort Mr. Bender to the police station and charge him with Obstruction. No phone calls for him."

Then, he turned his attention to a stubby, sandy haired woman with small lab rat eyes glaring at him. Patterson asked, "Your name, please?"

"I'm Mrs. Goddard my child is flunking out of school, and I demand to know why. I think it's because the teachers don't like my son because he doesn't go out for sports. It is discrimination that's what it is. I'm going to sue this district if they don't pass my son."

"Just out of curiosity, Patterson asked. "What grade is your son in?"

"A high school senior," she told him proudly.

"Then he knows how to pass his classes. It's time for you to let him grow up. Go to the high school talk with his teacher in a nice voice. The board office can't and won't help you."

"Don't you mean just won't, I demand." She spat at Patterson.

"Alex, will you please escort Mrs. Goddard to jail with Mr. Bender. Book her on the same – Obstruction of Justice."

J.T. and Alex walked towards Mr. Bender and Mrs. Goddard but, the two sprinted to their cars.

"Now, men. . . I need a brief meeting with you in the building." Patterson walked back to his truck and collected the donuts and coffee. Once inside, he told them their assignments. J.T. and Alex loaded up on donuts and coffee and headed out to pick up Nick Chase, again. Henry's assignment, explain to Ramon what the police department needed from him and his wife when they inspected Bunny Worthington's house.

"Henry, drive them take pictures of anything suspicious. Write down information about whatever they or you find interesting."

Patterson asked Ramon about the second door not locked last night. "Who locked the warehouse up last night?"

Ramon turned red, "I locked it and rechecked. It was locked when I left."

He trembled. "But someone for several months has been in the building going through things. And then leaving the building unlocked. Makes me crazy. . ."

This confirmed for Patterson that last night had been an inside job. He, also, knew that Ramon had locked up everything as he had said. Then who?

Patterson retracted into military mode. He called his second in command, Jim Murphy. "Jim, our department needs an IT person or hacker. Do you have anyone that can do that job? We are doing it first then asking permission."

"Already on it, sir, Gin is your IT. She got Worthington's phone records of for you, remember? What do you need?"

"Ah, Gin? Tell Gin that I need information on Mickey Sims financials and anything else she can find out about him. How does she know how to do this? What is her background? I thought she was a school Liberian."

"She told me she put herself through college hacking into banks and etc. for a very bad man. He had her family under his thumb. She did it to save them."

"Okay, she's has to be safe. She's what we need. Go for it." At this moment in time,

Patterson knew Samantha had corrupted him. Her motto: a little bad for the sake of good isn't bad.

Months ago when he explained the need for an IT person to River Bend's lawyer and city council showing them it would save man hours. And- that meant it would save River Bend money. It would make solving cases faster and more valid. Their comment was the old Police Chief didn't need one so that was that. One thing they did not want to realize was River Bend was a small town with big city problems.

48

POLICE CHIEF AT THE OK CORRAL

Vice Superintendent Mickey Sims dressed in his preferred style of Western causal, he swaggered into the make-shift conference room. He was well built, big shouldered from putting up hay each summer since he was eight years old. Mickey had boyish good looks, soft brown hair with a wisp of hair in the front that fell into his face all the time. Women loved Mickey; they always wanted to brush his hair back into the proper place and other things. His intelligent blue eyes and a lop-sided smile were his best features. Patterson knew Sims was well-liked by River Bends education community. But Sims had information that he needed now, how to convince him that he needed to share.

"Vice Superintendent Sims, we have a situation here."

Mickey Sims interrupted Patterson. Sims placed his hands on his hips in a no-nonsense stance. He looked the part of the basketball coach during the play-offs all puffed up red in the face and a smirk on his face. "You mean the holes in the walls. How in the h_ did this happen? I thought the police were here. Who's going to pay for this mess? Not the school district..."

Patterson let him vent before he started to explain again. "I said. We have a situation here. Someone entered the building last night, opened the service door using a school district's key and they knew the code to

167

the alarm. So you need to think twice before you try to sue the police department. We had people here. When the intruder discovered my people. He shot at them. Intent on killing them. I demand a complete list of people who have ever had a key this building. Plus, my men have orders to replace all the locks today. If this doesn't make you happy. Then I'll give your insurance a call. Tell them that a person used the district keys and code to open the building. Then shot it full of holes."

Patterson waited for Sims to make a decision of to tell the truth or let the truth deal with him.

Sims started to sputter and nodded at Patterson.

"Now, I need to know the truth. What were you after in the superintendent's office? What is going on here? I can't help or protect you or your staff if I don't know the truth."

Mickey Sims looked down at his boots. "I don't know what you are talking about. We had a well-run district until this past week. I left an important file in Worthington's office. I went in to get it. I forgot about the Do Not Enter."

"Mr. Sims, you are a poor liar. You forgot. Yet, you got tangled up in the yellow tape with Do Not Enter on it. Now take care of your insurance people. I need their number and claims person's name. When did you tell your Human Resource person to come in today?"

"Nine o'clock. . ." Mickey Sims leisurely rose and swaggered off to his office.

"Vice Superintendent Sims could you give me your business phone number and Superintendent Worthington's also?" Slowly Mickey Sims pulled out his phone found what he needed and in small pieces gave Patterson the information.

Patterson put the numbers in his phone. Under his breath. "Game playing will get you in trouble. Vice Superintendent Sims, you have moved up to number two in the suspects list. First place winner in the suspect category goes to -"

49

CHASING NICK CHASE

Agitated Patterson added more things in his notebook – have Gin check out Louisa Meeks, Nick Chase, all of the Worthington's and Mrs. Steinem's financials and background checks on all of them. Then he needed to compare what Ms. Meeks provided with what Gin finds. While he waited, he called Mrs. Steinem's ex-husband. That had been last on his list, but he called while he waited for Louisa Meeks.

"Good morning, I'm Police Chief Path Patterson of River Bend police department. Am I speaking to Mr. Bruce Steinem?" I know the Chicago police contacted you about your wife's death. I am sorry for your loss. She was an extraordinary lady. May I ask you some questions?"

"She was not remarkable. She was a lousy wife. I'm relieved she is dead. I don't want to know how." Mr. Steinem hung up on Patterson.

Patterson called him, again, but, spoke rapidly into the phone. "Do not hang up on me, or the Chicago police will be there in seconds to take you to their station. You're only one hour flight from here. You could have killed her. So talk to me or __"

"Fine. . ."

"Mr. Steinem, do you know of any reason someone would want your wife dead?"

"Besides me, no, but we haven't talked in some time." Bitterness edged each word.

"I know how you feel. I'm a divorced man myself. What caused your divorce? Hope you don't mind my asking?"

"Happy to tell you. She left me to go help her sister. A couple of years ago she moved into her sister's mansion and lives, I mean lived, lived there high on the hog. A lifestyle I couldn't give her. She was her sister's little call-girl. She worked at the school district's board. So, Judith could keep an eye on her niece and keep her out of trouble. That brat is h_ on wheels. Judith, my wife, I mean my ex-wife called me just last month. She begged me for a loan. Said Lana, her sister, needed a trip to get away from Bunny and Nick-what's-his-name. I, a poor old nobody, loaned the wealthy Worthington's a wad of money. That made my day, fact is, and it made my lousy life."

"Interesting. . . Do you know Nick Chase at all?" Patterson asked not sure what to expect.

"Sure, I know Nick. Nick is Timmons's son and also, his nephew. Nick is Susan's son. Susan, Lana and Judith are – I mean were sisters. Susan told her husband, Mr. Morgan Chase that Nick wasn't his son, but Timmons Worthington's. The old man said he didn't care, made him look young. They stayed together. Judith swore that Lana didn't know that Nick was Timmons's son. I think she knew or why would she let him live with them. Lana and Timm needed to send the boy home to his parents a long time ago. They couldn't afford Nick and his habits. The Chases had lots of money. But not anymore because of Bunny and Nick. Sounds like a soap opera, doesn't it?"

"Thank you for so much for the information. I'm sorry for your loss."

"Okay, just one question. . . She didn't suffer, did she?" Patterson heard tears in Bruce Steinem's voice.

"No, she died quickly." Patterson lied through his teeth. But, he felt Mr. Steinem had suffered enough. He still loved his ex-wife.

Patterson briefly wondered how he would feel if he learned his ex-wife had been killed. Nope, nothing, sad for her death but nothing more... He went over his notes again. Oh, so much, unexpected information. His phone rang.

"Yes, Alex. . ."

"Sir, J.T. and I are at Nick's. Nick has vanished. Didn't stay at his place last night. His car is gone. The neighbor next door said he saw Nick leave about ten last night. Said the fool almost ran over him and his dog. Nick has cleaned out his closets. The silver drawers and cabinets are open and empty. We have the photographs we took of everything in the house and can compare them with what he left behind. Even Mrs. Steinem's quarters that we locked yesterday has been broken into and searched, again. He could have taken Steinem's valuables, too. Or why else, search her place again?" Alex finished. He waited for Patterson to absorb the information.

"Do we know what type of car he was driving?"

"A sports car, sir. . ."

"I'll get the car information from the courthouse and call the state troopers to keep a look- out for our boy, Nick. Maybe we found our killer." Patterson hoped.

Patterson found Nick's vehicle information and called the State Patrol office. He gave them the license number and a description of Nick and the car.

"Yes, a white Mazda MX-5 sports, soft top, license plate N I C K# 1… cheesy, yup you could say that." Bemused Patterson thought, *now, they were chasing Chase. Sounded like a Charlie Chaplin movie.*

50

THE MEEKS' SHADOW

A shadow crossed the desk. Patterson looked up at Louisa Meeks. She was a mousey bird-like woman of about forty. Always a nervous whispered when she spoke. She easily distracted people by constantly swiping at her wispy brown hair that clung to her face.

"Just for my record, you are Louisa Meeks, the school district's Human Resource Person. Am I correct?"

Louisa Meeks nodded her head. Her hair swished. Her pallor face taunt caused her brown eyes and eyebrows to have a popped appearance.

"Please have a seat." Patterson pointed to the chair directly across from him.

Louisa sat with her hands in her lap. She bowed her head and prayed that the Police Chief asked only questions about the employees and nothing about her. She prayed that the Police Chief didn't find out that both she and Vice Superintendent Mickey Sims had talked about killing Superintendent Worthington. She day-dreamed about taking the blame if Mickey Sims did kill Worthington. How he would look at her, with love in his eyes because of her sacrifice for him.

She owed Mickey Sims her life. He had promised Worthington he wouldn't go to the board about her stealing money from the school district funds, if she hired Louisa. Louisa's role was to manage the staff's certification and all the forms that have to fill out and sent to the state. Things that school districts are supposed to keep records of, but, River Bend school district had not done so since Superintendent Worthington had taken over.

Louisa remembered how quickly she had gotten everything in order and all the reports up to date that the state required. The District's data was on target. Unfortunately, she had discovered some inconsistencies in the documents. She didn't want to bother Mickey, so she talked to Worthington. That had been a big mistake.

Louisa had discovered a serious problem by chance. One day she was adding an accreditation report to a teacher's file. Then a short time later, she had to add a warning letter for too many days missed for the same teacher. Louisa checked the most currant dates missed. They were the same days that teacher had been at a workshop that the district had paid for her to attend. What made it worse, the days were non-student days. She hadn't asked for a substitute. During Louisa's spare time she checked on other high absentees, she discovered more errors. She thought about telling Vice-superintendent Sims, but he was so busy. So she had told Worthington what she had found.

Worthington knew about the problem. She had caused it. Arrogantly she explained to Louisa, if she wanted someone fired or if she needed more cash or both, she filled out a form that charged the teacher for a day off that they didn't actually take. She then filed the form, which billed the substitute fund, collected it in a miscellaneous payroll account, and then pocketed the money. The teacher would then be in trouble for missing so many days of work and have no way to prove different. The computer showed that they were absent. It was their word against the school districts. No one, but no one in the district would go up against the superintendent and the board. It was impossible to find a teaching job if you had been fired by a school district. So the teachers quietly quit and hoped they could find another job.

The Monday before Worthington's death, Worthington called Mickey Sims into her office. She told Sims he had to fire Louisa because she knew the truth. If he didn't, she would destroy both him and Louisa. Wasn't his wife expecting, again? Mickey promised to take care of it. Then Mickey Sims had a meeting with Louisa about the situation and the threat against him and her. He promised Louisa everything would be all right. He told her, he would take care of it.

The file Mickey Sims tried to locate in Worthington's office was of the forms supposedly signed by him. But, Worthington forged them. If the police found the folder first, Mickey and she would be first on the suspect list. Nervously, Louisa sat there not sure why she had been summoned by the police. Mickey told her not to say anything about the folder. He would find it and destroy it.

Patterson watched Louisa Meeks twisting the button on her beige coat. Was it her shyness or something else? She had been more confident the last time he needed her help.

"Louisa I need information from the personnel files. Please write exactly what I tell you I need. Here is my search warrant." Patterson handed it to her to read. He continued, "Simple, I need the names of any staff member, just in this building, whose names first or last names begin with J. Okay?"

Relieved she nodded her head and almost smiled. "Okay, anything else?"

"Yes, I need the medical history on Steinem and Worthington."

"I don't have that information, only the health insurance companies have that it. It's against the privacy law for us to have or give out that information. We have the number of personal days used for medical leave. A person fills in sick or going to doctor, only, for their information, but that is it." She thought *I've done okay, so far so good.*

"Fine, I'll take that information, just the last names on that one, right?"

"Yes," Janet wrote down the last request.

"Are all the staff on the same health insurance policy? Is it a requirement of the district that you have to use district insurance?" Patterson had heard someone complaining about that.

"It is a requirement of the district for good reason. It is how we keep the cost down. But there are a few who have other health insurance policies."

"I need the 'who', please." Patterson questioned if it was the district's policy, then why did they allowed certain people to have a different insurance policy. And why weren't they in trouble? Or were they?

"Is that all?" She asked.

"No, wait. Can you get the beneficiaries for Superintendent Worthington and Mrs. Steinem's life insurance policies?" He absent-mindedly smiled at her. "Oh, you may use your office."

A shadow crept across the table as Louisa stood to leave.

A text message peeped on Patterson's phone. He read it, and a smile almost broke across his stern face. It was from Dr. Ackerman. "The cocaine found at both the crime scene at the board office and at Nick's house was from the same batch. Was it enough evidence?"

No, but it added to the facts. Nick didn't have an alibi. He fit the description – tall and thin, and he had a motive. Motive, he was one of the heirs to Timmons Worthington estate. Bunny Worthington was the legal heir, but, with her gone, Nick Chase would have it all. There was a problem with that theory. What was his motive for trashing the house he lived in, Janet Monroe's house, Bunny Worthington's house or the school board? If Nick received everything, then what was he looking for? Plus, he skipped town, blew his bail. Skipping town stamped guilty all over Nick Chase.

What was keeping Louisa Meeks so long? Had she skipped out, too? Patterson questioned his sanity for staying in a space with plaster dust and small pink insulation layered on everything. Any movement caused a storm of dust to swirl around like a tornado. He waited because the information Ms. Louisa Meeks collected might cement the killer to the crime.

51

MEEKS INHERITS

One nagging thought bothered Patterson. Actually, it was Samantha's nagging thought – Nick was lazy. His eyes started watering, and his nose started dripping. He had to leave. He walked outdoors to get some clean air and to clear his mind for just for a minute. On his walk, he noticed the gigantic football stadium, Worthington Memorial Field. Wow, it was impressive for a town the size of River Bend or any size of town. Then he noticed how ratty the board office building looked. The football field a corner-stone for the quad of remodeled and expanded buildings built in the last five years. A new elementary, renovated middle school and high school, from the highway it looked impressive. Then a short distance away – the school district's Board of Education office building appeared like an ugly step-child.

"Mr. Police Chief I have your information." Louisa Meeks had followed him outside.

He turned and nodded to her. They walked back into the office, and he held the door for her. He offered her a chair, then sat down and waited for her to start.

"All rightly, the people who work in this building with the first and or last name beginning with J are Judith Steinem, Janet Monroe, Jeri Jones and Jim Rodgers – that is it." She said.

Patterson poised his pen anxious to pin point a person of interest, but disappointedly wrote down only Janet and Judith names. To make sure, he asked, "What does Jeri Jones do? What does Jim Rodgers do?"

"Jeri is in our accounting department. Jim is in charge of payroll." Louisa waited for the next question.

Did anyone have a reason to threaten any of these people as far as you know?"

"No, not that I know of. . ." She answered too quickly.

"The ones with different health insurance are. . ." Patterson waited, and Louisa read the names.

Whispered words were heard, "Superintendent Timmons Worthington and Bob Boynton. . . Bob's the janitor at River Bend Elementary, he's on Medicare. Superintendent Timmons Worthington was on __"

"Why didn't Worthington have the same health insurance as everyone else?" Patterson questioned Louisa and himself.

"On her file by the line that says Type of Insurance, it reads – other. I don't know why. Maybe she had a prior health condition. Our insurance company will refuse anyone for a prior health condition. That happens sometimes. Or she just wanted something better than the rest of us. I would go with that reason."

Patterson picked up on the resentment Louisa had towards Worthington. Wondered why?

"Sir, I don't know why I brought this with me, but when I was going through things for you I found this note from Worthington on my desk." Louisa handed Patterson the note.

It read. *Contact Principal Moore at the middle school, fire Bob Douglass. Fire him because he took too many days off this year.*

Louisa knew why she brought it, and it had taken her some time to find where she hid the note. She hoped that Police Chief Patterson would ask questions. Then, she would have been obligated to tell him about Worthington's scam.

After reading the note, he asked. "Are there a number of teachers who are absent over the amount of days expected. I'm sorry I don't know how many days a month you can take off. What is the procedure?"

"The teachers have ten personal days per school year. They can use all of them or not. But over that amount, without a valid doctor's note or a family emergency, the district takes disciplinary action against the teacher. Bob has taken twenty days just this school year, and it's not even November, yet."

Patterson wrote this down. Didn't sound like the Bob Douglass that worked with Samantha? Need to text her after I am finished here.

"The beneficiaries for Worthington and Steinem are, Janet Monroe for Worthington. I need to point out that Worthington changed her beneficiary just two months ago from Nick Chase to Janet Monroe. I notarized it." Louisa pointed to her signature. "And – for Steinem it was Nicholas Chase."

Louisa was disappointed in Police Chief Patterson for not asking more questions about the note. She couldn't reveal the scam without being pressured into it.

Patterson just about bounced out of his chair. A motive – money. . . The big question, did Nick Chase know he was Steinem's beneficiary? And did he know that he was no longer the beneficiary for Worthington? Janet Monroe, why Janet Monroe?

"Thank you; may I have your copy of everything? Now, I need the names of teachers who have an unusually high number of absents this year? Will that take you long? I really want you out of this building as soon as possible. Not a healthy place to be with all the dust and muck."

"I can get that for you in a matter of minutes." Louisa spoke as she walked away and muttered under her breath. "Because I already have it, you big dummy."

Patterson watched her walk back to her area as he sent a text Samantha about the number of days Bob Douglas had missed. He needed to know the exact number and compare it to number the district had down for Bob. He rose from his chair, quietly and moved towards Louisa Meeks' office. He had planned to pick up the information and remind her to leave the building. Before he entered the hall, he heard Louisa talking to Mickey Sims. All he heard was – Mickey Sims said, "I didn't find it. But I plan to this afternoon after the Police Chief leaves. What has he asked so far?"

A soft voice answered but he couldn't hear Louisa whispered words.

Mickey Sims must have seen Patterson's shadow in the hall. He abruptly changed the subject and said to Louisa. "Oh, thank you for watching my kids so Annabel and I could go out. This pregnancy has been hard on her. Its baby number three, the last one, it's so expensive having kids. Going out was such a treat."

Patterson wrote down his latest theory. The message on the rock was meant for either Janet Monroe or Judith Steinem. Janet would gain with Worthington death and Nick would gain with Mrs. Steinem death. Janet and Nick were neighbors. They could have plotted together to kill Worthington and Steinem and made it look like someone else did it. Motive – to improve their lot in life. . . No one else gained from Worthington's or Steinem's untimely deaths. Patterson sensed Mickey Sims and Louisa Meeks were involved in something. Speculatively Mickey Sims and Louisa Meeks helped Janet and Nick. For their help, they received a portion of the inheritance.

The Meeks shall inherit. . .

52

DATE WITH A METAL DETECTOR

Four o'clock at Superintendent Worthington house was bedlam. Patterson had sent Henry out to the house with Angela and Ramon to look for missing or misplaced items. Henry called Patterson about noon. "When Angela opened the door she fainted. The house has been destroyed."

"List, I need to make a list to help organized my mind. First things call Doctor Ackerman and have him send his crew to help us collect evidence. Second the clean-up crew had shown up on time. Next have Henry, Ramon, and Angela start picking up and looking for what is missing. Last, get Samantha out there armed with her grandfather's metal detector." Patterson jumped into his truck and toddled out to Worthington's house.

Good news, Worthington was a minimalist in her decor. The bad news, the intruder, was an extremist and much of the furniture was slashed open and stuffing was everywhere. Angela and Ramon's little boy, Rey, was stuffing pick-upper person. Samantha showed up after school and started beeping around the house on the hunt for a safe. Searching for missing phones was Patterson's group job.

It appeared that Worthington did not have a wall safe. Since all of her art work had been ripped off the walls. Leaving white on white walls stretched out like sheets floating in the air on wash day. There were not any visible wall safes. Time to examine unusual places for a concealed safe. Samantha remembered her grandfather hid money in an ice cube tray in the freezer. Refrigerators are perfect for hiding things. Biscuit tubes have been known to conceal drugs, money, jewels and maybe phones. The inside of Worthington's refrigerator surprised Samantha. It was filled with everything from the Do Not Eat list – when on blood thinners. Lettuce, spinach, kale and tons of cranberries innocently snuggled side by side - all of them a big 'no – no's' for blood thinner takers.

Moving from the kitchen to Worthington's bedroom was a trip. When Samantha opened the bedroom door, the sun rays recoiled off the brilliant white walls and blinded her. She knew she should have waited until her eyes adjusted, but too late. She did not see the step up into the bedroom. She fell - splats. "Oh my. . ." Why in the world would anyone put a step up in the bedroom? Maybe, to hide a safe, no to make the room more exotic, no - it had to be hiding the safe. She moved all around the suite and stopped to investigate the on-suite bathroom's medicine cabinet, a perfect place to hide a safe. No safe, but she found a currant medicine bottle half full with blood thinning pills. The medication's date was currant and had been prescribed by Dr. Flanigan, with three more refills written on the label. But, the medical report said she hadn't had a blood test in eight years or more. Flannigan never tested Worthington's blood or at least he never reported it. Now, it was understandable why Patterson didn't want to use Flanigan on his cases. She put the bottle in her pocket to show Patterson. What was Worthington doing with aspirin also, a bad combination?

Samantha had saved the bed area for last. The moment she got near the bed, the detector went nuts. She slid the metal detector under the bed and moved it back and forth until she located the strongest sound. Something metal was hidden under the center of the bed, of course. Angela helped her move the bed over the thick carpet. It was a muscle building experience. Finally, Samantha crawled on all fours and felt around for the edge of carpet square placed over the safe.

Found it. She called Patterson before removing the carpet square. He appeared sweating and panting. She used the stethoscope to open the safe. He raced over and flung the safe's door open and lifted a box out of the safe. Gently he removed the lid. Their eyes intent on the mystery – what was so valuable it needed hidden in the safe?

"Clothing – baby clothing - she used the safe to hide baby clothes? Worthington wasn't pregnant, or Ackerman would have told me." Patterson eyed the clothing suspiciously.

Angela turned red. She turned to Ramon and told him to explain to all of us what she said. Ramon repeated her every word, exactly as she said it.

"Ms. Worthington asked me to have a baby for her. She wanted to pick the man. She offered me lots of money. Maybe she found someone to have a baby for her. I don't know who."

Samantha looked down at the cream color garments with delicate lace and tiny little buttons. Sorry. . . Poor Superintendent Worthington had everything, but what she truly wanted. Could the killer have been the surrogate mother who had changed her mind, or one of the men Worthington wanted as the father of her child? Strange, all of it strange. . . The clothes matched the bedroom next to the master suite, the only room with soft shades a lovely pearl colored walls and carpet. The pearl color was perfect for a baby's room, not like the Peacock Blue used in the baby's room at Robert's and Victoria's.

Hidden under the box of clothing was thin plain manila folder. Patterson opened the folder scanned the contents and made a mental note that the signature on the document was Mickey Sims. The front page contained information that Mickey Sims and Louisa Meeks would not want known by anyone. This had to be what Sims had looked for in Superintendent Worthington's office. Why hadn't Worthington turned this information over to the board? Why did she have them sign this document which showed their guilt and not give it to someone? Why did they even sign it?

Still no phones or USB drives. . . Samantha sat on the floor and questioned. "Where else would she put a safe or hiding place?"

Safes, different kinds of safes, think. Samantha remembered Pops favorite safe. "Where is Worthington's car? Was it at the board office and driven out here or what?"

Patterson looked back through his notes. "According to my notes. She had ridden to work with Sterling Bender. He lives close to her. She did that every now and then. Nothing unusual about it, why?"

"So, the car is here?" Samantha jumped up and started running to the garage. "I have an idea."

In the center of an extremely clean garage sat an older model Jaguar S series in British Racing Green. It looked like Robert's first expensive car. He purchased it the first months of their marriage. Samantha looked inside the car and saw the keys dangling from the ignition and the doors locked.

"Angela did Superintendent Worthington have a button thingy that she carried to open the doors." To help Angela understand what she said she pointed to the car door and pushed a pretend fob.

"Yes." Angela flew into the house and was back in a second. "Here…"

Samantha unlocked the doors and handed the lob back to Angela. She used the metal detector on the console some response, but not enough to be a safe. She turned the car on and checked the CD loader – nothing but a CD loader/player. Ah – remember the trunk. She slid out of the car and opened the trunk. Her grandfather put a car safe in every car he owned. Samantha had tried to get Robert to put one in his trunk, but he whined that his car had a large battery and CD changer. Even with a CD changer there was enough space for a car safe. She put the metal detector down, reached into the trunk and pulled the carpet back. It revealed a huge battery and a CD changer. Samantha pushed a button and the front of the changer flipped down and ta-da the safe. This one was digital combination, and she didn't have a clue how to open it. She noticed a key lock on the front under the combination's lip.

"Patterson, would you please get the car keys for me?"

He was gone and back in a split second. He handed her the keys. She found the small flat key like they used on the cedar chest. She slid it into the lock. Turned, clicked and opened the safe – inside she saw an iPhone and two USB drives. She backed out of the trunk and motioned for Patterson to take over the investigation.

A smile etched across his face as he meticulously put on his gloves after he photographed the scene and the items. Time to bag and itemize the found items. Then take them to the office tomorrow. He would spend the night going through each one to see why they were worth two people's lives.

Samantha stretched her neck to release some of the tension and noticed her old neighborhood through the glass windows in the garage. A tall, thin man in a black jogging outfit sprinted past. He looked so familiar, probably just one of the neighbors she saw before the divorce. No, she thought more recent, but where?

Thanks to Angela's hard work the Worthington's house was in better condition than when they arrived. She offered to come out on Thursday and clean it. Patterson agreed, but Henry and Ramon had to be there to protect and help her. Patterson loaded the evidence into the cab of his truck. When he turned to talk Samantha but, she had ambled down the street.

He ran after her. "What are you doing tonight?"

"Grading papers, talking to my contractor about my plumbing. I mean my house's plumbing. Oh, I forgot cleaning my Johnny-on-the-Spot. Why?"

"Want to go over this stuff with me? It would help. I have my men stretched out all over the place."

She jumped up and down, "Yes, I would love to, my place and you bring food."

Lucky is my Lady, thought the Shadow. He had been at the right place at the right time. The right place, Worthington's house just at the right time to witnessed the Police Chief leave with a couple of boxes. At first he had laughed at the futility of their search until he saw Patterson with the boxes. They found the evidence against him. What to do? He slinked closer and listened to Patterson's and Samantha's plans. He knew where to find his incriminating evidence it would be at Samantha Grant's house in the country - how perfect. He faded back into the shade and sped home. He had an appointment tonight – to save his life.

53

THE CHARGE OF THE SHADOW BRIGADE

On top of the hill, the Shadow sat in his car and enjoyed the late fall sun lower into the horizon. All the bright oranges, purples, and glowing pinks spiked with brilliant glow of the sun. Sunsets like this were only found in the Midwest. They were Ah –defining. He had studied sunsets for most of his life. The one true joy he had in his unimportant life. But, tonight he planned to have his life transcended. The M4 had changed him and his life. It had empowered him to be more than he had ever dared to be. When he mixed the gun with the white powder that Nick Chase sold him, he became invincible. He checked the time to make sure that most people would be home from work. He relieved himself in the wild and sniffed a touch of the white powder. When complete darkness had enveloped the earth, he began his dramatic descent.

It was all about appearance. He designed a plan for an awe inspiring appearance. His perfect plan involved background music the *William Tell Overture*. *It would play in the background as he recited The Charge of the Light Brigade* as he approached Samantha Grant's house. He planned a dramatic pause in front of Samantha's house. He planned to jump out of his 1972 MG roadster with his loaded M4, to storm the house and to demand all of the evidence gathered at Bunny Worthington's house. He visualized Police Chief Patterson and Samantha whimpering as they handed over the boxes to him. Grandly he would press the boxes to his chest as he dashed out to his car. The grand finale, he would jump back into his car, fire one shot into the air and blast the background music - the Finale Overture. The grand exit down the hill into the night.

He checked his watch, time to start and to put his plan into action. He placed the M4 in the passenger seat – *apparently it had called 'shotgun*. Music ready, gun ready, the Shadow ready, and his engine purred to life. The car moved along the newly poured gravel road. He slid the M4 into his lap as he began his descent down the seemingly gentle slope of freshly graveled road. As planned, he pushed button one and started the music– The Storm. The music built momentum as the car built momentum down the hill. At the top of his lungs, he quoted from *The Charge of the Light Brigade.*

> "Cannon to the right of them
> Cannon to the left of them
> Cannon in front of them
> Volley'd and thundered
> Storm at with Shot and Shell
> Into the Jaws of Death Ha . . . Ha . . . Ha . . ."

At the curve on the hill, he positioned the gun out of the window. He panicked when his right front tire hit a pothole. The car stopped, dropped and rolled around at the same moment he had moved the gun. He lost control of his vehicle, of his gun and himself. In his terror, he over compensated the steering wheel. The gun toppled and flopped around, landed barrel down in the passenger's foot-well. In the dark, the road became the Grand Canyon-like as the car's lights bounced from one dangerous ravine to another with a tragic ending cliff. With his eyes on the road he felt for his gun. Reaching across the seat he accidentally grabbed the gun by the trigger. When he pulled it up towards him, the gun fired through the roof of his car. Premature ejection had never been a part of his mental picture.

The car, the music and the gun increased their roar like a storm rolling across a valley -gaining speed with its unbridled fury. As the car raced to the corner – he spied Patterson's police truck located too close to the turn for comfort. He had planned to shoot the police vehicle just enough to take it out of commission. But- as the Shadow's vehicle vaulted around the corner, the gun wedged itself in the steering wheel. Now, perilously out of control, his feet tried to take control. He pushed the brake and clutch at the same time. He tried to tell his feet that wasn't a good idea. They didn't hear him.

The car skidded and slid sideways towards Patterson's truck. His hands fumbled around grabbed at anything. They clamped onto the steering wheel and the gun for dear life. This caused the gun to fire, again. The bullet hit the Johnny-on-the-Spot. Waste flowed. His car skated to a stop inches from the police truck. Yikes. . . His only hope of exiting without being followed was to kill Patterson's truck. He fired repeatedly at the truck and a few times at Samantha's house. One of his shots whizzed through the Johnny-on -the-Spot. It caused a waste waterfall and then a kaboom - Johnny-on-the-Spot exploded. A fierce fire followed the trail of waste product across Samantha's porch.

Stunned by the massive destruction he had caused. His next concern was survival. Was the fire enough to destroy the evidence? He hoped so. Calmly he pushed button two on his player. As he rode out of sight – the music blared – The Finale or more commonly known as the theme song from the Long Ranger.

He vowed as he drove out of sight to destroy the evidence and those who had it. His car reared up when he hit the huge bump in the road. He shouted "Hi-Ho – Silver and away."

54

Johnny Went Boom

Samantha and Patterson watched the sunset in all of its glory. Samantha photographed it from different angles. They ate pizza, drank beer, watched Bo chased bugs and laughed. It was a beautiful night to be outdoors. When the headlights darted over the hill; they looked over their shoulder and thought nothing about it. Samantha commented about Junior, the boy next door, getting home late from work. When they heard the newly applied gravel crunched followed by the avalanche sound of rolling gravel. Samantha explained to Patterson that fresh gravel put on a mud is similar to thick ice – very slippery until it settles into the mud. She made a comment that it wasn't Junior, he knew better. It had to be some fool that was now speeding on the road. They became curious when Bo started hissing. They walked into the house for a better look. A loud blink sound against Samantha's fireplace followed by the resonance of pieces of chipped stone tinkling down the chimney. Warned them, something was very wrong.

Patterson knew that sound and went into military mode. "Someone is shooting at us. Get Bo and your gun. Go to the barn." He stuffed the computer and the evidence into Samantha's computer bag and sprinted behind her.

He whispered, "If it's the same gunman from the school district's office shooting. I don't know where to go. His type of bullets cut through everything. That shooter is crazy or he acts as if he doesn't have control of his own gun."

"Why would anyone be shooting at my house? Could it be a kid with a new gun? Or could it be someone looking for the boxes we picked up at Worthington's today." Samantha prayed the shooter would stop shooting and leave them alone.

They watched from the hay-loft as the cloud of gravel spit out a small white sports car. Watched in amazement as the little white car skidded down the hill. It was like a tornado with four wheels, music blaring, rolled towards them. Then, they heard music associated with the Fourth of July's firework's grand finale. What did it mean? They watched. Like most Mid-westerners, they willed and prayed the impending disaster away. They were grounded, transfixed by the chain of events – unbelievable acrobatics performed by the midget car. Would a clown exit the car at the end of the show? Entertaining until the outhouse exploded and caught the porch on fire.

A scream erupted from Samantha as she climbed down the ladder and ran for the barn's door. Patterson seized her and held her close to him with her arms and legs still running. He tried to smother her pathetic repeated cries of 'No'. Every muscle in his body trembled as he contained Samantha in the barn. Hopelessly they watched as the shooter slowed down. Fear seized both of them at the thought he might stop and set fire to everything else. But the shooter just slowed down apparently stunned by the fire. Then, fired more shots at Patterson's truck. Finally, the car drove out of sight and in its wake the resounding music of the theme of the Long Ranger.

"I thought the Lone Ranger had been a good guy." Samantha spoke bitterly to the air. Her beautiful porch destroyed. "Pops said I would be safe here, but look."

Guardedly they exited the barn; the stench of gasoline burned their noses. They searched for the area of the most damage; the winner was Patterson's truck. Bullet holes decorated Patterson's police truck most of them located near the gas tank.

"Thank goodness our shooter was a lousy shot. He tried to hit my gas tank. Judging from the smell he may have punctured it. And, of course, I had just filled it."

In military mode, Patterson clicked his heels before he jumped into action. With his phone ready he took care of business, he started calling, first the fire station, next the tow truck company. He was afraid of an explosion if he had tried to start the truck. Last but not least he called the Johnny-on-the-Spot emergency number and told them about the explosion. Patterson reported to Samantha everyone was on their way.

They examined the truck and then Samantha's house. Their attention went back to the truck. Through clenched teeth, Samantha pointed out, "You know Patterson your truck has the peg-board look with all those tiny holes just like the inside of the school district's board office. Probably the same crazy shooter..."

"Yup, you're right." He started the search for a bullet. He remembered the clinking sound as something fell down the chimney. On the hearth next to a small chunk of rock laid a bullet. Holding it between his index finger and his thumb he studied it. Concluding it was the same caliber as the ones found at the board office; a 5.56mm caliber small center fire, common bullets, used both by civilians and military. Judging from the erratic firing the person wasn't military or ex-military, probably bought the M-4 out of a trunk of a car.

Samantha and Bo armed with a flashlight wandered up the hill and looked for tire marks. The fresh gravel prohibited tire marks on the road, but the skid areas showed tire markings. She found a large area where the shooter had lost control. In the muddy area, clean tire marks showed, she photographed the tire tracks on her phone and sent it to Patterson. She examined the tire thread, narrow in width, deep threads deeper than any American-made car tires. She knew a person with an older non-American-made car that was white in color. She and Bo gingerly walked back down the hill to Patterson.

"What do you mean the boys missed Nick Chase? He had to drive pass them." Patterson listened, "Nick Chase doesn't know the short cut I'm impressed he found Samantha's house. He had to follow one of us out here. J.T., you and Alex double around and drive to Chase's house."

Samantha tried to point out that maybe it wasn't Nick Chase, but Patterson gave her the look. So she changed the subject. "Where can we be safe, and go through this stuff?"

She patted the computer bag.

"There's a Motel 16 west of town on the highway. Pack your bag and don't forget Bo's things. We'll go there tonight. But, we need to wait until someone comes to help us before we leave here. I want the shooter to think he got us."

With some urging, the firemen called in a house destroyed by fire at Samantha's address. The tow truck driver asked the firemen to foam the gasoline by the truck to prevent another explosion. Finally, the Johnny-on-the-Spot driver hauled the charred commercial toilet onto his trailer, giggled about someone shot the Johnny. Emotionally drained Patterson and Samantha stared into the night as the last trailer vanished from sight.

Under Samantha's breathe, *with a Hi-Ho, Silver Away.* "Why the drama? It can't be Nick Chase, he is too lazy. He would have just burned the house down during the middle of the night. The shooter had decided to leave clues the first part of the *William Tell Overture, the Storm*; plus, I heard bits and pieces of the *Charge of the Light Brigade.* The clues from the music and the *Charge-* well, he stormed my house and then made us feel as if he surrounded us – *cannons to the left of them – cannons to the right---*with all of his shooting. The theme from the Lone Ranger, did the shooter feel he was fighting against evil? Did he feel we were evil? Or at least against him – now it's personal."

What else was needed to be added to help decode the clues? Well, the Lone Ranger – known for silver bullet and Silver, the horse. Samantha wondered did two *silvers* equal a Sterling -silver- Bender. No, not Sterling, he was too prissy. Wait, Sterling Bender was arrogant enough to assume no one would put two and two together. Motive, what was his motive for killing Worthington and Mrs. Steinem? Under the cover of putting Bo and luggage into her car, Samantha sent a text to have Gin run a check on Sterling Bender's financials.

She listened to Patterson talk to Jim about the evening's adventure. When he told Jim they needed to intensify the search for Nick Chase. Samantha laughed to herself. Logic and the study of human behavior dictated that the killer was not Nick Chase. She had a hypothesis about the identity of the killer. Now she needed to prove it.

55

FIFTY SHADES OF ANGRY

Patterson didn't say anything to Samantha, but he had recognized the car. The little white sports car belonged to Nick Chase. Nick never left the area. He wanted the phones to the point that he was beyond dangerous. Patterson called Jim and told him the situation and told Jim that he had sent Alex and J.T. out to snag Nick Chase.

"No problem, Patterson we're out by Pretty Prairie on Highway 5 not far from Seven Sister's Road. Nick has to come by here. We're waiting for him." And T.J. and Alex waited.

"I think when we see him rolling along, I'll step out with my gun aimed at him. That old white Mazda MX5 with Nick#1 on the vanity plates will skid to a stop. Nick will tumble out and beg for mercy." J.T. laughed.

Alex shakes his head, "No-o-o, I'll tell you what we need to do. Done it before, you go across the road. We have our guns drawn and aimed at the tires. Nick not a complete idiot. He'll stop. He'll know if his tires are shot out, his car will roll. It's sure death for him. He'll slow down. Put his hands in the air and smoothly exit his car."

Both men decided to check and clean their guns while they waited. Thirty minutes later and still no Nick Chase. They called Jim not wanting any more contact with Patterson in case Nick Chase had a way of eavesdropping to police calls. Patterson wanted Nick to think he had killed them.

"Jim, he hasn't come by here. Wonder if he went out on Oak Creek Road further west of town and then cut back. Okay, for us to go and look in that area?"

Jim told them it was okay to leave the area that Patterson would understand. Off they sped, sirens on, flashing lights in the opposite direction. If they had waited ten minutes longer, they would have caught the Shooter. The Shooter sped past the corner where Alex and J.T. had waited.

Some distance from Samantha's the shooter stopped. "That was wicked. Not like I planned. But I finished them off and destroyed that evidence."

He opened his glove compartment, licked his index finger and touched the white substance and then sniffed it. "Better now."

What had taken the Shooter so long to reach the corner where T.J. and Alex waited? Well, excitement always caused him intestinal problems. He had stopped to relieve himself along the Seven Sister Road. Then, he carefully placed the gun in his trunk and hopped it didn't fire on its own, again. Tonight's experience had wiped out his memory of how to work the safety. *Oh, well,* he thought.

After the sniff of the white powder he became careless and completely oblivious that he needed to be vigilant. Obsessing about the evidence and how he destroyed it, he drove past the point where the police had waited for him, the Shooter. He replayed the scene of Patterson telling Samantha Grant that they would investigate at her house. He knew it was perfect location, because her house was in the country and that made it easy to stage his dramatic attempt to retrieve the evidence. He laughed as he relived the scene of fire destroying the evidence as well as Samantha Grant and Police Chief Patterson. Bouncing from fantasy to reality, he started worrying about his car.

"Off to the car wash to clean and vacuum you." He patted his pride and joy. In his mind, the dirty car pointed its finger at his guilt. The dirt confirmed his presence on the road by Samantha Grant's house. Since he was his own alibi, he needed to get rid of more evidence of his transgressions.

The Shooter drove peacefully off into the sunset, while Samantha battled with her obtuse home owner's insurance agent. Unfortunately, for Samantha, this was her second call to River Bend Insurance Company in the last six weeks concerning damage to her home.

Samantha explained, "Someone shot at my house and burned my porch. Why? I don't know who or why. They aimed at and shot the Johnny-on-the-Spot. It exploded and caused a fire that burned my porch. Why do I have a Johnny-on-the-Spot on my porch? My septic tank backed up into my house. Remember, no, you don't remember, I don't know why my septic tank back- up. Remember, you helped me with the remodeling project and when the septic tank backed up in my basement you sent a nice person out and helped me decided what to do. Don't you remember our long detailed talks?"

"Sorry…" Slipped slowly out of Samantha's mouth… "You don't any notes on your computer about my past business calls. Denial is bad karma."

Patterson couldn't stand it. He asked Samantha for the phone. "I'm Police Chief Path Patterson of River Bend. What Ms. Grant missed telling you. She had an intruder that tried to break into her house? He couldn't because of the locks and the alarm she installed in the house. The intruder got so angry that he shot Ms. Grant's house trying to scare her. I'm in hot pursuit of the shooter as we speak. I have my men, the county sheriff's department and the state patrol after this person. It would be helpful in our case against this person if you had an inspector at her house tomorrow to give us an assessment of damages."

"Okay, thank you." He smiled at the phone. "Your insurance company will have someone at Ms. Grant's home tomorrow at nine in the morning. Great."

Samantha bit her lip until it bled. She didn't want to cry, but she had never been this angry. Not even when she found her husband in bed with their dog sitter. The shooter burned her porch. The Johnny-on-the-Spot had angered her beyond words, but the fire. She counted and she had at least fifty shades of anger. When she found the shooter she planned fifty ways to hurt him.

56

EVIL

The Night-Manager at Motel 16 teased them about the two beds. Patterson pointed to his badge. Then, the Night-Manager pointed to the No Dog sign. Again, Patterson pointed to his badge.

"She is under protective custody, not a romantic evening out. Now give me the key, or we will go elsewhere. Also, if you tell anyone we were here, I'll have you arrested for endangerment of my two witnesses." Patterson clicked his heels, and with the robot like motion, pointed to Bo and Samantha.

The Night-Manager handed him the key. Once in the room, Samantha and Patterson spread everything out on the small table. Patterson armed with his notebook. Samantha armed with her crime notebook. They started with Worthington's personal phone. They started the videos, just school district activities on the first four. They fast forward to the fifth video were they found motive for one of the multi-suspects. Worthington's voice penetrated the air with a sharp enunciation of each word.

"Your refusal to have an affair with me will cost you, Mickey. I promise, you will live to regret your decision." The video had been aimed at her door with the mirrored surface that showed the entire room. They watched Worthington slowly undress in front of Mickey Sims as she spoke.

"I hope Mickey Sims children didn't have a rabbit." Patterson tried to add humor to a painfully humorless situation.

In a disinfectant smelling room with a noisy room heater, they watched snippets of different people caught on video doing something corrupt. Each time Worthington seemed to be the one orchestrating the situation. Some of the people were unknown to Patterson. Samantha filled him in on their names and a brief history. Nick Chase had been videoed accepting her keys and the building code. One video showed Sterling Bender snatching pieces of paper from Worthington.

Bender appeared angry, but, then turned on his double dazzling smile and said through clenched teeth. "I can't forge any more documents for a while my partner is getting suspicious."

A long silence punctuated with Worthington's throaty laugh…

Different events and different people same subject each video had been taken while the person performed some act that would cost them later. Apparently, Worthington kept all of her incriminating videos. The last video they watched involved Janet Monroe, Worthington, and three men at Worthington's house. The video showed Worthington flaunting the pill as she put it in Janet's drink. Then the video showed Worthington maneuver an inebriated Janet into a bedroom. Worthington videoed each man with Janet. She made sure that the men's face and pertinent body parts were clearly identifiable as well as Janet's. Worthington moved in close, so the video clearly depicted how incapacitated Janet had been through the whole thing.

Patterson needed to do something else to help erase the nightmarish video he had just witnessed. He switched to view the pictures Worthington had saved on her phone and at last he listened to her voice messages. He stared at the phone.

"How could anyone be that evil? She ruined people's lives. She –she – poor Janet didn't deserve what happened to her. If Janet had killed Worthington, it had been in self-defense. I would testify on Janet's behalf. This only proves all of my suspects had reasons to kill Worthington." A tear slid down Patterson's chiseled face.

Samantha listened to Patterson as she plugged the USB devices into her computer. She scanned the files. Copies of accounting ledger sheets, contracts for weird things, employee files, and Worthington's personal files were on USB one/of three.

"Patterson, I think after you look at this, you'll need to show it to Robert. Aren't we lucky that my ex-husband happens to be a big time forensic accountant?" She had tried to be funny, but a painful look twisted her face.

Patterson noticed the look and wondered if the sadness was for the loss of Robert's love or something else. Women… He commented. "You are right the police department is very fortunate to have a person of Robert Grant's expertise to help them."

On the USB two/ of three, Samantha discovered images of school related activities. Then, a file titled My Daddy's other children. She clicked it open and found it full of pictures. She recognized pictures of Nick Chase and Janet Monroe. Samantha didn't know the other people. They were all in their twenties and thirties. *Sorry,* no wonder Superintendent Bunny Worthington was crazy. A file named *Important* had a folder named *Send to Police* if I die before my parents. Samantha handed the computer to Patterson so he could witness it first.

"I didn't know that Janet Monroe and Worthington were half-sisters? I wonder who knew that besides Worthington." Samantha asked. "Oh, before I forget, did you find USB device at the scene when you investigated Worthington's death?"

Patterson turned to the beginning of his notebook and read. "No, nothing mentioned. We didn't find keys, phones, or any electronic devices, except her computer. We looked carefully because she had been on the computer when she was killed. Remember you always said look for what's not there that should be and what's there that shouldn't be. So we looked for the things that should have been there. There wasn't an USB in or near the computer."

"Then her killer has it?" Samantha asked.

Tears flowed down Samantha's face as she collapsed on the bed. Patterson moved next to her, wrapped her in his arms and talked softly to her. His tears fell into Samantha's hair. Bo snuggled down on Patterson's side with his paw on Samantha. Patterson needed the comfort as much as Samantha. He saw hideous things in the war areas, but nothing as odious as what he witnessed tonight.

His mental list consisted of calling Robert Grant about going through the school district's accounts and asking Gin, the hacker, to check Worthington's computer, again. He needed to interview two of the three men involved in Worthington's indecent situation. Talk to Janet, first. Find Nick Chase and have him hung. Have Gin check-out Worthington's money problems. Timmons and Lana Worthington's daughter said in her file that they planned to hire a hit man to kill her. They hated her for her part in their financial ruin. They wanted Nick to be their only child. Another reason Nick would have to want Bunny Worthington dead. Patterson could see the headlines in the papers read *A Chase Kills Bunny.*

Samantha's mental list consisted of one thing – talk to Katherine and Gin.

57

LIFE WAS GOOD

The next day after the attack on Samantha's house, she asked her co-hearts to join her during their planning time. Three teachers were huddled in a room with their backs straight, legs crossed and their hands clinched as they focus. Katherine and Gin sat stunned as they listened to Samantha tell the account of last night's events. Like little girls during a scary movie, the three women held hands and wept as Samantha skimmed over the horrific video of Janet Monroe.

Katherine started the imaginary lint removal before she spoke. "It is time for us to make a list of prime suspects. Lately, I became a social butterfly attending anything where teachers meet and talk."

Katherine opened a notebook. "The people who stand out the most among the large number of abused and angry teachers are the following: Bob Douglas, Principal Devora Moore, and Mary Pierce. Bob went to a teacher's union meeting, drunk. He cried on my shoulder and told me that Worthington had called and demand that he come to her office at the end of the school day. She told he wasn't a good visual wanted him out of the school system. He said he waited for the ax to fall and nothing happened for weeks then she would repeat her belittling and threats. Then, we have Principal Moore. She was being blackmailed by Worthington after Worthington covered-up her affair with a parent at the school where she was the principal. Worthington batted Principal Moore around like a tennis ball. Bouncing her from one school to another with little notice. If Moore started to say anything Worthington played the video and threatened to show Mr. Moore. It is my humble opinion that Principal Devora Moore is a sex-addict. Last, but, not least, Mary Pierce, sweet little Mary Pierce, she is not so sweet. Her son is a lawyer. He told her to record everything that Worthington said to her. Mary ranted on and on about getting even with Worthington for calling her ugly and not a good visual. I have another one. Bess Burton is not on my list but should be on it. She was only one who bragged recently at a meeting that Worthington told her that she had been nominated for the <u>Teacher of the Year</u> award. Which is odd because she was at the same meeting as Bob Douglas and Mary Pierce. And they were both told they were not good visuals by Worthington and they would be replaced. Maybe she couldn't handle being told they were getting rid of her."

"In truth about fifty percent of our school district is over forty, over-weight, not attractive or lacking style. They hated Worthington and wanted her *gone*. Samantha, you were on Worthington's *Not a Good Visual* hit-list. So, you, too, could be a suspect." Katherine just shook her head and brushed the piece of lint into an imagined happy place.

"I know that I was on her list. I found out when Patterson showed me a bright green sticky note with my name on it. He found on Worthington's desk while investigating her death. He informed me then that I was a suspect. I figured what's new."

Gin had listened as Katherine went through her suspects. Gin closed her eyes and waited for them to ask about her group of suspects. Tired of waiting Gin was proud that she was essential part of the ongoing investigation. She blurted out, "I can't tell you what I found out. Patterson had me check on the following people: Louisa Meeks, Mickey Sims, Mrs. Judith Steinem, Bunny Worthington, her parents, Nick Chase and Sterling Bender. That's my list for today. The only one with questionable financials was Bunny Worthington. Her house payments are low; she had a sizable down payment, thanks to her parents or somebody. But, still, her payments are extremely low, like less than two hundred dollars a month. I did the math and she must have blackmailed the loan officer. Maybe, Bender, but his income fluctuates because he sells real estate. The one irregular items were the large amounts of money deposited to his account from an off shore account, which I am still checking out. I think it would be easier to find out who wasn't a suspect. That includes us. Think about it. I know how to find and how to lose things with the help of the computer. Katherine was on friendly terms with Worthington or at least that's what Katherine says. I know that Katherine was a Worthington's spy. Why did you spy for her, Katherine? Little Miss Samantha was on Worthington's hit list. Any one of us had the opportunity and maybe the need to kill her. Now, I must go back to my hole in the wall office and work. Love you…"

Katherine and Samantha stared at the retreating Gin and nodded. Samantha said, "She's right, everyone has secrets. We can do surveillance on the most obvious suspects. In my opinion that would be Principal Moore, Mickey Sims, Louisa Meeks and Sterling Bender. Mr. Bender was the one who was supposed to pick her up after work. Maybe he went into her office, they argued, he killed her, and then left. What do you think Katherine?

Lost in thought, Katherine said. "What? Oh, the names you have are fine."

"Okay since you are in an interesting mood. May Bo and I stay at your place for two reasons; I don't have any place to stay until they fix my house – insurance's orders. The second reason, I want to keep an eye on Bender."

Katherine smiled with relief that Samantha planned to stay the night. Katherine hadn't told Samantha about someone lurking around her house. She had a gun loaded and tucked away in every room and a Taser in her pocket. Nervousness or female intuition had never been a part of her personality. If she thought there was someone outside lurking, then there was someone outside lurking, plain and simple.

They changed the topic to the dance at the Club. The Country Club had planned a special pre-holiday dance, a Tom Jones night. Disco – so everyone planned puffy hair and white shoes. Johnny Jones had several pairs of white shoes. It was his trademark for his television commercials. Katherine glowed. There was a dance, Johnny Jones coming home early and a gig at spying. Today, life was good.

58

PATTERSON HAS A HEART

The sun was not up yet, but Patterson was wide awake. He inhaled the smell of disinfectant, Samantha's shampoo and Bo's doggy breath. He closed his eyes, smiled, felt safe and at peace. Mental scream followed – emotions – he didn't need any more emotions. He had homicides, rape and embezzlement issue to solve. He needed truth, facts - real facts and evidence that would put people away for a long time.

Patterson thought of himself as a straight forward, no emotions type of guy. In the military things were by the book based on facts. To him his two big mistakes were getting out of the army and marrying Jillian. He realized too often that he was a military man, He liked the order, the logic and the non-emotional environment. To him emotions messed up life. Facts equaled truth, plain and simple. And- right now he needed truth in the worse way.

The Worthington/Steinem case had deteriorated into an emotional mess. He hated mess of any kind. What facts he had - had been compromised with emotions. For example, he had not liked Nick Chase before he watched Worthington's videos. Now, he hated the man. His emotions had clouded the facts. He had to stick to the facts that could be physically proven. His emotions clouded his perception. He needed his head clear and to be dispassionate. Especially after last night's harrowing events.

But, for this minute in time he needed to feel the peace of having Samantha asleep on his numb arm. And the safety Bo scrunched up next to him. All fourteen pounds of killer dog. Patterson smiled.

Later that morning Patterson called the FBI and gave them all the information concerning Nick Chase. That started the nationwide manhunt for Nick. Next, he made an appointment with Robert Grant. Robert told him to bring in everything he had on the case. Robert promised to exam it immediately. Then, Patterson buzzed Jim told him to step into his office.

"Jim, we have a situation. We found the phones and thumb drives. Now, I need you to go through videos, voice mails on Worthington's phones. Then, we need to talk."

Nervous energy prompted Patterson to have a one-on- one with Sheila. They talked about weather, her police time with Janet Monroe, and finally about hiring Mrs. Murphy part-time. Sheila's narrow face crinkled up to a smile. Her bright red lips smiled then closed up into a pucker like they wanted to kiss him. He slid into his electric slide movement got out of harm's way.

"I take it, that's a 'yes'. Write up a serious – fact driven job description for to show the need of having a part-time dispatcher. Pinpoint the need, not 'I want'. I will take it to the city council and hope they will pass it. Don't forget to list who would do what and when? Here is her number talk to her. She takes care of Jim's children, so you have to work with her schedule, too."

When Patterson entered his office, Jim was there red-faced. He shook with anger as he pounded on the desk. "Scum, all of them, scum… Gin told me Janet's life story. How could anyone hurt that young woman like that? And- didn't get through all of it. Did you look at all of it?"

Patterson let Jim pound. "Yes and no. Samantha was with me. She identified everyone. When she couldn't stand it anymore. We stopped. I wanted you to see them so you would be on board for what we have to do. Let's divide and conquer. I'll interview Drake Armstrong's parents. I have to have them here when we interview Drake. You get to call Sterling Bender. Tell him you are looking for a house today. Go to Bender's office, let him drive around. You look at a few houses. Then, tell him you need to stop by the police station. Next, you tell him that he needs to be interview and why. That way he saves face. It will be easier to get truthful answers from him. I'm betting it was Armstrong kid who threw the rock through the board office door. I'm taking the video with me and show it to Armstrong's mom. Just his part."

Jim went off to 'look' for a new home with a very congenial Sterling Bender. Patterson solemnly left to talk with the Armstrong's. The principal, at Drake Armstrong's school, briefed Patterson on the family. Drake's dad had lost his job a couple of years ago and now, drank heavily. The mother worked nights at a truck stop. Life had been hard on all of them. Their only pride was their son Drake.

On the way to the Armstrong's, he stopped at the Board of Education office. At first, Patterson thought he had walked into the wrong building. Even before the shooting the interior of the building was old, dirty and nasty looking. He walked outside and checked the address. Then he went back inside. He was amazed at the change. It had changed in appearance from the shooting range decor to the clean stylish professional decor. It was miraculous. The bullet-hole dotted walls of yesterday were gone. Today the walls were repaired and painted, floor cleaned and everything neat and orderly. The old ugly worn-out and bullet ridden furniture had been removed. Nice attractive and clean furniture had replaced the old.

He walked up to Janet. "Remember me? I need to talk to you in private for about three minutes."

She got up and walked to the conference room, turned on all of the lights and motioned for him to have a seat. Patterson thought *this is strangely similar to my talk in this room with Mrs. Steinem.* He informed her that the police had found Worthington's personal phone and USB flash drives. Janet's thin shoulders trembled. She dropped her head embarrassed.

Janet whispered. "Did you watch all of the video?"

"Yes. I'm picking up all of the men involved in that situation. I will do everything I can to protect you."

He explained his planned procedure – all very legal. Patterson quietly asked if that was okay.

She nodded in agreement.

"Why did Worthington select you for her sick little party?"

"Worthington selected me because we are- were half-sisters. She showed me the DNA proof. She had taken the sample of my DNA from the special meals we had together in her office. She wanted a baby with the Worthington's looks and none of her mother's genetic problems. I asked how she could be so sure I had gotten pregnant. She explained about the hormone testing and how she had kept a cycle record and I don't remember what else. The three men were the best men she knew to breed with me. It was like I was her pet show dog. She took me to a doctor. He confirmed that I was pregnant. Worthington was like a kid in a candy store. We went shopping for baby things. Finally, she took me to her house and showed me the room I would stay in until the baby came. She told me I would be the nanny. It was then that I realized this beautiful brilliant woman was insane." Janet looked away.

Janet tears flowed, her face raw with emotion and shame. "I know it was wrong to have an abortion. I just couldn't have a baby out of wedlock. Worthington made me a whore just like my mother. Worthington violated and disrespected me just to get what she wanted. Yes, I hated her enough to kill her, but, I didn't. I have proof, an alibi. The Wednesday night that she was murdered. I had an abortion in the city. You can check with Dr. Ackerman. He will tell you all, who, what and when."

"Do you want to prosecute the men? I can have them arrested but, there will be a trial." Patterson rushed this question. It stressed him to have to ask this type of question to the victim of such a hideous crime.

"No! Worthington had something on all of them. She laughed about it. Said they didn't want to be a part of her scheme. So, she blackmailed them into it."

"Okay, thank you. You do realize I still have to interview them because this puts them higher on the suspects list."

A rattled Patterson thought about asking Janet about Worthington's misuse of public funds. Then, he decided he couldn't ask her. She might think he thought she was involved in it. Yes, he, too, had to protect Janet.

Off the subject, he said, "Thank you for your time. I have to ask who. No, how did this place get fixed up so nice and so fast."

Janet smiled for the first time. "Ramon and his lovely wife, Angela, did it. Isn't it wonderful? We should send a thank you note to that shooter fellow."

They both laughed. Patterson headed out to his nine o'clock appointment at Samantha's house with the insurance adjuster.

59

JOHNNY-ON-THE-SPOT DILEMMA

Patterson showed up at Samantha's house a few minutes after the insurance inspector. He studied the inspector for a few minutes to see how to handle him. Average height, thin, black goatee, balding and intense! Patterson watched and gagged when the inspector had cut a section of the burnt porch, smelled it and tasted it. Somehow, a person tasting something that had Johnny-on-the-Spot's fluid saturated in it, didn't qualify as healthy. But what did Patterson know?

Patterson walked up and held out his hand.

No handshake. The man stayed bent over the porch floor and looked at it with a large magnifying glass. "Well I hope you're here to arrest the homeowner. This was arson, without a doubt."

"How do you know that?"

Gasoline taste in the wood, the owner probably wanted a new porch and put gasoline in the Johnny and set it on fire. The good news for us is there's water in the Johnny and not a lot of room for gasoline. So minimum burning, which doesn't matter, we don't pay on arson fires."

Inspector Nils informed Patterson.

"Okay – sir I'm the Police Chief, I was here when this lunatic lost control of his car while shooting at my police truck. My truck had been in front of the owner's house. Call and check with fire department about what happened here last night. Also, call the Johnny-on-the-Spot people. They showed up and hauled the Johnny off with them last night. Here are their cards call them. Wait a minute – look there's trail of gasoline heading off. Let's follow it."

They followed the oily stream right up to the Roth Renovation truck. Sitting on the tail gate sat a burnt red gasoline can with two holes low on its side.

Patterson made Inspector Nils found him to find the workmen. They found them hard at work in the basement putting the plumbing together.

"Hey who's in charge here?"

They looked over at the short wiry built man with a pipe wrench in his hands ready for whatever.

"I'm Police Chief Patterson. I need to ask you about your gas can out on the truck."

"I'm Gabe, Roth's chief plumber . . . When I came to work today; my brand new gas can was on the porch burnt. It's the city sewer crew guys. They won't leave us or this house alone. They let air out of our tires. They steal our tools and our lunches. We didn't put gasoline in the Johnny. Is that the reason you're here to talk to us?"

A tall lanky kid raised his hand. "I did it. Those Jokers are always coming over here and using the Johnny. They make a mess like smoking and putting their cigarettes out in the Johnny. So I put gasoline in the Johnny and hoped it would explode and burn them on the butt."

"Billy is a bone head, but in his defense our bosses Steve and JR told us to keep this place clean. Said that Ms. Grant was a friend of theirs. No smoking or we get canned. Ha, ha" He laughed at his Johnny- on-the Spot joke. "Well, the town's sewer rats smoke on the property and leave their cigarettes all over. Billy has the honor of picking up their mess. We need our jobs."

"Okay, do you know the name of the foreman on the city sewer crew?"

"Lard butt Moore"

"Is he there now?"

"Yup"

Patterson and his new friend Nils walked over to the city's sewer crew. "We need to talk to Moore."

"What do you want?" This guy looked like he should have his picture in the dictionary under the word burly. Patterson had interrupted his sexting. The man's large hands moved skillfully over the phone, sweat slipped down his face, and his perverted smile revealed three missing teeth. The man had been sexting.

Patterson asked, had to, "Do you know Devora Moore, a principal for River Bend Middle school?"

"She's my honey. Why? Is she okay?" Then he looked at the text message and at the police officer.

"Just met her she seems nice. Very handful, I mean helpful." Patterson smirked at pun.

Patterson talked to Mr. Moore about harassing Roth's men. Inspector Nils explained property damage laws and told him that a citation would be sent to his employer. That his insurance company lawyers would be getting in touch with his employer – the city of River Bend.

Mr. Nils looked around, wrote something on his computer. "Okay, I'll take pictures. Have your wife get estimates for repairing the porch. Plus, I want to check and make sure you two don't have any other damage. We advise you to wait to repair the porch until after the plumbing has been finished."

"Ah this isn't my house. Samantha Grant isn't my wife. I'm just helping her by meeting with you today." Patterson explained.

They shook hands and exchanged cards. Patterson collected bullets embedded in the porch. Maybe there were finger prints on them. Patterson had one more stop to make, the Armstrong's, the worse one of the day.

60

The Armstrong's

Patterson drove into the oldest poorest neighborhood in River Bend. It appeared much like the pictures from the late eighteen hundred. The area was built to house the coal miners, river boat worker and the other hard working low income people. The Armstrong's house was small white clapboard with a white picket fence across the front of the yard. Their yard neatly cut it had to be the envy of the block. Hard times may have hit them hard. But- they took good care of their home and took pride in its appearance. Or maybe the Armstrong's hadn't lived in the house long.

Through the door's window, Patterson watched a swiveled up man laboriously walked towards the door when he rang the doorbell. As the man slowly opened the door, his thin face wadded up in distaste.

He asked. "What do you want?"

"It's about Drake." Patterson saw the panic on the man face and quickly added. "He is fine. Nothing has happened to him. But, I need to talk to you about something personal."

Patterson saw fear in the man's eyes. Fear that the only thing of value in this man's poor life had been still hurt or dead.

"Is your wife here?"

Mr. Armstrong nodded and slowly shuffled to the bedroom door. He knocked three times. "Liz, the police are here. Drake is fine."

A skin and bones woman entered the room. Tears of fear simmered in her deep set beautiful grey eyes. She had eyes similar to Bunny Worthington. Rollers were in her grey streaked hair, hands were red and chapped, an old house dress hung on her and she hadn't put shoes on her thin feet. Her feet were white and dainty with pink polish.

"Yes may we help you?" She spoke softly and her eyes were locked with Patterson's.

"Yes, I need the two of you to sit down. I'm sorry, but Drake's in trouble." Patterson looked away as the tears fell from Liz Armstrong's eyes. It didn't help him that every wall and shelf had pictures of Drake playing football or football trophies. Patterson thought *this will kill them.*

"Did you know your son was friends with Superintendent Timmons Worthington.?"

They mumbled. "No>"

"Well he had been friends of sorts with her. Then she blackmailed him into doing something that could ruin his football career. I need to show you a video. She used this to blackmail him."

Patterson played the video with Drake stealing computers from the District's board office. Patterson moved to the part were Worthington had video herself telling Drake that he had to do something for her or she would show this to the police.

"Now I'll show you what she made him do." Patterson played only a small part of their son with Janet Monroe. It showed clearly that Janet was not a willing participant. In the video it clearly showed her hands taped above her head and that she was unconscious. He stopped before they had to see things that parents don't want to see. The mother cried softly. The father trembled either in fear or anger or both.

"Are – you going to arrest my son?" He asked.

"The young lady doesn't want charges brought against your son. She wants silence from your son. I need to interview him at the police station. It depends on him. Do you drive?"

He looked at both of them.

Mrs. Armstrong shook her head. "We don't own a car. Please, we don't want the police to pick up our son at school. We know what he did was wrong, but the other kids might make our son a hero for being arrested. The video clearly shows our son is not a hero."

"Today is your lucky day. My police car is in the shop, I have my personal car. One of you can go in and get your son with me. I'll put a jacket on over my uniform. Will that work?"

They thanked him. Mrs. Armstrong got up and went back to their bedroom. In minutes she came back with her hair combed and wore a touch of make-up.

"Jack you stay here. We will be alright." She smiled and kissed the air in his direction.

They walked to the car. Patterson got a jacket out of the back seat and off they went. "I don't know if this is significant or not. I'm Bunny Worthington's aunt. Her father is my brother. We grew up poor. Our dad had money but lost it. Timmons made money. Jack, my husband didn't. My brother and I weren't close growing up. After we left home, we never saw each other or even talked to each other. I didn't know that Bunny Worthington even knew that we existed. She was –"

Patterson added the missing word. "Evil"

"No - strange…" Said Liz and nothing more.

Stiffly she walked into the school and in minutes she came out with her son. She refused to look at Drake.

Patterson drove them in silence to the police station. His office served as an interview room and everything else room, as needed. Special rooms were expensive and not in the police chief's budget.

"Drake, we will start with a video. Then I will interview you. Say 'yes', if you understand and agree to have it videoed." Patterson waited for a sign.

Drake nodded. His sandy brown hair fell into his deep-set grey eyes with long black eyelashes. His eyes were like his mother's. Patterson turned on the video of Drake, the same section he had shown his mother and a touch more. "Is that you?"

"Yes, but—"

"No buts, right now. Just answer the questions. It will be easier on you. Did this young lady do anything that indicated that she wanted this?"

Drake shook his head, 'no'.

"Was she aware of what was happening to her?"

Again he shook, 'no'.

"So this was done without her consent?"

A nod 'yes'... "But she wanted a baby."

"Answer the questions only. Did you know this young woman before that night?"

"No...."

"Have you had any contact with her since then?"

A pause, "I left her a note on a rock."

"So you were the one who threw the rock through the District Board of Education's office door?"

A nod 'yes' . . .

"Please talk clearly into the camera and explain your side of this story."

Drake explained. "I met Superintendent Worthington last summer. She started coming to our practices. One night she gave me a ride home. We talked about my plans for my future. I told her I wanted to go to college. She saw where I lived, and promised me she would help me get a scholarship and an entrance into the private college where she had gone. But, I had to help her with things. She kept coming by practice and then driving me home. We became lovers."

Patterson summarized Drake's story in his notes, similar story to Janet Monroe. Worthington took the special interest in him. Promises were made, then she videoed a compromising situation. Used it for blackmail in order to get what she wanted. Worthington was truly evil. Murder was too good for her.

"Drake, I need to ask you one more question. Where were you Wednesday night after five-thirty?"

"I had practice until five and then I walked home. I got home about five-thirty. Dad was home, but. . . He won't remember - he was -" Drake stopped. His handsome face distorted from trying not to cry. "Did you walk home with a friend or at least part way home?"

"No..."

Patterson knew how Drake felt. He had been in that situation with his alcoholic father. He needed to check with the neighbors to verify his alibi.

"Janet, the young lady in the video, doesn't want any trouble. But she wants you to sign a contract. The contract states, if you ever tell anyone about that night she will go after you with all the lawyers she can find. Do you understand me?"

Drake turned pale. "I won't tell. Did she get pregnant like Worthington wanted? Am I a dad?"

He turned so pale Patterson thought the boy was going to pass out. Patterson decided to keep quiet about the baby thing. "No, she didn't get pregnant."

Patterson realize that Drake would have done the right thing and offered to marry Janet if she was pregnant. Drake was a decent hormonal young man. Never the less Drake had to pay for some of his crimes.

Patterson wrote in his notebook. Then looked at Drake. "One thing I need you to realize. You need to work off the cost of replacing the glass door at the Board Office. I will help you get back on track for playing football in college."

Patterson couldn't believe he had said what he said. He had gone soft. Drake, his mother and Patterson made arrangements for their next meeting and drove them home.

On the drive back to the police station Patterson called Janet Monroe. Explained the note on her desk was from the high school boy involved with her situation. Patterson explained his motive had been fear that she would go to the police. That he promised to leave her alone and would not say anything about that night to anyone.

61

BENDER GOES BONKERS

Patterson heard the smile in Janet's voice when she responded. "Oh, I'm keeping it. I liked what the note said. It reads 'keep quiet or die'. There are times I could use it here."

As he drove into the Police station parking lot, Patterson heard ranting. After he entered into the building he asked Sheila. "What's going on his Jim's office?"

Sheila scrunched her entire body and with a diabolical smile. "Oh, that's old Sterling Bender. How dare we take up his valuable time? He was a pain in the butt when we were in high school together. He hasn't changed one bit, except now he's well built."

Jim came out and asked Patterson to join him.

Patterson enter the interview room clinched fists, every muscle in his body was ready to fight. Intimidation was the name of Patterson's game. "Bender, you are living on borrowed time. You should be in jail. But, first, you need to tell me about the day Superintendent Worthington was murdered. You gave her a ride to work, yes or no."

"Yes."

"Were you her ride home?" Patterson wrote down his answer to the first question.

"No." Sterling Bender squared his shoulders.

"Judging from videos I saw of you and Superintendent Worthington. You two were involved. Yes, or No" Patterson wrote down every muscle movement made by Bender.

"Yes." Bender squirmed.

Patterson paused, stood and paced in front of Sterling Bender. "I think - you were the last person to see her alive. I think - you were her ride home. I think - you stop by her office wanting to have fun before you took her home? She said no. You got angry. You stabbed her?"

Distaste filled Bender, "Bunny and I had been lovers for years. So no, I didn't have to force myself on her. I will say this very slowly. If you don't get it. My lawyer will explain it to you. I took her to the Board Office on my way to work in the morning. As usual when we rode in together she would call me if she needed a ride home. She didn't call so I went home alone. You can check with my secretary and with Mrs. Steinem they know our routine. They will tell you that it was common for me to take Bunny Worthington to work, and then she found another way home. Just do your job – investigate. Let me go back to work. You are costing me money with your stupidity."

"First let's go over some things. We have enough physical information on you to put you away for a long, long time. Now keep quiet and answer yes or no, only."

First, Patterson showed Bender only his part in the Janet Monroe incident. Bender smirked while he watched it and giggled during one section. During the interview, he answered only yes or no and sometimes he answered the question before it had been asked. Patterson and Jim looked at each other. Jim pulled out the keys to the cell. Patterson shook his head 'no'.

When Patterson explained to Bender he needed to sign Janet Monroe's contract. Bender ranted he would not. "Does that little bitch want me to sign a child-support contract for her illegitimate child? They will laugh her out of court. I had a vasectomy when I was twenty years old."

With that announcement Patterson wanted to sucker punch the Bender. But, calmly he said. "Mr. Bender, please listen to everything I say before you open your mouth. She doesn't want anything from you. Just for you to sign a contract stating that if you ever tell anyone about that night. She, her lawyers and I will go after you. Do you understand me?"

Patterson continued, "You know Bender we could have and should have interviewed you at your office. We felt that a man with your community standing deserved a chance to save face. When you go back to your office everyone will assume you were showing Jim Murphy some homes."

Patterson waited for Bender to apologize or thank him. Instead, Bender straighten his clothing, brushed his hair and glared at them and said. "I'll be talking to my lawyer."

Patterson knew the second the idea came to him that he should not do it. But, Bender, the nasty arrogant fool, deserved some of his nastiness back. Patterson scanned his notes, then he slapped his forehead. "Oh, I forget to tell you. There is one more thing. Dr. Ackerman discovered in Bunny Worthington's autopsy. That she had a new strand of STDs. After viewing the video, we tested Janet. She has it, too. That is the reason she has been in the hospital. Apparently one of you guys is a carrier. So, we will be checking all the men involved and their partners. The AIP- STD strain is vicious. Your hair falls out. You go blind. Certain body parts rot."

Patterson did a quick scan below Bender's belt area. "It's a smelly nasty way to die. You and your wife need to be tested tomorrow. If you don't show. Or if you show- up without your wife. I will send a parole car to get you and/or your wife. Understand? Or do I need to call your lawyer? So he can explain it to you."

Patterson noticed that under Sterling Bender's immaculate effeminate exterior his muscles rippled under his shirt. In panther like movement as Sterling Bender smoothed his silver hair and adjusted his shirt and slacks. Everything needed to be perfect including his teeth. They radiated. Patterson thought. *Lick your paws and smooth your hair, Bender.*

Patterson explained to Bender the forms he needed were located at the front desk. That he needed to ask Sheila nicely for them. Then he had to fill them out, have a witness sign them and have them notarized. And – finally, tomorrow - Bender, his forms and his wife had to be at the police station. Patterson marched out of the interview room and into his office. He called Dr. Ackerman and explained about the fake lab tests. Ackerman loved the idea and promised to show up without any speeding tickets.

A door slammed seconds later. Jim waltzed into Patterson's office. "What in the world was all of that about? What is AIP- STD?"

Patterson leaned back with a shocked look on his face. "Jim didn't you get the notice from Dr. Ackerman about AIP-STD? Well, sir, AIP-STD is a rare strain of STD. That only Arrogant Idiot People can get."

Jim freaked out. "You made it up? What about the doctor part? If that man finds out you messed with him. He will sue you and River Bend police department. He's always looking for ways to get rich, quick."

"Yes, I made it up. But, Dr. Ackerman will be here to administer the test. Then, we will have his DNA. Just in case we need it."

Patterson checked his messages. It was late afternoon and he hadn't eaten. But, Bender had left a bad taste in his mouth. Patterson thought. *The only thing that would get rid of that foul taste would be a great chili dog with lots of onions and a drive to clear my head. Both medicine for my soul.* As he drove around he thought about the Armstrong family and how much they reminded him of his own family. "This job is making me soft." He muttered to himself.

62

SURPRISE

Surveillance time. . . Samantha and Katherine were back on track to their delight. Samantha chatted with Katherine as they walked to their cars. "Patterson denies there could be anyone else besides Nick Chase that killed Worthington and Steinem. By all appearances Nick is a reasonable candidate for the master killer. Except for two things, one thing Nick is lazy, the second reason he doesn't fit into my galaxy theory. Neither Worthington nor Steinem had power over Nick nor does he have power over them. The only motive Nick had to kill anyone was Mrs. Steinem, she left him money in her will. I don't think he knew about the money. We have people of interest to keep our eyes on, let Patterson watch Nick Chase."

In the soft breeze Katherine's hair stayed in place and now so did Samantha's hair. Katherine touched her hair, brushed a piece of lint for her camel coat and questioned. "Who would have thought that Principal Moore was a church goer? The Wednesday night of Worthington's murder she sang in the choir with fifty or more people as her alibi. I'm glad Mickey Sims had an airtight alibi, too. I think it's cute he's a soccer coach for his daughter's team. I believe that coaching a winning team to its victory on the Wednesday night in question counts as an airtight alibi don't you? I bet the whole team went to eat pizza together. That's what I used to do with my son's team. I love soccer."

Shocked Samantha asked. "You coached? And you have a crush on Mickey, I'm going to tell."

"No, I was an assistant coach in soccer. And don't be silly about Mickey."

Samantha picked up Bo from Katherine's and went to Click's Photo Shop. Click reopened his shop in his garage after his store had been bombed. He still blamed Samantha for it. He cringed every time she came in for any reason. Today she bought infrared and regular film, again. She tingled with excitement as she walked through the door into the photograph shop. She made her purchases and loaded the film. She needed to practice since it had been a couple of months since she had used her camera. She sang to herself. *To the park to the park, hi, ho. . . .* Bo jumped around as they neared the River Bend's River View Park. As she walked and Bo scented twigs and blades of grass. Shih Tzu's may be small but they think they are mighty. The trees were rich jewel set against the deep harvest blue sky. The wind danced through the leaves caused them to shimmer as they twirled.

Treading carefully down the path to the river's overlook with the camera attached to her face. She witnessed a sad, but beautiful sight through her camera's lens. She watched a copper – headed mother wash her small child in the park's fountain. Then the mother chased the child with a dripping cloth. The car near the family appeared to be a home on wheels. It was filled with bedding, clothing and books. Then the mother handed each child a sandwich with wax paper that only Ms. Millie (River Bend's middle school cafeteria's cook) used any more. Samantha recognized the younger boy as Edward Wooten's brother. Why did he and his family live in a car in the park? She photographed them. They were a beautiful family. Not wanting them to see her, she and Bo left the park.

Back at Katherine's house, Samantha needed to think and prepare for their surveillance job. She put Bo on a leash and walked around her old neighborhood. She needed to find the best place to take pictures and write down Sterling Bender's activities. Staying a block away from Bender's house as she analyzed which angle worked the best without being caught by him. The right side worked the best. But, it was next to her ex-husband's new in-laws house. She could break into their house and watch Bender from any room on the left side of their home. While she stood there thinking. Victoria waved at her, then started yelling for Samantha to come over for a visit. To stop Victoria from drawing more attention to Samantha's stalking Bender's house, she walked over to Victoria. Samantha thought *on the plus side, if Victoria needed help with something at her parent's house, it would be a golden opportunity for her to watch Bender and his activities. . . Just think - all in one block - Worthington, Bender, Robert and Victoria and Victoria's parents.* Samantha bet at certain times of the year witches migrated to this block for the World Witches' Conference.

"Robbie is sleeping would you please come in and have a cup of coffee with me. I get so lonely here with just the baby."

She and Bo sat down at her old kitchen table, now Victoria's kitchen table. She needed to be nice to Victoria in case she or Katherine needed to use Victoria's parent's house. Victoria made her black coffee and with cream. Samantha hated cream. But she wanted a connection to the Bender house. She drank it. *Nasty* she thought. And then the room tilted back and forth. She had been drugged. "*Victoria, no-o-o.*" Samantha tried to stand up and hit the top of her hand on the edge of the table.

Through twirling movement Samantha watched fascinated as the bruises appeared all big blue and swollen on her hand. She stared at it. Movement out of the corner of her eye caused her to refocus her attention. Victoria sprint towards her with a small pair of scissors in her hand. She held it like a dagger. Samantha tried to run, but her rubbery legs felt cemented to the floor. She called Bo through what seemed like a tunnel. He couldn't move. Victoria had chained him to the stove and had dyed him blue. Hate filled Samantha. Her arms lashed out, but her feet stayed stuck to the floor. Her legs wobbled, yet she fought off Victoria. Victoria slashed the bruise on Samantha's open with the tip of the scissors, blood squired all over Victoria. She screamed repeatedly at Samantha for messing up her house and her life. Each blood droplet caused a new scream and a wave of hitting on Samantha.

Robert heard his wife screaming when he entered the house. He ran to help her. To his disbelief he saw Victoria attacking his ex-wife with scissors. Samantha, nearly bald with blue sprouts of hair. A whimper came from the stove area. It was poor Bo chained to the stove shivering and blue. Bottles of blue food coloring scattered on the floor.

"Victoria what have you done?" Robert asked. Victoria giggled and jumped around the room.

Samantha slurred. "Robert, you look dashing. Victoria put something in my coffee."

She thought. *Got to focus.* "Robert, you are wearing the last suit I got for you."

In her befuddled mine Samantha remembered she bought it for him just days before she found him in bed with their dog setter, Victoria, the bitch.

"I gave her coffee – look." Victoria pointed to the cup on the table.

"What did you put in the coffee?"

"I put Unisom in the cream." Victoria giggled jumping around. She had lost it.

Robert shook his wife's shoulders. She looked up at him and spat on him. "You and your precious Samantha, I hate her. Get her out of my house."

Shoulders slumped Samantha stumbled in an effort to leave, stopped, and said. "Sorry, Robert but, your wife needs medical help."

63

SAMANTHA'S BAD HAIR DAY

Samantha and Bo limped back to Katherine's house. Still drugged Samantha tried to explain the events that happened at Robert's house. She almost felt sorry for Victoria. Poor Robert had his hands full with a needy wife and a tiny baby. But a smile still managed to spread across her face. Samantha reported her findings for their Sterling Bender surveillance.

Katherine sent a text to Lisa, Samantha's hairdresser extraordinaire. "This is Katherine Jones, we have another emergency. Can you come? I'll feed you. You won't believe what happened to Samantha this time."

Lisa showed up minutes later. She shook her head.

"Oh my, Samantha, you are going to be a very light blond for a while. Just trust me and I'll take care of you and your little man."

Everyone turned their eyes to a cringing blue Bo. Samantha sat, drank lots of coffee and watched Lisa work her magic. Samantha chattered to Katherine about Edward Wooten's family living in their car at the park. Also, hadn't seen Mr. Bender maybe he wasn't home yet.

The three women talked about the weather and local gossip. They finally asked Samantha about Victoria. All Samantha said was Victoria needed help. Robert needed to take care of it. Finally, Samantha had enough coffee and felt better. She saw that Bo was alright.

When Lisa left, Samantha and Katherine pulled out their surveillance list. Bender, Moore, Mary Pierce, Bob Douglas, and Mickey Sims made up their list of primary suspects. They checked off Moore, Pierce and Sims because apparently they had solid alibis. That left Bob and Bender. Samantha said. "Katherine we need to focus on Sterling Bender. Remember he is a jogger. Plus, he wears a black jogging outfit like the man I saw talking to Roger and like the shooter at the Board office. Plus, Sterling Bender had a major role in Worthington's videos. Another thing his motive might be the legal document found on Worthington's phone with his signature on them. I feel we do need to check out everyone on our list."

As Samantha and Katherine discussed their surveillance plans a roar of a car sped down the road. Samantha remembered something that had sounded similar and interrupted Katherine. "What is that sound?"

"Oh, that Sterling in his old MG, he loves that car." Katherine told her.

Samantha stopped Katherine. "How big is a MG? The sound sounds similar to the roar from the storm that drove down my road and shot at me and Patterson."

Katherine a bit miffed by Samantha's rudeness started dusting off her imagined lint particles from her black shirt. "It is small, white and very clean. Sterling Bender would never take his car out on your road. Never happen – so it's back to Nick as our killer."

Samantha speculated, "You and Patterson have a problem with Nick Chase. I'm telling he's too lazy. But you do have a point. If he has to have a clean car, then my road was the wrong road to go down. He always so snobbish and uptight, usually killers aren't uptight, snobbish people. Or are they? If it was Bender that shot at Patterson and me. Then he took his car to a car wash. Right?"

Samantha looked at her Escalade and knew it needed cleaned. "Ah, Katherine there can't be more than two or three car care places in the River Bend area. Ta-da... Let's clean my car."

"Are you going to tell Patterson what we are up to? And what Victoria did to your hair and Bo? Oh, he will kill Victoria over what she did to Bo." Katherine danced in delight at the thought Patterson shooting Victoria.

Samantha ignored Katherine's chatter. The sound of the car reaffirmed her conviction that Bender was the murder. "Patterson is so sure it's Nick Chase. My gut tells me it's Sterling Bender. Plus, Sterling has more to lose than Nick. Sterling is smart. Nick is lazy. Let's check out the car wash places."

Later - Samantha smiled, "Well, the Clean Me car wash owner thinks he remembers Bender."

Samantha opened her phone. "Katherine look at my phone. See. I still have the print of the tire thread from the shooter's car. If I could get into Bender's garage and photograph his tires. Patterson could check them for similarities."

"Do you really want to hang-out at his house? Just remember what Victoria did to you last time you were there." Katherine held back a giggle.

64

BENDER'S TOOTH-BRUSH

Samantha watched the Bender's house off and on all night from the room over Katherine's garage. Bender's house stayed dark all night. Bo didn't growl once during the night. So no one had jogged by Katherine's. Katherine told Samantha about the times she saw someone slinking around in the shadows. It was impossible to see who it was.

Samantha thought, it had to be Sterling Bender. Hypothesis. Logical reasons for Bender jogging by Katherine's house. Reason one, he wanted to see how involved Katherine was in the helping me. Reason two, Mrs. Anderson's dog chased him from his usual normal routine, but dog chased anyone going by Anderson's house. No Bender would sue Mrs. Anderson. He sued everyone. Had to be he had been checking on Katherine's involvement. Katherine was endanger.

She was easy prey. She lived alone during the week. There were blind spots close to her doors no one would see him entering her house.

Six o'clock in the morning came too early, the alarm buzzed, and Bo growled at the window. Samantha turned on her side looked out the window. She saw Sterling Bender dressed in his black jogging suit driving off in his shiny bright white sport's car. She squinted her eyes and wondered. *Did I see a hole in the top of his car?* Samantha hurried and got dressed. She ran Bo outside to do his business. She kept an eye on the Bender's house the entire time. A swift glance at Robert's house out of fear, all quiet there. As Samantha walked into Katherine's house

226

the garage door at Bender's went up. Susan, Bender's wife, drove off. Wow, she left early for work.

"Katherine do I have time to go to the Bender's and get DNA from something of Sterling's? And- compare tire tracks in his garage to photograph of the shooter's tire tracks. He left already."

Katherine looked at her watch; the diamonds sparkled as the sunlight touched them. She checked her nails before answering. "I do need to buff my nails before we leave for school. And – I get to be the lookout."

Samantha jogged over and through the neighbors' yards slipped between Victoria's parent's, the Kant's and Bender's houses. All window coverings were closed at the Kant's. Their dog had died just before Victoria had baby Robbie. So no dog alert…Great, Samantha with her lock pick did a quick click and the door sprang open at the Benders. The great thing about breaking into a house in Pretty Prairie no one, but no one had alarms, this was a safe community. All the men had great jobs, the women were skinny, and the children all looked alike.

Once in, Samantha scurried upstairs. The master bedroom's door was opened at the top of the stairs. A stripped man's bathrobe rested on the bed, male slippers beside the bed. Only one person had slept in the bed. She jogged to the on-suite bathroom. A comb, brush, or spit, Yuk, have to have something. Her evidence bag fell; she bent to pick it up. There tossed in the trash can was his tooth brush. Was it his? Neatly placed beside the sink was a new – still in the plastic toothbrush, perfect. . . She bagged the disposed of toothbrush just like Patterson taught her. Her phone rang she answered it.

"Get out of there Sterling is driving into the garage in his company car."

Samantha scurried to the next room. She heard Bender come in slammed something on a hard surface and headed up the stairs. *Great she thought he will go into his bedroom and I'll be gone.* But no, he headed to the room where she hid. She slipped further behind the door and watched through the slit in the door. Bender stalked over to the bedside table, opened the drawer, removed a handgun, and emptied the bullets into his pocket. Strange thing to do. . . Then he went to the dresser, opened a drawer ran his hand around and pulled out a check book and left the drawer open.

Through the crack in the door, she saw his smile as he walked through the door. No attempt to hide he had been in the dresser. He wanted his wife to know. He trotted down the stairs. Samantha slid down the stairs right behind him. She watched him drive off before she ran to Katherine's and jumped through the open car door.

"Well . . ." Katherine gave Samantha an arched eyebrow - look.

Smiling, Samantha held Sterling Bender's tooth brush in a plastic bag.

"Now what?" Katherine asked.

"I'm calling Dr. Ackerman and asking him how I can get it to him, today. I need to check on Bender's car I think he dropped it off someplace to get the top fixed. I think I saw a hole in it."

The not so congenial coroner knew Samantha helped Patterson on cases, well; on a case. Hopefully, there wouldn't a problem. But she knew Patterson should be in the loop on this. She would text him – later.

Samantha's extreme makeover spread through the school like a wildfire. Speculation on, why went from her being on a reality show for the *worst hair cut* to her joining an *online dating* group. When the teachers bombarded Katherine with questions she just smiled and said Samantha needed a change.

Arrangements were made with Dr. Ackerman's assistant to pick up the DNA sample during Samantha's planning time. Amazed that he didn't question her about who requested it and accepted it was Patterson's request. She guessed he assumed that it was like the other time.

The assistant showed up right on time and took her information and Bender's tooth brush. Said they would have the information back to her later today.

65

PATTERSON'S BUSY FRIDAY

At six o'clock in the morning, Patterson's phone rang and woke him up from an exhausted sleep. At first he thought it was his clock and hammered it to shut it up. When that didn't work he answered his phone. No one ever called him that early for a good reason.

"Yes, Patterson here."

"Kip Kipling here, the Worthington's are returning today. I'm picking them up at the airport this morning. You need to be here to tell the about their daughter. Like you said. . ."

Patterson cut Kipling off. "What time?"

"Call you when I know they're an hour or so out."

"Thanks owe you one." Patterson got up, made coffee and started to write what he needed to say to the Worthington's. Patterson wandered. *How do you tell people their only child was dead? In the military I personally informed parents about their child's death. It was hard. But those parents had lived in fear that it could happen. These people had left angry at their daughter. Now, they would live to regret that anger.*

When the call came Patterson drove to designated place and met Kip Kipling. He got into Kip's car. On the ride to the airport they talked about this and that. Finally, Patterson steered the conversation around to the possibility of Kipling working for his police department as a consultant. Kipling smiled and told Patterson, he'd think about it. They pulled on the road that led to the private planes area.

Patterson assumed they knew about their daughter and had taken a private plane to have privacy on the way home. "Apparently the Worthington's know about their daughter's death. So they hired a private plane."

Kipling replied, "No they always travel by private plane."

Their plane slowed down and Kipling jumped out of the limo. He gently guided the Worthington's to the limo and opened the door for them. Patterson had been in the back seat when the Worthington's entered the car. He introduced himself. The travel worn couple stared at him bewildered.

"Police Chief Patterson, although it is kind of you to meet our plane and introduce yourself to us. What's wrong?" Timmons Worthington leaned toward Patterson his dark grey eyes drilled into Patterson.

Be strong, Patterson mentally snapped into military mode. *These people need to be told someone murder their only daughter. Then inform them that someone had murder, Mrs. Worthington's sister also. Make it quick and to the point.*

"You are correct. It is my duty to inform you, your daughter Ms. Timmons Worthington was murdered last Wednesday night. To add to your burden I must, also, inform you, Mrs. Worthington, that your sister Judith Steinem was murdered on Monday of this week."

Inhale, prepare for the storm. He waited for the crying and walling. Nothing. . . They stared at him..

"Have you arrested the person responsible for Bunny's death?" Mr. Worthington asked.

"No, but we do have a person of interest for her and Mrs. Steinem's death. He has fled the area. We've involved the state and County Sheriff. Plus, the FBI in the search."

Mr. Timmons Worthington wrapped an arm around his wife and looked at her as if for her approval. "So you have nothing on who killed Bunny. Am I correct?"

Patterson nodded embarrassed.

"I will call a press conference and offer a large reward for anyone providing information that helps us find our daughter's killer. Rats will turn out in droves to get money."

"Sir, I don't think that is a good idea. You'll send the killer into hiding. We feel the deaths are related. We found patches of cocaine powder left at the scene of the second murder and at your home in River Bend. We had a search warrant in hand to examine your home, Nick Chase opened the door with coke powder on him. We took a sample. It matched the cocaine found at the scene of the first and second murder."

"What would his motive be for killing Judith?" Mr. Worthington asked.

"He was the beneficiary on Mrs. Steinem's insurance policy for a sizable amount of money."

Patterson paused and thought about telling them about him being involved in a shooting rampage at the Board of Education office. Before he continued Lana Worthington crumpled in the seat, released a bitter sob.

"It wasn't Nick. He couldn't. He's a good boy."

Patterson wondered. *A sob over Nick Chase, but nothing over her own daughter.*

Mr. Worthington turned to Patterson. "Where do you have Bunny and Judith's bodies?"

"We had Dr. Ackerman from City General take them to Rockwell Funeral Home. We were told you were friends of Mr. Rockwell. That you would want him to handle things."

"Yes, now for the Press Conference, do you want to arrange it or me?" Worthington pulled an iPhone from his pocket ready to do business. Business was his safe mode.

"Would you consider making an announcement tonight at the Country Club dance? Many of the people your daughter blackmailed will be there. Let my detectives and I keep an eye on everyone. Also, this will give you a chance to work out any kinks for the press conference that you can hold on Sunday morning."

"Excuse me are you saying my daughter blackmailed people, our friends? And- that you think one of our friends may have killed her? Impossible, our kind do not kill. We pay and we pay dearly." Mr. Worthington looked at Patterson with distaste.

"Sir, you need an open mind to all possibilities. There are some facts you need to know about your daughter." Patterson became stoic. He didn't like Bunny Worthington, but these people were her parents.

"Yes, she blackmailed people. Your friends and others… She knew the person who killed her. She trusted that person. There wasn't a fight. And, your daughter was a fighter. So yes; your kind could have killed her. I'm sorry I need to show you something unpleasant. A brief section of a video your daughter made. I believe you know the men." Patterson showed them a section of the video of her doctoring Janet's drink and then the men following her to the bedroom with Janet.

"Yes, I know all three men, Sterling Bender, Nick and my sister's boy. I don't remember his name. Bunny knew Nick and Sterling they all ran together. I can't believe she would do something this-."

"You need to understand there will be several people at the dance that your daughter had blackmailed. She even blackmailed Nick." He stopped before he called her 'evil'. "I am sorry to meet you under such circumstances. I am sorry for your loss."

Solemnly Patterson nodded and exited the car.

Worthington told Kipling to have Patterson wait while they talked to Kipling.

Patterson waited while they talked. Finally, Kipling came around the limo to speak to him. Kipling updated Patterson on the Worthington's plans.

"They want to go to the funeral home. Then to their home in River Bend. Tonight I'll be in the parking lot at the Country Club. I'll keep an eye on any activities out there. If you need any help text me. Okay old man?"

To Patterson the 'old man' comment stung. "Hey, Kipling, I'm surprised you know how to text? Old man – back at you."

66

THE SUSPECT LINE DANCE

Katherine appeared twenty years younger when she entered the living room. Katherine, yes, Katherine wore an above the knees short formal, like she had worn back in the '80's. A black strapless dress with a ruffle skirt, the form fitting top covered in sparkles. She had added large rhinestone earrings. She literally sparkled.

Samantha had to say, "I have never seen your knees before. Wasn't sure you even had them."

"I'm glad one of us looks beautiful." Samantha wanted to stay home she was embarrassed about her looks. Before Victoria's vendetta, Samantha had planned to wear her hair in its normal fizzy way. She had planned to order an easy to dance in dress. Before she clicked on the 'Place Order' square, she showed Katherine what she had picked. Breathing fast, eyes bugged out – all Katherine could say, "No, not that granny looking thing. I'll find something for you."

Katherine hands shook as she waved Samantha away from the computer. Katherine ordered the dress, ironed the dress and had not let Samantha see or touch the dress before the dance. The night of the dance Samantha held up a sophisticated satiny-sheen red dress with a boat-neck that settled just off her shoulders, the full skirt gathered tight with a tiny black belt accentuating her small waist. Best of all the sleeves were ¾ arm length and gave Samantha the illusion of long sleek arms. The satin like material reminded her of something Grace Kelly had worn in one of her movies. Katherine had Lisa stop by to do Samantha's hair. She styled Samantha's new short hair into a smooth style and it finished her Grace Kelly look.

Katherine and Samantha stared at each other's transformation. Katherine hugged Samantha and spoke rapidly. "Samantha are beautiful. The dress is perfect for you. Johnny's a half an hour away so we will be on time. What about Patterson? And – what did you hear from Dr. Ackerman?"

Katherine's fast forward chatting meant she was nervous. Her husband of twenty – five years still made her nervous. It had been said that Johnny Jones made espresso nervous.

"I haven't heard from Patterson. I'll just meet him at the club. There should be a crowd tonight. Have you talked to Gin?"

"She and Jim are going. She was very excited about her dress. I feel just like I did in high school. Oh, I think it is so great they're doing a Tom Jones Night. Fun, fun, and more fun. . . . Then back to sleuthing tomorrow."

Johnny Jones threw open the front door, slid into the house, ran upstairs, put on the outfit that Katherine selected for him and slid down the banister.

"Ready to go, Doll?" Then he stopped, ran his fingers through his oily black hair, and did a side glance to appraise Katherine. His mouth dropped open. He smiled, "Lookin' good."

Then swung his arm out for her to take. . . With a big smile, Katherine seized Johnny Jones's arm and she danced to the door.

"Lock up and make sure Bo has water."

"No, dogs allowed in the house." Johnny Jones stopped.

"Bo is a guard dog. I've been having trouble with a peeping tom. Okay?" Her eyes flirted with him as she pulled him through the door and out to his latest swanky car. Johnny Jones proved yet again that he wasn't the brightest bulb in the light fixture. He never questioned about the peeping tom or why a Shih Tzu for a guard dog.

It was past time for Samantha to leave for the dance, but she felt nervous about leaving Bo. The thought that Katherine's voyeur or Johnny Jones would bother Bo made her nervous. Johnny Jones had a history of being mean to Bo. She decided to put him the safe room,

Katherine's sewing room. No windows and it was a 'no Johnny' area. That worked perfect for Bo. He had a place to hide under the sewing table.

She left a message for Patterson telling him to meet her at River Bend Country Club. With three inch black heels on for the first time in a year, Samantha practiced walking in them for a few minutes. Then she daintily stepped into the Escalade and headed across town. First, she drove by the Bender's to make sure they were going to the dance. As she stalked by the Bender's she saw them settling into Sterling's MG. Samantha honked and waved. Sterling proudly smiled and waved from the driver's side of his sparkling white sports convertible. His smile matched his car. His wife, Susan had on a shimmering silver floor length dress with a back that dropped well below her waist. Samantha thought *Susan Bender cleaned up very nicely after teaching all day. And Sterling Bender had to be a sociopath or evil as Worthington, he seemed so nonchalant. On his defense he didn't know that she had figured out that he was the killer, the crazy shooter and worse.*

Samantha parked in an easy exit area and walked into the club. Itsy, the country club president greeted her at the door. His son-in law swaggered around in skin tight pants and Tom Jones frizzy hair style as he crooned Tom Jones' version of *Begin the Beguine*.

Samantha surveyed the room. It was just like she imagined the dances had been like in high school. Each table had a different group of River Bend's cliques possessively attached to it.

A man in a white suit waved at her, she strained to identify the good looking man. It was Patterson. Her breath stopped and her body shut down. He was. . . The effect reminded her of when a magician puts a cloth over a rubber band and when he lifts the cloth – a diamonds bracelet appear. "Sorry" slipped out as a compliment. Patterson was no longer a grey rubber band; tonight he appeared as beautiful as a diamond bracelet. The disco ball cast lights and shadows that played magically across Patterson's muscular body and magnified his chisel facial features.

Their eyes locked. Patterson's mind was caught in a memory. He used to love to hold his sister's snow globe. He had turned it over and watched the glitter land on the love of his life. He imagined that the beautiful young woman was trapped in the globe by an evil witch. The girl in the globe wore a red dress, just like Samantha had on tonight. Destiny. . . Patterson turned to the band leader and pointed. The band leader nodded, stopped the song they were playing and moved into a new song. Patterson moved toward her as they started the song, *She's a Lady*. His walk glided into a fluid disco movement. He held out his hand to her. Mesmerized, she touched his hand, a visible spark snapped in the air. The music penetrated their normal up-tight souls. They discoed as if she knew how to dance. His mind, voice and eyes told her what to do and he skillfully moved her around the floor. Everyone stared at them as they danced completely oblivious of all others.

Before the next dance, Patterson had several requests for line dancing lessons. He agreed and the floor filled with dancers swaying, stepping left then right forward and back. Even Johnny Jones and Katherine were on the floor and line danced. Patterson with Samantha carried the crowd over the dance floor. The Tom Jones impersonator sang and danced along with them. Body movement and laughter filled the air. The cool fall breeze energizing the crowd. It bemused Samantha that the line dancing group was a moving line-up of suspects in a murder case. Janet Monroe, Mickey Sims, Sterling Bender and herself followed Patterson's every move, one of them would be in line for a murder trial. At least, this dance would help that person in the police line-up with all the practiced stepping forward, turning and backing up.

Exhausted, the band begged for a break. River Bend Middle School people had been invaded by the Roth Reconstruction group, the young people. JR Roth moved in beside Janet Moore and continued a conversation they had started days earlier. Gin, Katherine and Samantha gave each other 'the smile' when they watched Janet and JR talking together. Everyone at her table was drinking and talking about this and that. Samantha's phone dinged. She looked a text from Dr. Ackerman. She read it. "DNA matches the poop – tell Patterson."

Instead she showed Katherine the text. They read it together and then scanned the room for Bender. When their eyes met his, he saluted them. He had been watching them. 'Sorry' came out of Samantha's mouth somehow she knew this wasn't going to end well.

Patterson picked up on their stranger than usual behavior and asked to see the text. He read it and asked who? Samantha whispered Bender.

"So what – he pooped by the Board of Education building that doesn't mean he's the killer."

He kissed Samantha on the head. "You're a good detective, I'll give you that. I'm telling you, it's Nick Chase."

"No, it's not. He's too –"

Patterson ended her sentence. "Lazy. . . I need to ask you something. Remember I asked about Bob Douglass' missing lots of work days. You told me he hadn't missed any. Well, Mickey Sims handed me a note while we were all out on the dance floor. I need to read it to you and Katherine."

Patterson opened the small folded piece of paper. "Part of the scam that Worthington blamed on Ms. Meeks and me was charging people for missed days when they weren't absent. She charged for a substitute teacher against certain teachers but the subs were never hired. Worthington pocketed the money. I'm willing to help you in any way I can. I talked to my wife she knows everything."

Patterson whispered, "What do you think of that? How much money does a substitute teacher get?"

"Around a hundred dollars a day, unless it's for long term then it's more."

"That doesn't sound like much but it could add-up." Then Patterson did some quick addition on the number of days Bob Douglass had supposedly missed. Shocked at the amount of money, all he said was "Oh, my…"

"Plus, Patterson you have to realize it wasn't just one teacher or one school. It was several teachers and all of our schools. Think of what you could do with extra hundred dollars or more a week." Katherine responded.

The band came back and the crowd danced, sang and had a great time. Until – Timmons Worthington and Lana Worthington walked on to the floor and asked to have the microphone for a minute. Timmons cleared his throat and gave his message – short and demanding. He wanted information about who killed his daughter given to Path Patterson, the police chief. Anyone who provided useful information that brought the killer to justice would be rewarded with fifty thousand dollars.

Samantha watched Bender while Mr. Worthington talked. At the mention of the large amount of money, Bender turned pale. Then a smile slithered across his sullen face. Samantha nudged Katherine.

"Look at Bender. I bet he's going to frame someone for the crimes he committed and then collect the money. When he leaves I'm going to follow him. Keep your phone close."

Samantha stood up and excused herself. All, but Katherine, assumed Samantha had gone to the ladies' room. JR, Janet, Anna and Steve begged Patterson to teach them to disco so off he went to show the kiddies how to dance. Gin and Jim trailed along for more fun. Johnny Jones had found a friend at the bar named Jim Bean.

The band stopped for another break but turned on their DJ box and played a tango. Patterson raced back to get Samantha.

"Katherine, where did Samantha go?"

"I thought she went to the restroom, but, I think she went to her car. When Sterling leaves she plans to follow him. She's convinced that he plans to plant his incriminating evidence at someone else's place."

"Do you agree?" Patterson asked Katherine. She wasn't as convince as Samantha that Bender was the killer.

Katherine explained. "Bender turned pale when Worthington mentioned the reward then seconds later he smiled. Samantha thinks that means he figured how to plant the evidence on someone, police find it and he claim the reward."

"But first Bender would have to destroy his sections on the videos." Patterson's face turned to stone. If that man was the killer, he had already tried to destroy the evidence and everyone with it. Now, more desperate because of the money, Bender needed the evidence, in order to destroy his part. Patterson thought it was a matter of life and money to Bender. Everything Bender wanted was locked in the police station, but Bender didn't know that. Patterson had to stop him before he hurt someone else.

"Tell Samantha to stay and wait for me. I'm coming with her."

He ran to his car and searched for Samantha's car. It was gone.

He called Katherine. She told him that Bender and his wife had left the club. They were heading to Pretty Prairie.

"Call her back tell her to stay on the line and to keep talking to you. Tell Gin everything she says and have her relay every word to me. Okay?"

67

Remodeling at
the Bender's

Lives changed that night, some for the better and some for the worse. Patterson headed in the direction of the police department. He called his office, and Mrs. Murphy answered. Oh, no, he thought. Calmly he explained to her. "Go to my desk, open the locked drawer. Removed the large envelope full of evidence. It says Worthington on it. Lock up everything. Check that no one is outside waiting for you before you walk to your car. Go home. Be careful."

He did an *all call* to his men, told them the situation, to meet and to gun up at the office. He put the little blue flashing light on the top of his car. Boy, did he miss his police truck with its rack of lights.

He had to make sure they weren't after the wrong person. So he checked with Sheila. "Sheila did you hear from anyone today about Nick Chase."

"You told me to call the town with the runaway girl, Nick's little milk-jug friend. Well, I got a call back about five-thirty. Their sheriff told me he had Nick in custody for the last two days."

"Thanks, Sheila needed that information." Patterson thought that didn't mean a thing. Nothing has happened since Wednesday.

Nick Chase had been a free man the Monday morning when someone murdered Mrs. Steinem.

Samantha knew she was on the right trail. Logic identified the killer as someone close to Bunny Worthington. Sterling Bender had been physically close to Bunny. His body's shape was like the Shadow's. His smile reminded her of a jack o' lantern smile and finally his ego. Still all circumstantial evidence, she needed proof - physical proof. She followed Bender's car, staying several blocks back, she hoped he wouldn't know someone had followed him. From a distance, she watched Bender pull into Pretty Prairie. His car continued to race down the road. Samantha squealed to a stop when she saw his car slammed into his closed garage door. Wood fragment flew everywhere. Susan Bender screamed, "No". Samantha heard her two blocks away.

Samantha inched down the street with her car lights off. The Bender's house was dark except for the blinking light from the motion detector flashing on the splintered garage door. Surprised that the Bender's had a motion detector light, she thought that Pretty Prairie was a safe place to live. Finally, a light snapped on in the upper window, from a block away she recognized Susan standing at the window. Bender stood behind her with a gun at her neck. Samantha's phone rang. The ID showed unknown number.

"Yes,"

"This is Susan Bender. Sterling wants you to bring all of the evidence that you collected from Bunny Worthington's house to him, or, he will kill me."

"Okay, I will call the Police Chief because he has the evidence. Tell Sterling to give me time, please."

She called Katherine and told her about Sterling demands and threats. Tell Patterson, please, I'll keep a watch on Bender."

Katherine said. "Patterson said to wait for him. He will be there in ten minutes and don't get close. He will bring only the phone. What does that mean?"

"The USB flash drives have incriminating information on them, also. But, one is missing." Samantha murmured.

While she waited, she looked around the moonlight reflected off a shiny thing moving along the sidewalk. Samantha moved her mirror so she had a better view. There toddling down the street walked Mrs. Kant, Victoria's mother. She had taken little Robby out for some air. As she pushed the stroller along, she sang to him. The baby still cried. He must miss his crazy mother. Somehow she had to get Mrs. Kant away from this area. She rolled down her window and whispered.

"Mrs. Kant, come here."

Mrs. Kant was lost in the moment trying to soothe her grandchild and didn't hear. Samantha rolled her car back to get closer to Mrs. Kant and that meant further away from the Bender's house. Samantha used no brakes, so there wouldn't be brake lights and hoped that Sterling didn't notice her car moving. She finally got even with Mrs. Kant.

"Mrs. Kant you need to take Robbie out of the stroller and get in the backseat of my car. Mr. Bender has had a bad day and has a gun and will shoot anyone."

"No, you made my daughter crazy. I will not get into any car with you."

"Okay, then do you see Mrs. Bender in the window? Now do you see the gun to her head? You don't? Alright do you see their car crashed into garage door? Then get in the car and I will back you around safely to Robert's house. I mean Victoria's house."

Mrs. Kant nodded her head but kept walking toward the Bender's house. Her inner brakes and reverse were malfunctioning, apparently. "What about the stroller I can't leave the stroller. Victoria would kill me."

"If you don't leave the stroller Mr. Bender will kill you and Robbie."

A ping, a loud cracking sound as a bullet crashed through Samantha's windshield and one zipped past Mrs. Kant's head. She and Robbie were in the backseat, in a flash.

"Now drive like a bat out of hell." She said.

Samantha backed around the block with flying bullets dinging everywhere. All the while, Mrs. Kant and the baby hid on the floor. What possessed her to get the old woman and baby out of the way and to a safe place. She pulled into Robert's driveway, backed in where

Bender couldn't see them. She instructed Mrs. Kant to take the baby and Robert to the basement.

"Oh, I can't take little Robbie to the basement, it is dirty down there." She said very primly.

"Fine, it's up to you. Do you want him dirty or dead?" Samantha drove off. Craziness . . .

Samantha hated sounding dramatic, but that was the situation. She pulled forward when she saw Patterson's headlight heading in her direction.

68

BENDER GETS THE POINT

Patterson left his three deputies, Henry, J.T. and Alex, guarding the police station and more importantly the evidence that provided motive for murder for several suspects. He raced to Pretty Prairie, like a knight in a white suit charging off in his old truck to save Samantha. Armed only his.45 police pistol. He slid to a stop when he detected Samantha's car. Her car lights were off, but she was inching her way towards him.

He cut his lights and pulled up beside her and asked. "What is going on here?"

"It's Bender. He has Susan as his hostage in the upstairs window. Told you he was the killer." Samantha curtly reported.

"Where can I get a good shot?"

"Go into Katherine's garage and up the stairs to the bedroom window. But not with that gun. You need to call Katherine and tell her you need her rifle. When you get it and you are ready call me. I'll sneak up to the Bender's house and cause a distraction. When Susan is out of range, shoot him. Don't kill him just shoot him."

Patterson smirked. "Who is the police chief here?"

"Go to Katherine's. It's me." Samantha smirked back.

He handed Samantha his gun. As he drove off he heard Bender yelling threats and shooting. He knew they didn't have time to wait for back-up. Patterson called Katherine about her rifle and proceeded to the Jones's house. He ran back of the house to the sewing room and opened the door. Bo bounced out. Patterson grabbed Bo and the rifle.

"Who hides a guns in a sewing room? Only a scary person."

He phoned Samantha, "I'm here and have Bo. I see Bender and his wife."

Only a few seconds passed before he heard Samantha yell at Bender. Her voice bobbed around he wasn't clear where she was. Patterson noticed as he stood at the window there were bullet holes in the frame. He thought, *I need to evacuate the neighborhood, but there isn't a safe way to do it right now.* In military mode he scanned the area to assess the situation. A shadowy shape moved in front of Bender's door causing the motion detector lights to flash on. It was Samantha.

Dressed in her red dress and three inch heels, she planned on saving Susan Bender and mess with Bender's mind. She yelled in the direction opposite of Patterson. "Do you see him from there? Good – now shoot him."

Patterson thought. *I can't yell at her. That would tell Bender my location. At least he can't get a clear shoot from that angel. But, damn, she's crazy taking that chance. Bender has lost it. Dangerous situation when a person slips over the edge."*

Bender started shooting at shadows again. Samantha took advantage of the noise to dash through the door. She left it opened. Patterson watched her climb the stairs.

"No Samantha don't." The words slipped out of Patterson. His heart raced as he wondered. *How can I stop her? Civilians watch too much television. The idiot will get herself killed. Oh Samantha.*

What Patterson could not see was Samantha stayed next to the rail. She knew that Bender couldn't see her from that angle, plus he was too busy shooting up the neighborhood. She was safe until she reached the bedroom door. Silently she stood at the door and pointed the gun at him.

"Bender let your wife go, and I won't shoot you nor will Patterson." Her voice soft and smooth, she didn't want him to feel more threatened. Bender gave her a sideways look, smirked, and tightened the grip on his wife. Samantha kept the gun pointed at Bender. She nodded at another house as if to say see the SWAT team over there. For a split second, Bender looked in the direction Samantha nodded.

The second, he looked away from her. She yelled. "Susan drop. Now." And she shot Bender in the leg.

Susan went limp and slid out of Bender's grip. Bender bent and grabbed his leg. The second bullet hit him in the shoulder and exploded. Pain ripped through Sterling Bender's body. Pain incensed him more. He turned and aimed his gun at the crumbled body of his wife.

"Drop your gun . . . Tell your boyfriend to get over here or I'm shooting both, you and my wife." He yelled at Samantha. He slid to the floor and leaned against the wall. Blood flowed out of his shoulder and leg onto the once perfect white carpet.

The moment Patterson saw Samantha shoot Bender. He shot Bender wounding him more. Methodically he clicked his heels and sprinted down the steps. In combat mode he darted down the street blending into the shadows as he edged his way to Samantha. From street level all Patterson saw was a bullet torn window no civilians were visible. To better assess the situation he climbed a tree what he saw made his blood turn cold. His heart stopped. He saw Bender aim at Samantha and fire. Then, there was no visual of Samantha. Patterson radioed Jim as he ran. He told Jim of the hostage situation at Bender's asked for back up and ambulances. Patterson crouched, foreword rolled into the Bender's house with the rifle aimed. Yelled Samantha's name. He listened. She didn't respond.

Bender yelled down the stairs. "You want to see your girlfriend alive? Then bring all of the evidence upstairs. Your gun stays downstairs or I'm killing both of them."

"Okay . . . Give me a minute."

Patterson planned to use his phone, an identical phone to Worthington's. Plus, it has some of the evidence on it to show Bender. He had clips from the different videos. Maybe he could fool Bender into thinking it was Superintendent Worthington's phone. Then, maybe he would release the women. If not, at least Bender would be distracted long enough to miss the knife flying at him.

"I'm coming up . . ." Patterson banged the rifle on the floor a couple of time so Bender could hear it hit the floor. He released the knife he always wore and stuck it in the belt behind his back. Slowly he ascended the stairs with his hands high and holding the phone. At the top of the stair, he saw Samantha and Susan on the floor under the window. Bender leaned against the window frame blood flowing.

"You girls okay?" Patterson inquired.

They nodded.

"Here is the evidence, now, let them go."

"Show me something, first."

Patterson started one of the videos and showed it to him. "I'm giving you to the count of three. Then I'm sending the evidence down the stairs for the police to find after you shot me and whoever. One . . . Two . . . Thr-"

"Fine, women get out of here."

Patterson didn't breathe. Couldn't trust Bender not to shoot the women when they passed by him. Bender's shaking hand held a gun on Samantha with his eyes focused on Patterson. Susan scurried past Bender and then Patterson. Samantha limped as she moved towards Bender. Bender looked down to see why she was limping.

Sterling Bender noticed Samantha's hand flayed uncontrollably as she limped towards him. Had he shot her or had she had a stroke? He wiped the sweat out of his eyes with his bloody right hand. Samantha neared Bender slowly she limped and slowly she raised her left arm with the three inch heel shoe in it. With the point of the heel, she whacked Bender in the side of the face. The air was knocked out of him. He hit the floor. She flew past Patterson.

"One . . . Two . . . Three . . ." Patterson counted slowly.

Bender scowled up at Patterson with a "Say what" look on his face. He bowed his head to spit up blood.

"I said, one . . . two . . . three . . . drop your gun, Bender."

Bender just glowered at Patterson. In a swift movement, Patterson aimed, threw, and his knife caught Bender where the neck and the shoulder meet. Bender lost the grip on his gun. Patterson dove, and in one critical swoop Patterson held the gun on Bender.

"Samantha and Susan go to Katherine's house. I have Sterling's gun. I called an ambulance. Just go."

Both women ran barefoot down the street to safety.

Patterson and his men searched the house for more evidence and guns. They seized videos of young children, but no guns. They boarded up the house. Patterson left a message for Dr. Ackerman. Humbly Patterson told Ackerman that Samantha had been right, Bender was the killer.

69

No One's on First and Watts is Out

It was Saturday morning and a killer was brought to justice, alive, well sort of. To top it off, it was a bright and sunny day in River Bend. Sheila had volunteered to help in the office; homemade donuts were delivered by Mrs. Murphy. Then, metaphorically, a cloud covered the sun. The cloud's name was Sean Watts, an attorney, who at one, time had been a big name lawyer in River Bend. That was until someone discovered he embezzled money from his clients.

He sauntered in the police station dressed in a navy blue stripe suit, not pin striped, but, loud striped, plus red tie. He looked like a stylized flag from some newly started third world country. With his thumbs in his lapels, his chest puffed out, he announced to Patterson and Sheila, "My client, Mr. Sterling Bender is innocent of Superintendent Timmons Worthington murder. Sterling Bender is a fine citizen. I was at the Chamber of Commerce meeting with him on the night in question. Dealing with city development issues of which I cannot discuss. I demand Sterling's release."

Patterson had Mr. Watts go into his office. His normal straight lips were arched in contempt of Watts. The man was a total scum bag, Watts had stolen from Patterson's dad, from Al Roth, Patterson's second dad, and many others.

A subdued partially mummified Sterling Bender entered Chief of Police office with his arm, shoulder and leg bandaged using a thin cane. Patterson helped him to a chair. Bender turned to Sean Watts and explained, "Sean, I didn't call you. I don't need a lawyer I have confessed to everything. I deserve what I get."

Patterson jumped in and added. "We will not release Sterling. We found his DNA at the scene of a murder. Mr. Sean Watts, I need to inform you, your non-client has elected to co-operate with us concerning an ongoing investigation."

Patterson stood up and walked Sean Watts to the front door. Opened it and shut it, but not before Sean Watts had placed his Italian made loafers in the doorway and jammed the closing.

"May I inquire as to whom you suspect in your on-going investigation? They may need my services."

"Can't tell you. . . FBI has taken over the case. And that means - *Watts is out*."

Patterson accidentally stomped on Sean's foot and slammed the door shut the second Sean moved his foot.

"Idiot . . . Shame, I can't lock the police station's door."

Patterson walked a docile Sterling Bender back to his cell. Worried about Bender, he asked. "You never mentioned the Chamber Meeting. Why? I'll check it out. Off the record what happened to you?"

Bender inhaled then looked Patterson in the eye. "I've been in love with Bunny Worthington since she was five and I was fifteen. I had a vasectomy because of her. She talked me into doing things. Things that I knew I shouldn't do. But, it meant money, power and Bunny. I've learned things in the past few days. First, I'm weak, Mrs. Steinem almost beat me up. I killed her in self-defense. Then, I got that big grand gun. I thought it would make me strong. It did for a while. But then, your girlfriend almost killed me with her shoe. Nick Chase got me hooked on cocaine. It started when Bunny asked me to go to one of his parties with her. She gave me some of Nick's coke. I thought she has some, too, but she hadn't. We went into a bedroom, oh, the sex was good, the best ever. When I woke up Bunny was next to me, she asked me if it was as good for me as it had been for her. I told her, yes. Then, she showed me the video of my love making – it was with a man, not her. Then she told me that she now had me and I would do whatever she wanted or else. Bottom line - I'm weak, and I deserve prison time. I hope it kills me. Patterson, you could have and should have killed me, but you didn't. I owe you, there is something that I can do for you. You have to find that one missing USB drive. Bunny put the information concerning finance on it. I will go through all of them with whomever and uncover all of the hidden documents. You showed me some of the stuff against Bunny, but there is lots more."

Patterson patted Bender on his good shoulder. As Patterson walked away, he called Samantha and asked her and Bo to come by for a chat. Yes, a chat.

When she showed up they went into his office and shut the door. Of course, Sheila had a glass against the door before it had fully closed. She sounded like an old baseball announcer announcing *who did what.* The detectives in the office were bright and curious young men, so they listened to her broadcasting all the information.

Patterson sat on one side of his desk and read his notes. Samantha and Bo on the other side, she twisted, wiggled, and tried to see what he was reading. Had he written down all illegal things she had done on this case. Had he asked her here so he could arrest her?

"I want you to know you were right about Bender. And – you were right about there being more than one killer. The person that killed Worthington is still out there. I would like for you to write down your suspects. I'll write down mine. Then, we will compare."

They both had, Janet Monroe, Mickey Sims, Ramon Reyes, and Drake Armstrong. The ones that Samantha had that Patterson didn't – were the teachers attending the meeting with the Superintendent, Devora Moore, her beloved principal, Angela Reyes, and Bob Douglas.

Patterson reminded Samantha. "Oh, let's not forget Nick Chase and Worthington's parents. Oh, I forgot, can't be Nick. He was in jail."

"This is off the subject, but important. I've been thinking about Worthington's autopsy report and health information that I accidentally read in your truck. Let me show you, what I'm talking about."

Samantha showed him the bruise on her hand and explained how a little poke from scissors popped it open, and it bled everywhere. "Remember we both thought the killer had to be a male. I'm beginning to think it didn't have to be a male all big and strong. It took very little to cause my bruise and even less to break it open. The killer had to be strong enough to break through the skin. If I had been on blood thinner as long as Worthington had, I could have bled out very quickly and easily. When I went through Worthington's house looking for the safe, I accidentally looked in the medicine cabinet. In the cabinet I saw a recently filled medicine bottle for blood thinner prescribed by Dr. Flanigan. Yet, in Dr. Ackerman's medical history, it said she hadn't had a blood test in twelve years. That meant Flanigan never did a blood test on her. The autopsy report showed her numbers were extremely off. Her blood was too thin and that's the reason she kept her office so hot. She was cold all the time."

She dug in her purse the entire time she talked. She finally found the bottle of blood thinner with Timmons Worthington's and Dr. Flanigan's name on it. She handed it to Patterson. He made a note in big letters about Flanigan and underlined it – *get rid of Flanigan.*

"What I'm trying to say is it wouldn't take an abnormal amount strength to poke Worthington in the neck and have her bleed out. I've been experimenting on things that are sharp but small. Plus, the item needs to be something simple that a person carries with them all the time, like a pair of small scissors. The kind of scissors that older women carry in their purses to trim their fingernails and stuff. Plus, some of our suspects are the older women teachers who were at the Board office that night. Right? Anyway, the scissors I am talking about are about one and a half inches from the fulcrum or screw to the point. Or like the ones Victoria tried to stab me with and used to cut off my hair."

Patterson nodded and sent a text to Dr. Ackerman to confirm if a small pair of scissors could have been the tool used to kill Worthington.

"Well, I still think its Nick Chase, somehow. I would put money on it. I'm concerned about Mr. Worthington's plans for his press conference tomorrow. He's announcing the reward for information on the death of his daughter. I need to find the killer before he announces information about the reward. Or I will have an office full of money hungry nuts. I won't have time to investigate. Just time to deal with nuts."

"I have an idea." Samantha smiled and wrote. While Patterson read it. She tiptoed to the door and opened it. Sheila fell forward the glass dropped, and her skin-tight pants ripped. One of the men yelled "home run". Sheila jumped up and sashayed back to her desk as if she always showed her lime green underwear.

"I gained a pound or two doing police undercover work for Patterson." She swaggered, readjusting her pants and wiped her nose, a female Barney Fife.

70

QUIET BEFORE THE STORM

Edward Wooten stood, determination in his eyes, in Samantha Grant's usual parking space and waited.

Late, as usual on Monday, Samantha sped into her parking spot. Edward backed up as she drove in. She saw Edward standing there she wondered why. Edward faced the sun so she didn't see the tears in his eyes. She pulled up beside him and tried to determine his mood. Impossible he faced the sun and caused his face to scrunch up. "Good morning, Edward, can I help you?"

"You're the one that turned my mother in aren't you?"

"Yes, I told my friend who knows what to do in any and all situations. She took care of it. But, she did it in a way your mother wouldn't get in trouble."

"I want to thank you; my brother slept in a real bed last night. They found my mother a job. We have a place to live, I took a real bath. Now, the kids won't make fun of me for stinking."

Samantha did a quick pit check. "I know what you mean about being able to take a real bath. I'm glad you're okay about what happened."

"Thanks for always trying to help me even though I was a pain."

"When I was eleven my mother and I had nowhere to live. I know what you are going through... Let me know, if you need anything."

Edward looked off to the side for a second, and then turned back to her. "I need a Thanksgiving Dinner somewhere, anywhere for my brother, Joseph. He has never had one in his entire life, and he is seven years old."

Tears filled her eyes. "Okay I'll see what I can do."

Later in the day, Edward watched Samantha leave and knew she was up to something. He considered calling the police to help her, but knew she would get arrested.

71

THE STORM

The storm clouds had gathered, the thunder rumbled across the fields towards River Bend. Lightning danced in the sky. Electrifying air put everyone on edge. The stage was set. The suspects were in place. Show time...The suspects, mostly teachers nervously chatted with each other. They waited to see why they had been called by Police Chief Patterson to attend a meeting at the Board Office.

Gin Walker, the unofficial police IT person, had salvaged most of the deleted files off Worthington's computer. The one Patterson was particularly interested in was the 3R file. The file listed the names of the teachers who Worthington wanted *removed, relocated or retired. It provided the* Who's-. So the Who were invited to the Board of Education office for the special meeting.

"Now, who else do we need to invite to our party." Patterson prepared to write down their names.

"Shouldn't Janet Monroe and I be on your list?" Samantha asked.

"But, you play Worthington, the victim. And Janet will be doing her job as usual. Just like it was that night. Just like you wanted."

"Sorry... details, just make sure I don't get killed or that I don't kill anyone, accidentally."

Four o'clock and everyone on Worthington's hit list had shown up. Wearing a dark wig and tight clothes Samantha stepped out of Worthington's office. In her best imitation of Katherine, she said,

"The reason you have been asked here is to inform you, that the late Superintendent Worthington's plans for reconstruction of the school district has been approved by the school board's members. Therefore, the 3R's relocate, replace or retire decision must be enforced."

Samantha returned to Superintendent Worthington's office and reflected in Worthington's upside-down stiletto shaped chair. To no one she said. "Remember, two weeks earlier these people had entered Worthington's office with hope. Then, they were told they were expendable. She died. They had hope once again. Now, they enter, again, hopeless about their job. Emotional roller coaster. I need to stay focused someone in this group could be a killer. Ready or not here goes."

Samantha wore her killer three inch heels. She was trying to channel Superintendent Bunny Worthington. Samantha sauntered out of the Superintendent's office and pointed at a teacher. Impatiently she motioned for the person to follow her into the Worthington's domain. Once again, the poor suspect/teacher had to revisit the hot stuffy – a freak show gone bad - room. Samantha reminded the teacher of the fact she didn't fit the River Bend School District's new image. The School Board had decided that she had to be relocated or retired by the end of the school year. The Board needed to have she decision within two weeks or the board would make the decision for her.

Time ticked away as teacher after teacher came, interviewed and left. All had entered quietly and left downcast. Deputy Henry herded each one as they came out of the building to the side door and into the conference room where J.T. and Alex stood guard.

Discouraged Samantha sent a text Patterson, "I'm afraid I have wasted your time."

A rumble and lighting struck outside the building. The smell of wood burning filled the air. The lights dimmed then, flashed off and on. Another clap of thunder vibrated the building at the same moment a large man dressed in combat boots and jogging pants stomped into the building. Janet rushed to him and spoke softly as she guided him back to her area. "The Superintendent called a special meeting this afternoon. Right now, everyone is busy, but the district values your time. Let me reschedule an appointment for you at a more convenient time."

Defiantly he said, "I have information that the new superintendent needs. If I don't get to see her, then you will be sorry, little missy." He slammed his fist on the ledge of Janet's reception station, snap, the corner of the top broke and fell on the floor.

"Tell her my wife's a teacher and she is here." He lowered his head and peered through his bushy eyebrows that stood straight out covering half of his bulging eyes. He shuffled his feet and looked at the superintendent's door. In a blink of an eye, he charged the superintendent's room.

Janet chased the bull, cornered him and talked quietly to him. "Sir, you will either sit down, or I will call security. Then two things will happen; first you will not get to speak to the superintendent now or ever, second you will be sent to jail for threatening the superintendent. Your choice. . ." Janet had her hand on the phone ready to use it.

Grudgingly, he nodded. Lucky for him, he saw his wife half hidden by a large green plastic plant. Aggravated he flopped down next to her. She smiled sweetly at him, patted his arm and in a sing- song voice. "Oh, Buddy, I have everything under control. I know this superintendent will listen to me. I will receive the <u>Teacher of the Year </u>award. You need to wait for me outside, dear." A smug look changed her normal mousey appearance and a dreamy stare filled her small beady eyes.

Harshly he roared, "I'm not here for you, you old cow. I'm here to talk to the Superintendent and I'll be coming home with a wad of money. No, thanks to you."

He laughed, howled and moved away from her.

72

THUNDER ROLLS AND LIGHTNING STRIKES

Embarrassed by her husband's behavior, Mrs. Burton peered around to see who noticed. She prayed. *I hope no one saw him. Why did he show-up tonight? Tonight is my night. I know one thing; this new superintendent will listen to me."*

The new Superintendent, Samantha Grant, walked out and motioned for her to follow and even said to her. "I saved the best for last, Mrs. Burton."

A good omen, gleefully the woman chattered as she toddled into the Superintendent's office. She tottered onto the chair next to the new Superintendent Worthington. Bess Burton started her speech about the Teacher of the Year award and how she was value as a teacher. "I want to thank you for this opportunity. My test scores are the best in the state. You know I have never been in this room before, yet I have nightmares about it. I get so confused lately. This room makes me feel like I am an object placed inside the kaleidoscope's cylinder and then I'm converted into a geometric image on the walls."

Mesmerized by Bess Burton's lilting voice redundantly telling how valuable she was as a teacher had almost lulled Samantha asleep. A crack of lightning jerked Samantha awake. Enough was enough, time to end this. Samantha in her heart knew that Bess Burton was not killer material. She was just a sweet little old teacher. Samantha raised her hand in the stop position. "Sorry, but, for district purposes. I need you to answer this. Your name is Elizabeth Burton, right."

"I prefer Bess. I don't want to be confused with that actress Elizabeth Taylor Burton. I want Bess put on the award, please. *Bess Burton. . .*" She held her red wrinkled hands up, to show exactly how it needed to look.

Flippantly Samantha said, "Oh, Bess you know the <u>Teacher of the Year</u> award was given to one of our high school teachers. Sorry, but back to business. You've been with the district thirty years. That is a long time. I have asked you here to discuss your options for next year. As I said in the reception area we are all here to discuss plans for next year. I want to remind you, there are only two choices, relocate or retire. Do you have any questions?"

Graciously, Bess Burton bowed her head and said 'no'. She stood up, she reached into her handbag and pulled out her gloves. She paused and said. "I need to discuss my decision with my husband. Thank you again for your time and consideration for the award."

The thunder rolled, lightning struck and the lights went out. Samantha stared and waited for the lights to turn on or lighting to light up the reflective wall in front of her and the desk. She felt around the desk. Nothingness surrounded her. She said. *"Mrs. Burton just wait for the lights it will be just a minute."*

Not a sound, Samantha thought, poor Mrs. must be lost in the middle of this black hole of a room. Another flash of lightning lit the room. Samantha saw Bess Burton not in the middle of the room but standing beside her. The feeling of being trapped and scared filled her. But this is sweet little old Mrs. Burton. Channeling Superintend Worthington – Worthington had trusted dear old Mrs. Burton. Then, Samantha remembered. *Mrs. Burton's left hand is behind my back. Left-handed - Worthington's killer had been left-handed.* The light vanished and everything went dark. Another flash. Samantha saw a spark of light illuminated Bess's red crazed eyes. She thought. *The chair was useless as protection.* When the light disappeared Samantha stood up. She tried to not touch Bess Burton so she wouldn't know Samantha's exact location. How to exit? She assessed the situation, sound was the only constant source of knowing where Bess Burton stood. Intently she listened to Bess's rapid breathing and the rain drumming on the windows. The breathing was behind her and to the right. The rain tapped on the window to her left. To escape she needed to move left - to the windows. The breathing volume increased, Samantha's short hair bristled; as warm puffs of air hit the back of her neck. Bess had moved closer and now she totally blocked Samantha's exit. A small flash of lightning briefly lit the room. Samantha searched the reflection. The light flashed off something a small and shiny in Burton's raised left hand. Samantha smashed herself away from Burton. A crash of blinding light Bess Burton plunged towards Samantha. The sharp point touched Samantha's face, she jerked away. In the afterglow Samantha locked eyes with Burton in the mirrored wall. Burton's beady little eyes stared through her. Bess Burton moved closer until she pressed against Samantha and smashed Samantha against the hard edge of the desk. This was not a feeling now, she was trapped. Burton's body trembled with tension as she waited for the next lightning strike. Samantha felt Burton's left arm lift ready to attack with the next lightning strike. Mrs. Burton's plan was two strikes and Samantha was out of the game.

The thunder rolled, Samantha had three second to escape. One thousand, one-thousand-one, Samantha did what Pops had taught her to do when cornered, one thousand-two and -. The lightning struck and illuminated the room. Bess Burton leaned back and lunged with all her might at the same moment. Samantha slid to the ground and rolled under the desk. Bess Burton smashed onto the desk and released a piercing shriek. Then a gurgling sound.

In the dark Samantha opened her phone, pushed and held just one button and hoped it called 911. The storm had rolled on leaving River Bend in darkness. Samantha crawled out from the desk and into the black hole of a room.

Samantha heard a faint, "911- May I help you?"

Samantha woodenly spoke, "There's a fire at River Bend's Board of Education. I'm trapped. My name is Samantha. Help please... Cough, cough..."

Samantha knew if a person needed help, they yelled fire. The fire department, the paramedics and Patterson would respond to the call.

Patterson better respond since he was in the next room. All were needed to help poor sweet Mrs. Burton.

BANG – the glass in the window shattered. Samantha crumpled to the floor. A second later Jim and Bob Douglas shattered the door frame and the door opened. Bob Douglas bent down beside Samantha and gently patted her hand. "There, there…," he cooed.

She shook her hand free. "Mrs. Burton is over there, help her."

Patterson shot through the window shattering the glass. Henry helped him leap through the window. He dashed to Samantha and scooped her into his arms. "I didn't shoot you, did I?"

The emergency lights were on in the reception area which cast light into Worthington's office. For once the reflective walls were useful, they help light the room. Samantha pointed to Mrs. Burton slumped on the desk. "Watch her, she is armed, dangerous and your killer."

A pool of blood surrounded Bess Burton's body and flowed onto the floor. Patterson felt her thumb for a pulse. She was dead. He reasoned. *When she fell she stabbed herself in the throat with the murder weapon.*

He didn't want to upset Samantha so he whispered. *"Bess Burton is dead."*

73

THE NOT SO GRAND FINALE

Resolutely, Patterson clicked his heels and went into an at-ease stance. He turned and faced Samantha. "What happened?"

Wide eyed, a long cut down the side of her face, blood mixed with tears smeared across her face, Samantha stood ready to be arrested. Tightening her jaw, she answered, "Sir, I had just finished interviewing Bess Burton. She rose to leave, lightning struck and the lights went out. She stayed, moved behind me, and then tried to kill me. She had me pressed against the desk. Then she raised her left arm ready to stab me when the lightning flashed again to provide light. I slid to the ground and caused her to fall forward. She fell on her scissors didn't she? I killed her."

Samantha tightened her lips a tear slipped down her face. "I'm so sorry, poor sweet Mrs. Burton."

Patterson said, "She tried to kill you."

"Yes, but, if you had listened - you could have stopped her. Didn't you hear the screams?"

"No, the room is sound proof. It never dawned on me that the room would room sound-proof. I should have checked before the reenactment. Plus, we were busy with her husband. He demanded to see you. We chased him around the office. Then, he charged the door. While we were handcuffing him against the door. We heard noises coming from the office. At the same time the 911 operator called me.

She said there was a fire here. We tried the door. It was locked. I went through the window." Patterson talked in robot mode.

Tears were in Jim's eyes, "I can't believe Mrs. Burton was the killer. She couldn't hurt a fly. She was my favorite teacher."

In the reception area, the man in the jogging pants sat handcuffed to a desk. Petit Janet Monroe nervously sat holding the gun on him.

Bleary eyed the large man looked up at Samantha and spoke. "Superintendent I came here tonight to see you. I – I have information about the killer. I found this in my wife's purse. It had blood on it." He held a small rectangular thing in his huge filthy hands. It appeared to be a flash drive. Samantha walked over, held out her hand and smiled. "Thank you."

He dropped it in her hands.

"Now, I want my money." Bull-like Buddy Burton postured at Samantha.

"I have to give this to the Police Chief. He will handle getting the money for you."

Samantha still had blood flowing beside her eye; as she stood with the other suspects. Patterson explained about the reenactment. He told them that the police had caught Superintendent Worthington's killer and they were free to go home. Mickey Sims added a *thank you* to Patterson for his dedication to school district. Sims also, added a thank you to the teachers for their part in solving the case and they had the next day off with pay.

The harvest moon hung low and created a soft light in the parking lot as they walk to their cars. Superintendent Sims interrupted the quiet. "Ah – excuse me one more thing I promised all of you that everything will stay the same for a long time, don't worry. We are not changing any of you."

Patterson stood in the door way and watched the traumatized group of teachers wobble to their cars. Samantha and Bo came up behind Patterson. She reached out and lightly touched his arm. "Patterson, Bo and I are leaving. Here's the weapon. I bagged it the way you taught me when I don't have gloves." She handed him the bag containing a pair of small long-nosed scissors in it.

A side-ways smile appeared on Patterson's face. He reached out and removed the black wig that had slipped to the back of her head and ruffled her very short hair. "You did a brave thing back there. I just couldn't believe it was a teacher."

"I know but, they were the only ones left with a motive and without a solid alibi. They were the last people to be with Worthington. Some remembered who went before them but no one remembered who went after them. I knew from the 3R's list that eight people had been called to Worthington's office that night. The one high school teacher came at two-thirty and left at three. She had a bowling game alibi along with Bob Douglas. Principal Moore's alibi was church. That left the five elementary teachers. A few of the teachers were still here after Mrs. Steinem and Janet Monroe left. It was unclear which ones so that meant this group didn't have an alibi. Worthington caused her own death. Her idea of perfect River Bend school district consisted of only perfect teachers. When Worthington threatened to remove Bess from her job. Bess panicked. She was being ripped out of her galaxy - the only place she felt safe and loved. Oddly, no one remembered Bess Burton being at the meeting. Yet, she was the only one who admitted being there. She told me she had been nominated for Teacher of the Year award. To be honest I should have suspected her earlier, but she was the one teacher who really deserved the award. I thought maybe they really were giving it to Bess. I should have remember a high school teacher got the award, a male teacher, of course. But logically it added up that one of the elementary teachers did it."

Patterson wrote in his notebook. "I see."

"What are you going to do about that her detestable husband of hers?"

"He is going to jail for some time. Not long enough."

The harvest moon hung low and created a soft light in the parking lot as they walk to their cars. Superintendent Sims interrupted the quiet. "Ah – excuse me one more thing I promised all of you that everything will stay the same for a long time, don't worry. We are not changing any of you."

The moon dipped lower covering Patterson and Samantha in a soft silvery light. Patterson wrapped his arms around Bo and Samantha. Their shadows entwined, stretched across the parking lot and blended into the dark. Samantha looked up at Patterson, the moon reflected in her eyes. They kissed.

EPILOGUE:
DEAR CRIME NOTEBOOK

Samantha opened her Crime Notebook and wrote. Success on my second real case – the summary. On this one there were two murders and two different killers: Sterling Bender murdered Mrs. Steinem accidentally while under the influence of cocaine and fear. Bess Burton murdered Superintendent Worthington and for that, she should receive the <u>Teacher of the Year</u> award. I am beginning to understand Patterson dislike of emotions when it involves a case. I let emotions steer me away from my first premise. The premise was Worthington's murderer had to be someone she trusted. And it was – someone that Worthington thought was so harmless - so insignificant that she ignored/trusted her.

I realized at the end of this case that life was a river of denial. Each one of us denies things like a how we feel about a special person. And sometime we denied about serious things like the Worthington's denied their daughter had serious problems. Their denial over-flowed out of control and caused two deaths.

Samantha paused, reflected and continued writing her summary.

Thanksgiving Day marked the end of fall, the end of the Worthington case and for me real traditional Thanksgiving dinner. This Thanksgiving Patterson and I decided to co-host a Thanksgiving dinner. I had promised a first Thanksgiving dinner for Edward Wooten's little brother, Joseph. I asked Mr. Bruce to cater, a proven caterer extraordinaire. Once his magic turned a nasty old warehouse into a stunning setting for a memorial service. I knew he could turn Patterson's barracks-chic house into something cozy and welcoming.

Filled with the holiday spirit, Katherine and I made pies for the dinner. What a lovely way to spend the Wednesday night before Thanksgiving. We baked aromatic apple and pumpkin pies, while we shared a bottle of wine and the latest gossip. We had just started on the juicy stuff when we were interrupted by the door-bell. Bo took off running so excited he slid into the door. Katherine looked through the peek hole. "Oh, Samantha, it's for you."

Patterson staggered in, his eyes bugged and his military length silver hair stood out straight. He reminded me of one of those rubbery stress dolls when you squeeze them. Stuttering he told us his problem. "Your friend, Mr. Bruce took over my house. Then kicked me out. I didn't know where else to go."

Katherine elegantly flitted around refreshing wine for us and getting a beer for Patterson. We resumed our 'talk' about Bess Burton's husband. We bullied Patterson into telling everything. He hesitated, and then informed us Bess's husband was still in jail. Also, Dr. Ackerman had text him Bess Burton died of a heart attack and not by the stab wound I had caused.

Great news, since I thought it was my fault that she died. Katherine and I have another bit of good news to share with Patterson. The teacher agreed to have engraved on Bess Burton's headstone - Bess *Burton Teacher of the Year* everyone is chipping in some money to pay for it."

Thanksgiving morning, we loaded pies into my Escalade and drove to Patterson's house. Mr. Bruce beamed as he opened the door for us and helped with the pies. The transformation was amazing. He turned Patterson's sterile abode into a rustic retreat, included an electric fireplace that added to the ambiance. Chairs were wood logs. Pine boughs and pine cones sprinkled with cranberries and mixed with burnt orange, reddish browns and gold colored foliage. Fall runners flowed down the tables, like a liquid autumn. Mr. Bruce had created a magical retreat.

Thanksgiving with a house full of adults, children, baby and a Bo created a lively magical atmosphere. Jim Murphy's family with Gin Walker added constant merriment. Gin involvement in the Worthington case had been done under the police table. She hacked into accounts for the police department via Jim's supervision. Which lead to the recouping of hundreds of thousands of dollars embezzled by Superintendent Worthington.

Gin commented on the reason for the embezzlement. "I feel, Bunny Worthington needed the money to clone children to look like her in her diabolical scheme to take over the world."

Everyone stared at her then kind of giggled. It was a bizarre theory but Worthington was a bizarre kind of person.

Jim's mom shared about being hired as part-time dispatcher. Sheila told us she had decided to take classes to become a real police officer. Hopefully, Sheila will not use her drinking glass against a door to help solve crimes. We discovered that her door listening skills was the reason she arrived wearing a Native American outfit. She 'heard' Patterson and me talking about the first Thanksgiving. She missed the part about it being Joseph Wooten's first Thanksgiving. She arrived dressed in an interesting looking leather dress and moccasins. She wore her usual bright red lipstick and added a feather in her wooly hair to finish her thematic appearance.

When Patterson first saw her and her outfit he bent over in laughter. I had never heard a sound like that before. His laughter needed oiling, it was a bit squeaky - lack of use. He ran and searched for Joseph Wooten. Excitedly Patterson explained, "Joseph Wooten I would like to introduce you to Sheila. She really is a real Native American from the First Thanksgiving. You are one luck young man. Sheila took time away from causing fights just to meet you."

Patterson pointed Sheila's lips. "That bright red stuff is her war paint. Yup, that's war paint. What do you think?"

Joseph's blue eyes wide with fear as he looked from Patterson to Sheila and back again and then he darted to his mother.

Sheila ambled away her bony body hunched as she mumbled something about looking a dull knife with Patterson's name on it. She planned to scalp him. He reminded her, "Better be nice to me or I won't let you have a bullet for your gun. Think about that."

"Don't you mean bullets?" Her scrawny arms tensed up ready to fight.

"No, I mean one bullet." He winked at Sheila and ran. She chased him in hot pursuit. Envision, robot Patterson being chased by a stick woman with Brillo pad hair.

The prime suspect, Janet Monroe inherited a huge life insurance policy and a house from Superintendent Bunny Worthington. Only there was a problem, because Bunny Worthington had absconded with a considerable amount of money from the school district the house and the insurance money were being held for collateral. Once the school district received all of their missing money Janet would then receive her inheritance. Most of the money, my ex-husband Robert had located in an off-shore account. It would be enough to pay back the school district. Janet planned sell the house and divide any remaining money with her father, Timmons Worthington. She said she had to help out dear old dad.

Janet laughed. "And to top it off, Drake Alexander's mother is my aunt. She is Timmons Worthington's sister. My family is like something out of a bad *Hee Haw* joke book."

Patterson and I invited J.R. Roth, his sister Ana Roth and her friend Steve Kovacev. They were my contractors on my house and their father had been a second father to Patterson. This was their first Thanksgiving since their parents passed away. I felt their pain – I missed Pops so much today.

The main reason for the Thanksgiving dinner had been for Joseph Wooten; a seven year old who had never had a Thanksgiving dinner. His brother Edward had started the school year off on a rough note. And I thought he had caused of my migraine headache, or so I thought. He turned his life around, now, he is an A student. Their mother has a job. The story behind their living in a car was not shared with anyone but Police Chief Patterson. Is it a matter he has taken care, or could it be our next case?

Patterson, Katherine and Gin have spent the past weeks making fun of me for inviting Robert, my ex-husband, and his wife to our Thanksgiving dinner. I reminded them it was a time to be thankful. And- I was thankful he was Victoria's husband. Kidding aside they were alone; both of their parents had abandoned them. Victoria had that effect on people. I touched my head with all the glue like products needed to not look like a scarecrow. I had always wanted an 'every hair in place' style. I have it now. Beware of what you wish for, a useful cliché that I need to remember when I'm in a wishing mode.

Thanksgiving was a beautiful day where golden sunlight and hope filled Patterson's house. The crisp smells of autumn blended with the aroma of turkey, corn bread dressing and pies created a cornucopia of pleasure. The hum of talking and laughing provided the background music of the perfect day.

About the Author

Lea Braden is a retired middle school teacher. When she is not creating compelling mystery tales, she enjoys walks along the Missouri river with her two dogs. River of Denial is the second book in the Samantha Grant mystery series.

Printed in the United States
By Bookmasters